THE
HIGH
RANGE

The High Range

Douglas King

E~PRIDE Books
Beaumont, Texas

ISBN 978-0-9882671-0-7

First Edition

The
High
Range

Douglas
King

E~PRIDE Books
Beaumont, Texas

Copyright © 2012 Douglas King

ISBN 978-0-9882671-0-7

First Edition

For Jerome, David and Keith, with love

CHAPTER 1

Parker White down-shifted the rented Range Rover as it climbed the tortuous, winding, former logging road higher into Rocky Mountain National Park. The windows were down, and Parker deeply inhaled the rapidly cooling air. His suitcases tumbled about in the back seat and the airport luggage tags snapped in the rush of air.

The narrow road divided suddenly as a small feeder exited toward the sheer drop-off of an overlook. Parker whipped the powerful vehicle into the turn and came to a stop in the turnout. He shut off the engine and climbed out onto the broken granite gravel that defined the narrow path up to the small rustic, wood-beamed pavilion that perched on an outcropping of rock. He was still wearing the khaki Dockers plus light blue, cotton polo that comprised his "flight suit," and he reached into the Rover for the mauve silk windbreaker in his carry-on.

His muscles ached from the confinement of a long, uncomfortable flight and he stretched his lean, muscular body, letting the stiff, cool breeze penetrate to his skin before setting out toward the outcropping. He felt better already, and knew then why he had driven right through Estes Park, past the small motel holding his reservation, and headed straight for the mountains.

He stepped up into the small pergola-like structure and leaned slowly over the safety barricade. The familiar wrenching in his gut began immediately, and he tried to fight off the beginning of hyperventilation. Forcing his clenched eyes to open, he looked down into the gorge below. He pulled away from the safety barricade with a hoarse word of profanity. The unexplainable fear still gripped him, and he backed a few steps from the edge. Silently, he tried to convince himself not to rush things. He would conquer this just like he had every other unreasonable fear.

He had driven up well above the tree line and the only vegetation surrounding him was small, gnarled shrubs and assorted moss-like flora. He squinted against the brightest sunlight he had ever bathed in to survey the range of mountains and valleys stretching out before him. The air was so clean he could literally see for miles to the horizon of more jagged, rocky peaks.

He nodded at the expanse. This was a good idea no matter what. The burnout he had been feeling for so long would soon be a memory. The Great Outdoors was not usually his cup of tea, but the opportunity for some vacation time was last minute, and there hadn't been enough money for his dream jaunt to Scotland. That would have to wait. He had consistently spent most of his reserve funds on the ravenous monster that was his home computer network. It had not been satisfied till accumulating more RAM than God and every peripheral known to Microsoft.

What drew him to Estes Park, Colorado, in June were

the Highland Festival, the mountains, and the cooler climate, which would be a close second to Scotland. It certainly fit his budget better. The FBI expected much, but paid for very little. Still it gave him the needed outlet for his other two great obsessions, small arms and serial killers. He considered his computer and his CD collection to be passions, as opposed to obsessions. The Bureau paid for the obsessions and Parker paid for the passions. His was a balanced life.

The winds cascading down from the glaciers stood Parker's short-cropped, brown hair on end. He found the grey, woolen beret in the pocket of his windbreaker and pulled the welcome cover down to his forehead, gripping the narrow brim to keep it in place against the icy wind. In sloping pockets above the gorge below were dark, almost black pools of water. It was hard to gauge their true size from the distance, but Parker guessed they were small lakes, cut out of the rock in the path of some ancient ice flow.

He made himself comfortable on a rough, redwood bench that spanned the support posts of the pavilion's cover. A smile broke through his day-old growth of dark beard and he pulled a small, silver flask from his back pocket. This wasn't Scotland, but it was certainly an occasion for a wee bit of his most treasured single-malt. He pulled the silver cap from the flask and unscrewed the cork seal, allowing the liquor's oaken perfume to envelope him in the stiff breeze. He toasted the mountains in a circling gesture before bringing the small flask to his welcoming lips.

Parker froze as a loud crack echoed from above and down through the gorge. He sat up stiffly, cocking an ear instinctively toward the sound's point of origin. He knew the discharge from a high-powered rifle when he heard it. Two more loud cracks sounded through the gorge in quick succession. Parker stood before the echoes died away. Who could be shooting a rifle in a national park?

He quickly resealed the flask and returned it to his back pocket before sprinting across the gravel walk to the Range Rover. He ducked his tall frame into the driver's seat and, in one motion, gunned the engine and swung the vehicle out onto the roadway.

He headed higher into the tundra, expertly negotiating the sharp s-curves. The air blowing in through the open windows grew even cooler. Parker could feel his heart rate accelerate slightly. He wasn't sure if it was the thinning oxygen as he went higher into the mountain range, or his well-trained sense of danger.

The road moved into a wide curve and the gorge was replaced by an expanse of sloping glacier and tundra. Parker more sensed than saw movement in the distance where the gently sloping mountain crests rolled one into another.

He pulled the Range Rover off the road into another small turn-out. As he turned off the ignition with one hand, he reached back into his carry-on with the other hand to retrieve the Smith & Wesson .40 caliber semi-automatic pistol that was his constant companion. He snapped a fifteen-shot magazine into the pistol's grip, and stuffed the light-weight, black weapon into his belt.

Parker squinted his eyes against the bright sunlight reflecting off the small glacier extending down over one side of the slope. He shook his head, unable to make out anything definite over the distance. Reaching down, he pulled the small release to pop the Rover's rear gate.

Parker moved quickly around to the back where his

suitcase was stored. He unzipped a compartment and rummaged about, cursing softly, until he pulled out a black binocular case. He pulled the powerful lenses from their nest and trained them on the distant tundra. There were four, maybe five dark figures moving quickly across the low vegetation, before they disappeared around a large outcropping of bare granite.

Parker left the road and ran out onto the tundra and down the edge of the glacier. About a hundred yards out, he trained the binoculars again but to no avail. He estimated the distance at a little over a quarter mile. As he was already breathing hard due to the short sprint from the roadway, he thought it best not to push it. He wasn't used to the thin air, and knew he was risking altitude sickness if he forced his body on before he had time to properly acclimate.

He pointed the binoculars in the direction of the outcropping once again, but discerned no further movement. He cursed softly under his breath and let the binoculars drop to dangle from the strap around his neck. The best course of action would be simply to return and report the incident to the nearest ranger station.

"You there?" An angry, baritone voice called out from the roadway. "What the hell do you think you're doing out there?"

Parker spun around. He squinted through the bright light at the figure standing back at the road. He caught the reflection of light from gun metal, and saw the bolt-action 12-gauge pointing at him.

"Just doing a little sightseeing," he called back innocently. He pulled his windbreaker closed, covering the pistol in his belt.

"Come back to the road now!" commanded the

stranger. The rifle barrel bobbed as if to emphasize the order.

Parker started to retrace his footsteps while at the same time snapping the lower buttons on his windbreaker closed.

"Keep your hands where I can see them," the angry voice demanded.

Parker held his hands out in front of him. He crossed the distance quickly, all the while feeling the mosses and lichens crunching under his feet. As he closed in on the figure, he recognized the ranger's uniform and relaxed a little.

"I said keep your hands out!" The young park ranger raised the rifle barrel slightly.

"Take it easy, ranger," Parker said, putting on his friendliest smile. "I'm FBI. I have identification."

The ranger did not relax his grip on the rifle. "Just keep your hands out and get up here on the road." He kept a sharp eye on Parker.

"Will do," Parker replied flatly. He stepped onto the road to face the ranger. "ID's in my back pocket."

Keeping the rifle at the ready, the ranger circled behind Parker. He dipped a hand into Parker's back pocket and extracted the wallet. He flipped it open and scrutinized the picture identification.

"What the hell were you doing out there?" The ranger's voice was less pissed-off.

"I heard some rifle shots. When I got up here I saw about four, maybe five figures move around that granite outcropping," Parker responded, pointing.

The ranger stared hard in that direction.

"Can I put my hands down?" Parker asked.

"Give me those binoculars," the ranger said reaching

for them.

Obediently, Parker pulled them from around his neck and handed them over. The ranger studied the distant tundra through them in silence.

Parker put his hands on his hips. "What's going on up here, anyway?" he asked.

"I'm not sure," said the ranger, lowering the binoculars. "We won't get to them from here anyway. Give me your keys. I'll drive."

"You'll drive? Parker raised his eyebrows. "What do you mean you'll drive?"

"They're heading down toward Bear Lake. We'll make better time getting to them by the main road."

Parker shook his head and pulled the keys from his pocket. This wasn't the way he planned to spend his long overdue vacation. He tossed the keys to the ranger who pushed ahead of him for the Range Rover. Parker studied the ranger a little more closely from behind. Though not quite as tall as Parker was, the ranger certainly carried more muscle mass. Parker admired the ranger's thick calf and thigh muscles which rippled with every step. He wore bulky hiking shorts above knee-high wool socks.

Parker climbed into the passenger seat of the Range Rover and smiled at the ranger's freckled, ruddy face. "An introduction would be nice," he said.

"Eric Borenson," the ranger responded, pulling back his parka hood. He smoothed down a mass of reddish-blonde hair with a freckled hand. "Park ranger."

"That I gathered," Parker said with a slight chuckle.

He reached out and accepted the ranger's strong handshake. Eric-the-Red, he thought to himself. Good Viking stock. He stopped himself from staring and held on as the Rover careened out onto the roadway.

"Seriously, Eric, what gives? Why were you shooting at those people?"

"I wasn't the one doing the shooting, Agent White," Eric responded. "I have enough sense not to discharge a firearm while standing under a glacier."

Parker suppressed a laugh. "I'm glad you told me that," he said, unsnapping his windbreaker to reveal the Smith & Wesson. "And it's Parker. You don't call me Agent White, and I won't call you Ranger Borenson."

The young ranger looked at him. Parker swore he caught a brief smile.

"Deal." Eric said, pulling the Rover sharply around a ninety-degree turn.

"Easy on the tires, Eric. I put a deposit on this thing."

"Put it on your expense account," Eric said, letting the wheels squeal through another turn.

"I don't have an expense account. I'm on vacation," Parker said, gripping the door. "How did you get up here anyway? Where's your transportation?"

"I'm on foot," Eric replied, trying to concentrate on his driving.

"You have a station nearby?"

"Down on the main road. You passed it when you entered the park."

"Damn!" Parker looked at the ranger admiringly. "That's one hell of a hike."

"You get used to it in the Park Service," Eric said. "You get up in the mountains much?"

"First time. I just flew into Denver a couple of hours ago." Parker responded.

"You'd better take it easy up here for the first couple of days."

"You're probably right," Parker said. He pulled his

eyes away from Eric's groin, and wondered if there was any part of the well-developed ranger's body that didn't bulge.

Parker shook himself. He had pretty much put his personal life on hold since being accepted to the Bureau under the new Congressional anti-discrimination policies. He had certainly not tried to hide the fact that he was gay, but solidifying his dream career had taken his full attention. He smiled, remembering he was on vacation now.

"How long you been in the service?" Parker asked.

"Since college," Eric said. His eyes remained glued to the winding road.

"So it's been about . . ." Parker's voice trailed into a question.

Eric shook his head, but kept his gaze forward. "I'm twenty-seven, okay?"

"Just wanted to be sure you were covered on the insurance," Parker said. He tested the security of his seat belt as the wheels screamed around another curve in their speeding descent down the mountain road.

"I thought you FBI guys were trained to assess a person on sight."

"We are, and I have," Parker said. "It's just nice to pin down some of the facts." He was still trying to decide if the younger man's hair was red or blond, but it kept changing with the shifting sunlight.

Eric's eyes darted for a second in Parker's direction. "Let me know when you've finished your assessment," he said, and returned his gaze to the road.

"Sorry . . . habit." Parker blinked. "Besides, I don't put much stock in instant first impressions."

Eric laughed again. Parker found it a pleasant sound.

"Yeah?" Eric pursed his lips. "I'd say you're early thirties, short, dark-brown hair, blue eyes . . ." He glanced over at Parker's amused expression, and quickly returned his attention to the road. "Electric blue, I believe they call it. About six-three. Two hundred pounds, maybe two-ten. You should work out more."

"Ouch!" Parker grimaced.

"You're from the South," Eric continued, eyes on the road. "Probably Texas, and your carrying a Smith & Wesson semi-automatic stuck in your pants." The Rover jolted over a pot hole. "And I hope the safety's on."

Parker glanced down self-consciously. "Thanks for noticing." He turned sideways in the seat. "And I'm from West Virginia."

"Born?" Eric asked with a frown.

"Well, the last four or five years, anyway."

Eric's perfect teeth flashed as his wide mouth broke into a grin. "Texas. I knew it." He pulled off the main road and shifted the Range Rover to negotiate the now rising slope of the roadway.

"Where does this head?" Parker asked.

"Bear Lake."

"Ah." Parker nodded at the sign which confirmed that fact as it flashed past the speeding Rover.

He reached back to retrieve the shotgun Eric had tossed into the back seat before commandeering the Rover. He admired its clean line and bolted the chamber to check its ammunition load. "Nice weapon. You expecting an elephant?" Parker asked.

Eric cocked an eyebrow. "Up here it's best to be prepared . . . for anything."

They pulled into an expansive, circular parking lot, filled with busses of arriving and departing tourists. Eric spun the Rover up to the front of a small information booth. He grabbed his shotgun from Parker and bolted out the door. Eric approached the booth and waved to a young woman inside. Parker followed tentatively.

"Got some possible poachers on the slopes above the lake, Alice," Eric called out.

"Need some back up?" She called back with a worried expression.

"Nah." Eric gave her a thumbs up. "Got a Fed with me. We'll check it out." He sprinted for the hiking path up ahead.

Parker stood planted, hands on hips.

"Come on, dude!" Eric called to him. "We might still have time to catch up to them."

"Slow down a minute, Eric." Parker trudged up the path toward him. "I think the lady's right. We should call some of your men up here to help. I'm hardly dressed to go crashing through the Rocky Mountains looking for poachers."

"We don't have time," Eric said impatiently. "And you know damned well they're not poachers. You should be prepared, dude. What the hell did they send you up here for? Now, come on. We've got a job to do."

Parker held up his hand. "*You've* got a job to do," he said. "Look, I'm up here on vacation. I don't know what the hell you're talking about," he said.

Eric stared at him wide-eyed. "Shit!" Eric almost spat. He turned and sprinted up the hiking path.

"Hey, wait a minute!" Parker yelled. He started after Eric. "Remember, I need to take it easy."

Eric slowed to let Parker catch up to him. "Don't worry," he said, patting a leather pack attached to his belt. "I've got a small oxygen inhaler. Taking a hit from it every fifteen minutes or so should stave off any altitude sickness."

Parker was already panting. "Well, don't go bounding around this place like a mountain goat. I don't have your legs."

Eric laughed and sprinted up the path ahead of Parker. "Thanks for noticing," he called back, mimicking Parker's earlier tone.

Parker did his best to match the pace Eric set. At least they were sticking to the trail. Their path was soon broken by a fast moving, shallow stream about ten feet across. He could hear a roar close by and deduced the water climaxed in an impressive fall not far downstream.

Parker bent over, panting. "How about a whiff of that oxygen," he managed to sputter.

Eric extracted a small silver canister from its hip holster. "Okay, now," he said. "You need to straighten up and breathe deeply." He put a hand on Parker's shoulder.

Parker obeyed slowly and, with effort, managed to get his breathing under control.

Eric held the canister under Parker's nose. "Now take a long, deep breath." He pressed a lever on the canister and it hissed softly.

Parker inhaled deeply. He could feel his head clear almost instantly. "Damn! That's good stuff," he said, exhaling slowly.

"You're keeping up pretty well for an out-of-shape, old man," Eric said without sarcasm.

Parker grabbed the hand holding the canister and forced another expulsion of oxygen sucking it in hungrily. "I tell you what," he said. "After I get out of the hospital, I'll go ten rounds on the mat with you any day you choose."

Eric ignored him, jerking the small canister away. He leapt across the running water from exposed rock to exposed rock. "You're on," he said, arriving at the other side effortlessly. He returned the canister to its holster. "Now get your butt in gear and come on."

Parker stumbled across the stream, cursing as the tip of his boot slipped into the cold water. He scrambled up the creek bank and stomped the water from his boot. Eric watched from a safe distance, shaking his head at the city dweller.

"What's next?" Parker asked, barely missing Eric with a twig kicked up with his wet boot. "Swing across a gorge on vines?"

"We're wasting time," Eric replied. He turned and bounded up the path again.

Parker started after, determined not to lag behind.

Eric suddenly veered off the main path and cut smoothly into the dense underbrush. Parker followed. He hoped the underbrush would slow them down a bit, but Eric leapt over fallen trees and swept through obstructing brush concentrations like a hart on the run.

"How much farther?" Parker called out to Eric who was now a good twenty yards ahead.

"We should be able to intercept the shooters on the other side of Bear Creek Canyon." Before disappearing from view, Eric added, "I hope you're not afraid of heights!"

Parker could hear the words echoing hollowly up ahead. "What the hell," he muttered under his breath. He stumbled out of the brush into open air and felt the ground beneath him give way.

"Fuuu—" Before he could finish the expletive, Parker felt a powerful arm wrap around his waist and jerk him back. The breath exploded from his mouth as he was pulled tightly up against Eric, whose other arm was wrapped securely about a small Aspen.

Parker stared wide-eyed down the sheer embankment of the expansive gorge, a good two hundred foot drop. Parker gripped the arm about his waist tightly and fought the panic that was beginning to envelope him. He shut his eyes tightly and tried to concentrate on the feel of Eric's breath, hot against his neck.

"Gotcha," Eric said, steadying Parker up on the dangerously narrow path that ran along the rim of the deep gorge.

Parker reached for a hold on one of the small trees and thrust his free elbow back into Eric's solar plexus. He felt the younger man's stomach muscles harden like a brick, but not before having a little of the wind knocked out of him.

Eric pulled back, half laughing, half gasping. "What was that for?" he asked, rubbing his stomach. "I saved your life."

Parker struggled to regain his composure. "You're the asshole who put it in danger in the first place."

"I'm used to moving about alone up here," Eric said evenly. "I'll have to get used to looking out after someone else."

"I can look after myself, mountain boy." Parker spat into the gorge. "A little timely warning and I would have been just fine."

"Now, stay still so I can get around you." Eric stifled another laugh.

Parker gripped the small Aspen tightly as Eric reached around him for another hand hold. The path was barely wide enough for one man, much less two. As Eric squeezed around him, Parker took the opportunity for a closer inspection of his younger nemesis. He knew the young man was well built, but he had no idea how powerfully until he actually felt the rippled steel that inched closely around him. He smiled at the thought of reaching out and pulling those narrow hips up against him, but the prospect of losing his handhold kept his urges in check. Eric's face brushed across his own and Parker breathed in the clean, warm scent of the younger man.

"All right, let's get going," Eric said, gripping the tree on the other side of Parker and swinging the rest of the way around. "Keep a hand hold on the trees as you move along."

"Some things I don't need to be told," Parker replied, following.

They moved with surprising speed along the embankment.

Eric kept a close eye on Parker's progress. "Doing good, old man," he called back, increasing the pace slightly.

"Bite me!" Parker answered with a smirk. He stumbled over a protruding rock, but didn't lose his handhold. "Goddamn it!" He rejoined the pace. "Now, how much farther?"

"The gorge narrows up ahead, and we can cross."

Parker squinted up the gorge and saw where the side walls seemed to curve inward on each other. As they neared the crossing point, he saw that a pine had toppled across the gorge, spanning the distance from one side to the other. Still, the distance across was a good fifteen to twenty feet.

Parker stopped in his tracks. "Boy, you've got to be

crazy!" he said, shaking his head.

"You'll make it," Eric said. He gave the tree trunk a few pushes with his foot, testing its resilience. "There. It's still plenty solid."

"When was the last time you crossed this thing?"

"Last Spring."

"Shit!"

"It's still in good condition," Eric said. "We won't have any problems."

Parker shook his head. "I'd rather swing on a vine."

"Now don't be such a wussy, Mr. FBI man." Eric stepped out onto the natural bridge. "Remember, Truth, Justice, and the American Way."

"That's Superman, you twit," Parker replied, taking note of each step Eric took out onto the tree trunk. "I'm just an underpaid civil servant."

Eric moved gracefully across the trunk, arms outstretched, in perfect balance. "You want underpaid, try being a park ranger." He stepped easily off onto the other side of the gorge. "Your turn."

Parker stared at Eric like the man was an idiot. Still he stepped up onto the tree trunk, taking a moment to find his center of gravity. It's just like the obstacle course back at the FBI's Quantico training facility he tried to tell himself. He had always raced through the obstacle course without a problem.

He looked down. "Holy shit!"

"Don't look down!" Eric called out.

Parker gave him another one of his looks. "No shit, Yogi."

"Come on." Eric shot him the bird. "Quit wasting time."

"Or is it Boo-Boo," Parker muttered under his breath.

He moved out onto the trunk keeping his eyes on his feet and narrowing his peripheral vision to block out the gorge depths on either side. "When I get over there I'm gonna shove that finger up your pretty little nose," Parker said, narrowing his eyes at Eric.

"That's assuming you make it over." Eric laughed.

Parker moved over the center of the tree trunk and could feel it give slightly.

"That's just the natural give of the wood to your weight," Eric called out as Parker stopped. "Keep moving."

"If this thing breaks," Parker said, taking a few steps. "I *will* live long enough to kill you."

"Quit whining and come on," Eric chided.

Parker ignored the last few steps and jumped the remaining distance to the other side. He landed on his feet, much to his surprise.

"Very impressive." Eric turned and headed toward a stand of pines. Parker caught his breath, and started after him. The ground began to slope downward and Parker found it easier to keep up with Eric's pace. There was little underbrush at the base of the pines and he was able to keep just a few feet behind the younger man.

Eric stopped suddenly.

"What is it?" Parker narrowly missed crashing into him.

"Over here." Eric broke into a run.

Parker followed him out of the trees toward a tower rock face. At its base, Parker spotted what Eric was headed for. They dropped to their knees together beside the bodies.

Parker checked for a carotid pulse on the larger male. "Dead," he said.

Eric rolled the other, smaller form over. "She's the same. Shot in the back of the head."

"Who are they?" Parker asked checking the man's pockets for identification. "What the hell are they doing out here?"

"Rock climbers." Eric said, fingering the collection of pitons and carabiners clipped to the dead man's belt. He stood up and looked about. "The rest of their gear ought to be around here close by."

"Well, now we know what the bad guys were shooting at," Parker said, also standing. "But why?"

Eric pointed to a set of tire prints running down to a clearing below. "Four-wheeler," he said.

"Listen," Parker said. He cocked an ear up and listened silently to the low hum echoing in the distance beyond the horizon of the tree line. "That's a helicopter."

"Goddamnit!" Eric stood, hands on hips, shaking his head.

"My guess is these two were in the wrong place at the wrong time." Parker looked down at the bodies. "They saw something they shouldn't have."

"Come on, we'd better head back," Eric said.

"Now?" Parker followed him a little way.

"We've got to get a team up here to retrieve the bodies," Eric said.

"This is a crime scene," Parker admonished. "I had better stay and secure the area."

"You're right." Eric nodded. "I'll probably make better time on my own anyway."

"I hope you fall on your ass in the gorge." Parker gave Eric's shoulder a hard shove.

Eric laughed and started for the trees.

"Hey, how about leaving me that oxygen," Parker

called after him.

"Try breathing this clean, fresh mountain air instead," Eric replied breaking into a run.

Parker watched Eric bounding toward the trees like a Viking warrior, khaki shorts straining against a butt that must have been carved out of Carrara marble.

"Damn," Parker said with a slight smile, watching closely after this vision. "I'm gonna chip a piece of that off before this is over," he muttered under his breath.

CHAPTER 2

"Sorry, guys." Parker studied the small group gathered around the rough-hewn table. "But you're overlooking one important point. I'm on vacation. I'm off duty."

The assembly of men and one woman showed no evidence of registering this point.

"Besides, most of the dirty work is already wrapped-up on this one," Parker said.

That much was true. Retrieval of the bodies had been accomplished in a Life Flight chopper from Valley Hospital in Denver. By the time the investigative team had assembled and arrived from the local sheriff, Park Service, and Denver FBI, Parker had already made a thorough ground search around the crime scene. All it netted was a few .308 shell casings, identification and motel key of the victims, and a clear set of tire prints for casting.

"Maybe things are a little different in Washington," Eric said from the corner of the room where he sat arms folded, growing more sullen as the conversation progressed. "But around here we don't consider things *wrapped up* until the killers are caught."

Parker sighed again and rolled his eyes. "Far be it from me to disillusion your fresh-aired naiveté, but shit happens," he said. "You don't have a single lead to pursue here. Denver FBI can look into the helicopter and four-wheeler angle and maybe, but that's a thin maybe, give you a direction of inquiry. This is not the usual neighborhood murder that you can wrap up by arresting the ex-husband."

"So we shouldn't even try?" Eric's sarcasm was palpable.

"Look," Parker replied sharply. These murders weren't premeditated. They were a matter of momentary necessity from the look of things . . . two people in the wrong place at the wrong time. They have no direct connection to the murderers. Unless you can open up some tangible line of inquiry, you'll just be wasting time, resources, and manpower. These guys will not be returning to the scene of the crime."

"Well, the newspapers will love that explanation," Eric said. "Sorry, some murder you *can* get away with."

"I'm afraid the ranger is right on this one," Sheriff Jenner said. "Tourism is the life blood around here. The public must see a concerted effort by law enforcement to investigate this crime. At least we have to be able to assure people that this won't happen again."

The only female in the group stood. "We have to admit here, gentleman," she began, "that neither this county nor the Park Service has the resources to mount such a criminal investigation." She straightened her lithe, well-proportioned figure and adjusted the braided bun in her honey blonde hair. "This is a Federal problem."

"Margaret." Sheriff Jenner looked her over. "You've been a federal prosecutor in this district for almost six years now. You and I both know that this may be Federal jurisdiction, but it's also a local problem."

"I won't argue with you there, Don," she responded, parting her red lips in a sparkling smile. "But Agent White needs to understand why the Bureau needs to handle the heavy logistics here."

Parker shook his head. "I think the Park Service might view that differently as they have the true jurisdiction in the matter," he said. "I'm sure even Ranger Borenson would prefer not to have FBI agents in dark suits stomping all over his precious tundra."

Eric ignored him.

"Besides," Parker continued, pacing over to the window, impatient, "Agents Stern and Avery can assist you from the Federal side."

"We're rather short-handed at the Denver office right now, Mr. White." Agent Stern shifted in his chair. "Everyone's been pulled over to Salt Lake to work that post office bombing."

Parker stared down at the baby-faced, rookie G-Man. He wondered if they had just been left behind to answer the phones. "Appearance is what counts on this one, Agent Stern," Parker assured him. "It's a chance to get your name in the papers."

Eric shot up and kicked his chair backwards. "Goddamn it, people!" His voice full of anger. "Instead of appearances, can we try for a little substance here?" He rounded the table to face Parker. "These killers are not going away. They've been up to something in the high range for some two months now." He poked a finger at Parker's chest. "They'll be back all right, just to a different area of the park."

Parker looked down at the finger and then leaned in nose-to-nose with Eric. He took hold of the offending finger. "Boy," he said low and even. "I'd be careful with this if I were you. I'd shove it up your ass, but I don't think there's room in there what with your head and all."

Eric jerked his hand away and glared at Parker. "Fuck you, White!"

Parker couldn't discern if what he was now feeling was anger or horniness. "Come on, kid." He beckoned with his hands. "You want a piece of this?"

Eric stood his ground. "You want to mess with me, old man?" Eric asked. His muscles flexed ominously.

Margaret pushed in between them. "Now, you two bucks just let all that testosterone cool down a minute." She wiggled in the tight space between their heated bodies and smiled seductively up at them. "Or we could just stay cozy like this."

Parker backed away from the table and took a deep breath to calm his racing pulse. He tried to glare at Eric, but all he could see was that tense, taught body poised and ready for action. He shook his head and turned to Sheriff Jenner. "What does he mean about their being in the park before? Have there been other murders?"

"No, no, no. Nothing but conjecture." Jenner stretched back in his chair with a shrug.

"Someone's been operating up in the tundra for two months now," Eric protested. "Everyone here has read my reports. If we had mounted an investigation when I first reported these incidents, we might have avoided all this."

"What incidents?" Parker threw up his hands. "What am I missing here?"

"What Ranger Borenson is referring to is most likely unrelated to these murders," Sheriff Jenner began.

"Bullshit, and all of you know it." Eric brushed past Parker to glare out of the picture window.

Sheriff Jenner raised a bushy, white eyebrow. "What's got the ranger so upset," he said, "are the dozen or so reports he's filed alleging various incidents of illegal access to restricted areas of the park by person or persons unknown."

"It's the same people," Eric said, pointedly keeping his gaze out the window.

"I really don't know how you can say that, Borenson." The Sheriff shuffled through some papers. "We get a ton of reports every season of stubborn or just ignorant tourists who wander, on purpose or not, off the main paths in the name of curiosity or just a better photograph."

"Those incidents I reported are different," Eric said. "They were not routine trespass events."

"Give some specifics," Parker insisted.

"Temporary camp sites far from any road or main path," Eric responded. He turned to eye the group in earnest. "There were vehicle tracks just like the ones we found at the murder scene. They would go a short distance and then disappear, just like the murder scene, like they were dropped off out of nowhere and disappeared the same way."

"You mean helicopter?" Parker asked hesitantly.

"You tell me." Eric pointed to the papers under Sheriff Jenner's hand. "It's all in the reports."

Parker paced about the room, ignoring Eric's hard glare. He stopped behind the two junior agents. "Be that as it may, the fact remains that I am out of this picture," he insisted. "Agents Avery and Stern, here, can—"

"We really have to be getting back to the Denver office," Agent Stern said, looking up at Parker nervously. "We were only authorized to come up, check out the problem, and make a report back at the office."

"I'm authorizing you differently," Parker said flatly.

"I thought you were off duty." Eric folded his arms again.

"Look people," Parker began angrily. "I'm on vacation. I deserve this vacation. I damn well need this vacation. I—"

"Agent White?" cooed a feminine voice.

Parker turned sharply to the attractive blonde DA. She was holding out a telephone receiver to him.

"I think you'll want to take this call," she said. "It's Deputy Director Phelps." She threw him a Cheshire grin.

"I didn't hear the phone ring," Parker said, glaring at her.

"It didn't." She cocked her head and pursed her lips.

Parker closed his eyes, trying to regain his composure. He opened them again hoping daggers would target her incessant smile.

She whispered, "The Deputy Director, Agent White. Mustn't keep him waiting." She waved the phone at him.

Parker assumed his own frozen smile. "Thank you, Ms. Curry." He snatched the phone from her. "Yes, Deputy Director, this is Agent White." He listened for a moment, already knowing what was coming. "Certainly, Deputy Director . . . I understand . . . No problem . . . Yes, Sir . . . I'll certainly do that." Parker stiffly lowered the receiver and walked slowly behind the demure DA. He put a hand on the back of her chair and bent ominously over her to hang up the phone, leaning close to her ear. "Thank you, Ms. Curry," he said between clenched teeth.

She drew up her shoulders as his breath tickled her ear. "Please," she said. "Call me Margaret." She turned to him with a raised eyebrow. "We'll all be working closely together on this. Why be so formal?"

Parker straightened. "No joke." He turned to the group. "As Ms. Curry," he smiled sweetly at her, "has so quickly gathered, I've been ordered to head this investigation."

Eric leaned against the window sill. "Head the investigation or assist in it?" he asked, warily.

Parker looked at him for a moment. "It all depends on how I feel at any given moment."

Eric started to object.

"Understand this," Parker continued forcefully. "The extent of FBI jurisdiction and involvement in this case is a matter of Agency discretion. As the senior agent on the scene, that discretion is mine."

"Unless over-ruled from higher up." Margaret smiled, even in the face of Parker's homicidal glance.

The group remained silent.

"Where do we go from here?" Eric took a seat at the table.

Chief Jenner spoke. "A low profile with the media is best until we have more information as to the circumstances and motive."

"We'll have to give the sharks something," Margaret interjected, clicking her peach colored nails on the table.

"True," answered the Sheriff. "But we need to remain in control of the information flow."

"Do we have anything on the victims' backgrounds yet?" Parker asked.

The Sheriff pulled a teletype from his hodge-podge of papers. "Students from Washington State University," he said. "Nothing out of the ordinary."

Parker thought a moment. "Tell the media we're investigating the possibility that a former boyfriend, lover, whatever, may be involved," he said.

"You can't be serious!" Eric slammed a hand down on the desk.

"Look." Parker sat down at the conference table. "First, we're telling the truth. Though it is a remote possibility, it's one of the many angles we will be looking at. In the meantime, it gives the press a focus away from our main line of inquiry."

Sheriff Jenner roared with laughter. "I like it," he said decisively. "We implicate a crime of passion. It will calm the tourist trade to the possibility that this was probably an isolated, non-repeatable event."

Margaret nodded. "It ought to dampen any potential fires," she said. "As long as the investigation stays low-key. No grandstanding."

"Agreed," the Sheriff bellowed.

"God, no," Eric said, rolling his eyes up. "We wouldn't want a murder investigation to impede commerce."

"Couldn't have said it better." Sheriff Jenner smiled at the younger man.

"All right." Parker stood and checked his watch. "It's getting dark out. First thing in the morning I want to have a look at those other areas of activity you mentioned, and then have a closer look at the crime scene."

Eric also stood. "That's a good seven to eight hours of hiking high up in the tundra." He gave Parker the once over. "Are you sure you're up to it?"

Parker straightened his aching back. "I'll manage," he said.

"Then I'll get the gear together." Eric stopped at the door. "Can I ask you what you hope to find up there?"

"A motive for murder." Parker looked him in the eye.

Eric shrugged and headed out the door. Parker grabbed up his jacket and started after him.

The two rookie agents stood to follow, but Parker stopped them with a look.

"I'll call you when I need something," he said icily. He kicked his chair under the table and started to leave. A hand rested on his shoulder and Parker spun around, annoyed.

"Fast reflexes," the lady DA said, smiling up at him.

Parker looked down at her in surprise.

She tapped his chest with a long, polished nail. "I should be glad you didn't instinctively karate chop me in the throat or something," she said, "knowing how well-trained you FBI men are."

"The thought had crossed my mind," Parker responded only half-joking.

"Now, you're not still mad at me about that little phone call, are you?" She pouted seductively.

"Oh, no." Parker shook his head. "This was my first vacation in three years. The fact that you ended it for me almost the moment I set foot in town . . ." He bit his lip. "What makes you think I should be angry?"

"Exactly," she said, linking her arm in his. "And there's absolutely no way I'm going to let your vacation be spoiled. First I'm going to take you to dinner."

Parker tried not to laugh. "Dinner!" he said in disbelief. "I'm the guy who wants to assault-and-batter you, remember?"

"Then as DA around here," she pulled him toward the door, "I'll have to take you into protective custody for tonight."

"Protective custody? You're the one in danger."

"To protect you from yourself," she responded.

They exited the office arm-in-arm.

"And, who pray tell, is going to protect me from you?" Parker asked, allowing himself to be led out into the brisk, evening air.

"Now, Parker, you're a big strong FBI man." She gave his biceps a test squeeze. "What does big old you have to fear from little old me?" Her laugh was boisterous.

Against his wishes, Parker found himself liking her brassy personality. They strolled along the brick promenade that followed the banks of the Fall River which meandered through and along the main shopping district. The sidewalks were crowded with tourists still hunting a bargain.

"So, Margaret," Parker said. "What type of caseload does a district prosecutor deal with up here in the wilds of Colorado?"

Margaret sighed. "A beautiful night," she said. "Moonlight, a stroll along the river walk, and G-Man here wants to know what my criminal case load is."

"Just trying to make conversation."

Margaret stepped in front of him, stopping their leisurely stroll. "Am I boring you?" She stood on her tiptoes and glared at his face.

"Anything but," Parker said, trying not to laugh.

She nodded and sank back to her heels. "You may talk to me about important things then." She linked her arm with his and they continued along the promenade.

"Like, is there anyone special in my life? Do I want children?"

"Oh, is that what I'm supposed to do?"

Margaret groaned. "No, it's not what you're *supposed* to do," she said. "For crying out loud, don't you ever do anything impulsively because you want to?"

"I see," Parker answered with teasing insistence. "So you're saying you want me to—"

"No!" Margaret stopped him again. "Look, I had four brothers. You may be too beautiful to kill . . ." She reared back with a roundhouse fist. "But, I can damn sure—"

Parker threw an arm about her waist and grabbed the fist before she could follow through. He hummed a tune and began to waltz her about the promenade.

She laughed with delight as they tumbled onto a park bench. The loose bun her hair had been restrained in was precariously close to unraveling.

"I've messed up your hair." Parker eyed it warily.

"Impossible," Margaret said. She reached up and pulled a pin from her loosening hair.

With a toss of her head a shower of glistening blonde cascaded down about her shoulders.

She laughed at Parker's surprise. "Yes," she said. "I was hiding my true beauty under that cold, professional exterior."

Parker cocked his head at her. "I don't think you could hide that, hair up or down," he said with a smile.

"How sweet." Margaret batted her lashes at him. "There *is* an impulsive side as well." She pushed her hair back off her shoulders. "And here I was beginning to think you were just full of federal red-tape."

"That's a nice way of putting it."

Margaret linked her arm through his and snuggled

against his shoulder. "I'm a very good judge of people, you know." She played with the ringless, third finger of his right hand.

"I don't doubt that," Parker agreed. He watched her with some amusement.

"It's just part of my job," she continued.

"Do tell."

"And I'm very good at my job."

"I can see that," Parker said.

Margaret turned his hand over and seemed to study his palm intently. "Let's see." She batted her eyelashes at him. "You waltz, you hum show tunes—"

"Show tunes?"

"Please . . . *The King and I?*"

Parker started to laugh.

"You're over thirty," she continued. "You're not married. Ever been married?"

"Nope," he said, trying not to have any eye contact with her.

"Hmm," Margaret droned. "Never been married. You wear boxer briefs."

"Now wait just a minute." Parker scooted across the bench from her in mock indignation, inspecting his palm. "How would you know that?"

"I felt you up."

Parker's hands went defensively to his crotch. "Bullshit!" He couldn't help laughing.

"I did . . . when we were dancing."

"Liar!" Parker reached over and gave her hair a good tug.

"Okay, okay." Margaret laughed and punched at his arm. "But I did manage to give your butt a little pat. I felt the panty line."

"Men don't wear panties."

"Some do." She gave him a knowing look. "Anyway, it all means you're either God's chosen messiah to all women, and I found you first . . . or—"

"Or what?"

She spun around on the bench and stretched out, laying her head back in his lap.

"Or you're gay." She looked up at him.

"Interesting." Parker watched the crowd milling about. "I see you're a connoisseur of stereotype, as well."

"Aha!"

"Aha?" Parker said, mocking.

Margaret reached up and poked him under the chin with a fingernail. "Exhibit six," she said. "You're not protesting loudly, scratching your crotch, and earnestly professing your expert ability to prove your manhood to me."

"Would you like that?"

"Well, yes," she said, wagging a finger at him.

"Mere circumstantial evidence, counselor." Parker looked down at her with a teasing smile.

"Confess, Agent White." She gave his stomach a playful punch.

Parker expressed a feigned moan, and rubbed his belly. "Confess what?" he asked.

"Damn!" Margaret rolled her eyes. "Am I or am I not the luckiest woman in the world tonight, or am I destined to go home frustrated and depressed."

Parker merely batted his own eyelashes at her. "There's no reason for you to be depressed."

"I knew it!" Margaret moaned loudly. "Life is so unfair."

"Certainly not to you."

She turned over into a fetal position, nestling in his lap. "Don't talk to me, I'm being depressed."

"I thought you were hungry." Parker laughed.

"Oh, yeah." She sat up quickly and gave him a kiss on the cheek. "Oh, well. A girl needs something to keep her warm."

"Oh, I'd say you were pretty hot already."

"Of course, it doesn't matter to me, you know." Margaret took his arm and pulled it around her shoulder.

"Oh, God." Parker rolled his eyes. "Here it comes."

"What?"

"Some of your best friends are gay," he said, shaking his head.

"Well it's true." She pressed her head against his shoulder. "I like gay men. Gay men are a woman's best friend, and vice versa."

"You can keep us as pets, and feed and—"

She hammered a fist at his stomach again. "Don't put words in my mouth," she said over his laughter.

"Okay, okay," he said. "No more hitting. If you prick us, do we not bleed?"

Margaret held up the hairpin she still clutched. "Keep it up and we'll find out."

"I'm shutting up," Parker said.

Margaret nodded satisfied. "Come on." She jumped up and pulled him with her. "This place has great manicotti."

"Looks like there'll be a long wait," Parker said as they entered the small restaurant's crowded foyer.

"Don't worry about it," Margaret whispered in a conspiratorial tone. "I know the owner." She pulled him along the wall circumventing the crowd into the dining room. "That table's empty," she said, pointing with one hand and pulling Parker with the other.

"Shouldn't we wait to be seated?"

"Lines are for tourists," she answered, taking a seat. She grabbed at a young waiter walking by. "We'll have the manicotti and a piece of Italian sausage for two," she ordered. "And a carafe of the house chardonnay."

The waiter nodded and left quickly.

"I like red with pasta," Parker objected.

"Don't confuse me."

"Oh, so all gay men drink white wine." Parker rolled his eyes.

Margaret laughed and shook her head. "You're not very good at this are you?"

"Not very good at what?" Parker's eyebrows went up.

"Being gay. You have a lot to learn."

"And you're going to teach me."

"Now don't get me wrong." It was her turn to laugh. "You're terribly tall, dark and handsome. But you're just a little too . . . too—"

"Stereotypically straight looking?"

"Yeah." She winked at him.

"I see I'm a miserable failure." Parker gave her his hurt puppy look.

"Let's examine the facts, honey." She patted his hand. "You did end up attracting me with your charms, and you really should have been attracting someone like . . ."

The young waiter brought them their wine. Margaret gave the nervous young man a good going over as he filled their glasses. Parker watched her examination with amusement. As the waiter turned to leave, Margaret's gaze appreciated how the tight black rayon trousers hugged the waiter's firm buttocks.

"Mmm," she said nodding. "Something like that."

Parker chuckled.

"Don't you think he's cute?" Margaret's eyes shot back in the young waiter's direction. "I think he's cute."

"He's a little young, don't you think?"

"If he's serving wine here he's over eighteen," Margaret said, finally returning her gaze to Parker.

"You don't think eighteen's a little young?"

"Hell, no!" Margaret took a sip of wine. She threw her head back to let the wine trickle down her throat. "They're just peaking then."

"I see, ripe for the picking."

"That one was damn ripe, if you ask me." She wrinkled her nose and shook off the chill of the wine. "I'd love to keep a few eighteen-year-olds in my stable."

"And what would you do with an eighteen-year-old?" Parker was beginning to think she was a lot of fun.

"Honey." She leaned forward and took his hand. "What could you *not* do with an eighteen-year-old?"

Parker laughed louder than he intended.

"Ah!" Margaret nodded her satisfaction. "Made you think didn't I?"

"Don't be ridiculous."

"You're on vacation. Loosen up."

"I *was* on vacation, you mean." Parker wrinkled his brow at her.

"Now, don't go getting bitchy again," she said, refilling his glass. "All is not lost. You're going up into the mountains tomorrow, hiking, camping. And with that dream-boat park ranger. God, what I wouldn't give to share a tent stake with him. And I've tried, let me tell you. He's always got an excuse, always . . ." She stopped herself, taking note of Parker's interested attention. "Aha!"

"What now?" Parker stiffened.

"You had me fooled."

"What the hell are you getting off on now?" He shrugged.

"You win," Margaret said. Her face broke into a big smile. "Queen-for-the-day. I am impressed."

"She speaks English and I still can't understand her." Parker groaned.

"Don't play the unspotted virgin with me, Bucko." She took his hand and leaned across the table. "You're gonna make a play for Eric, the mountain god, aren't you?"

"Who?" he asked, full of innocence.

"I thought there was a lot of . . . tension going on between the two of you earlier. She sat back and hugged herself. "Agent Dreamboat, meet Ranger Gorgeous."

Parker refused to take the bait. He sipped his wine with seeming disinterest. "How you do go on," is all he would say.

"Not as far as you apparently," she cooed.

He almost spit his wine.

"Exhibit 7!" She nodded excitedly.

"I don't even know this Ranger Borenson well," Parker insisted.

"I'm remembering it all now," Margret said excitedly. "Every time Eric would walk away from you, you'd be staring after him." She paused, eyes widening. "You were staring at his butt."

"Oh, please," Parker groaned.

"You did, I saw you."

They were momentarily interrupted by the arrival of the pasta.

"This looks good," Parker said when the waiter finally

left. He reached for his fork.

"Don't change the subject, Agent White," Margaret said. "This interrogation is not over. I want to know everything."

Parker pointed to his mouth full of manicotti and shrugged.

"I'll be damned," Margaret continued, ignoring him. "Eric Borenson. No wonder I couldn't get him on a date."

Parker almost choked. "Oh right," he managed to say. "He wasn't attracted to you, so obviously he must be gay. That's your reasoning?"

Margaret smoothed her dress under her ample breasts and looked at him from under long lashes. "If I were a man, could you resist all this?" she asked.

"If you were a man?" Parker chuckled. "In a word . . . yes."

"You could?" She looked crestfallen. "Why?"

"Too nelly."

They both reared back laughing. The other patrons began to look over at them.

Margaret shushed him and took his hand again. "All right," she said. "I'll change the subject if you promise me one thing."

"If you'll change the subject? Anything."

"When you come down from the mountain with the good ranger," she clutched Parker's hand to her breasts, "we have a dinner date."

"Done."

"I'm not through."

Parker rolled his eyes. "What else?" he asked.

"You promise to tell me everything."

"Everything?"

"Everything . . . and I mean everything."

Parker shrugged and took a sip of his wine.

"Oh please, please, please, please, please," she begged. "Girlfriends should share everything. It's a bonding thing."

"Everything?"

"Even the smallest detail," she said excitedly. "No matter how boring."

"What makes you think it might be boring?" He gave her a leering look.

"My, my!" She straightened and gave him a surprised look. "Aren't we the confident one?"

Parker reached out to flick the end of her nose with his finger. "I'm an FBI agent, ma'am," he said with his most southern drawl.

"So?" She kissed the tip of his finger.

"We always get our man," he said, blinking innocently.

Margaret almost fell out of her chair with laughter.

CHAPTER 3

Every bone and joint in Parker's body ached. He wished now that he had never asked to make the long trek in the first place. It certainly never occurred to him that retracing the path of the shooters he had witnessed would have taken an entire day of hard trudging, climbing, insects, and a particular close call with a large, antlered and horny moose.

Parker dropped to his knees in the soft moss and let the heavy backpack fall from his shoulders. "Couldn't we have brought a pack mule or something? This thing weighs a hundred pounds," he said wearily.

"You're carrying a standard load so quit whining." Eric hoisted the even larger pack from his back and eased it onto the ground.

Parker fingered a small smooth rock, mentally gauging the distance to the back of Eric's head. Instead, he sat back onto the moss bed and rubbed his shoulders. "This is the murder site?" He looked about them. Everything seemed different.

Eric pointed to a spot of higher ground. "The rock

face the climbers use is another hundred feet up," he said.
"This is the common camp ground, so I thought we'd set
up here before looking about."

"You allow camping up here?"

"By special permit." Eric rifled through his backpack.
"It's really just for the rock climbers . . . the real fanatics.
They'd probably try to camp out up here anyway so it was
just more prudent to set aside a small spot for tent and
campfire, and leave them regular supplies of firewood."

"Give them an inch so they don't take a mile." Parker
shivered slightly. "Speaking of campfires, how cold will it
get tonight?"

Eric busied himself connecting fly poles for the small
dome tent. "You'll keep warmer if I don't tell you," he
said. "Besides, it's not the cold so much as the wind you
have to worry about up here."

"How long before dark?" Parker watched the young
ranger deftly raise the tent and stake it down. "I'd like to
go over the murder site up there once more."

Eric looked up from his work. "I don't quite
understand why you want to do that again," he said.
"Surely you don't expect to find anything useful that the
sheriff's men missed?"

"I just want to be sure." Parker scratched at the soil
with a finger. "I'll sleep better after I've gone over
everything myself."

Eric finished the staking and moved over to the small
hole etched out of the hard soil and surrounded by rocks.
"What's bothering you about it?" He tossed a few pieces
of the cut wood stacked neatly beside the fire site.

"Well, you remember how the victims' gear and all
was thrown about and torn up? I'm thinking someone
was looking for something in particular—and in a big

hurry."

"I see what you're saying," Eric said. "But what? What would they be looking for?"

"That's the question. Perhaps either our rock climbers were not as innocent as we think, or else the murderers thought the climbers had found something that didn't belong to them."

"Sounds like a pretty deep fishing hole to me."

"Anything else we need to do to set up camp?" Parker asked. He stood and looked up the hill toward the rock face.

"Nah, we're in good shape," Eric replied. "I'll start a fire if you're ready to eat."

"If you don't mind," Parker said, "I'd rather take another look around up there." He started up the hill.

"Suit yourself." Eric stood to follow. "But I think this ground's been gone over thoroughly."

By the time they reached the small pebble-strewn plateau beneath the rock face, Parker was breathing heavily.

"Don't be in such a hurry," Eric warned. "You still haven't adjusted to the altitude."

Parker filled his lungs deeply. "I don't think I ever will." He tried to study the scene with a fresh perspective.

"I still don't know why you wanted to come back up here," Eric said. "Nothing's changed."

"Elementary, my dear, Watson." A sudden inspiration moved Parker closer to the mounded boulders littering the base of the rock face. "We really only searched a limited area up here, and then only from the perspective of a murder scene."

"Yeah. So?"

Parker climbed in among the boulders. "We didn't

look in here." He studied the ground around, between and behind the large rocks.

Eric stood by watching. "What the hell do you expect to turn up in there?" he asked.

"If you stop standing around gabbing, we'll both find out the answer to that question," Parker said, scrambling up onto one of the larger boulders.

"Where do you want me to start?" Eric asked.

"Down there." Parker motioned to the other end of the rock face. "We'll work towards the center."

Eric made his way to the appointed starting place. He inched his way among the boulders, carefully eyeing the nooks and crannies between the rocks and the visible ground below. His movements dislodged several smaller stones and Eric scrambled back out of the path of a zigzagging streak of brown. The scorpion's tail hooked over its back, poised at the ready, as it retreated into the dark recesses of the rocks.

"Hey, G-Man!" Eric raised his head above the rocks. "Are you allergic to insect bites?"

"Am I what?" Parker stood from behind a large boulder.

"Never mind," Eric hollered out, smiling to himself. He dropped back behind the rocks.

Two large boulders jutted from the base of the rock face wedged in a V formation. Eric stood up on a small rock near them and was just able to see across their top. Noting a deep well-like space formed in the center of the triangle of rock, he pulled himself up onto the flat surface of one of the cold, granite boulders.

The sun was down well behind the climbing face placing the boulder field at the foot of the cliff in full shadow. Eric tried to peer into the space between the rocks, but it was just too dark. Keeping a hand hold on the rock, he wrestled a match from a small pocket in his safari shorts. He struck the match head against the rock and lowered it into the small crevice, following the flickering light with his eyes.

Before a gust of cold wind funneled into the crevice to extinguish the match, Eric glimpsed a rough, brown bundle about the size of a backpack. "Hey!" he called out, wrestling for another match.

Parker raised his head up from among the rocks nearby. "Did you say something?" He saw Eric dangling, half on, half off a large boulder right at the base of the rock face.

"There's something down in here." Eric abandoned his one-handed effort to extract another match, and instead reached blindly down into the space.

"What is it?" Parker stumbled over the intervening rocks to Eric's position.

Eric bench pressed his entire torso up onto the boulder surface. "Grab my ankles, man," he cried out. "It's down deep, but I think I can reach it."

Parker grabbed hold of Eric's legs at the calves. He squeezed his fingers into the thick mat of coarse reddish-blonde hair that covered them. "What's it look like?" Parker asked.

"Some sort of bundle," Eric replied. Levered by Parker's weight, Eric bent head first into the crevice. "Looks like it's wrapped in burlap or something!" His voice was muffled by the surrounding rock. "It looks pretty big."

Parker stared up at the muscular buttocks straining against khaki twill inches from his face. "Just make sure it's not a rattle snake," he mumbled. He adjusted his hold

and felt the steel-banded calf muscles working beneath
his fingers, the curly hairs tickling the edges of his hand.
"Well?" he called out.

"It's stuck," Eric replied in muffled tones. "Hold on!"

Parker instinctively doubled his grip and bent his
knees to keep his weight low. He felt Eric's whole body
tense. The young ranger took a deep breath and tugged
with all his strength to dislodge the bundle. Without
warning, the heavy package shifted and the rocks released
it from its impaction. A backlash of momentum flung
Eric out of the hole, still gripping the large bundle.
Parker's knees buckled under the weight and he was
unable to adjust his stance quick enough to compensate.
He fell backwards, exhaling a loud grunt as Eric sat down
heavily on his chest.

Parker tried to catch his breath in the settling dust. He
opened his eyes facing a large jagged rock that his head
had barely missed.

"Sorry, G-Man," Eric said, dropping the heavy
burlap-bound bundle next to Parker. "Got it."

"Do you mind?" Parker slapped at the younger man's
calf. "I'd like to breath."

Eric climbed off Parker's chest onto his knees. "What
do you make of it?" He handled the large bundle, testing
its weight. "It's pretty heavy," he said, dropping the
bundle back on the ground beside Parker.

Parker sat up to take a look at the package. "I'd say
that's a motive for murder if ever I saw one." He poked
the package with his forefinger.

"What do you mean?" Eric grimaced at the package.
"What's in it?"

"Want to get high?"

"Drugs?" Eric's eyes widened.

Parker fondled the package. "Judging from the feel of the blocks inside," he said, "I'd say heroin."

"That explains a lot." Eric shook his head.

"You got that right." Parker replied. He stood, shaking the dust from his clothing. "Let's get this down to camp for a closer inspection."

Eric grabbed up the large bundle and the two men made their way through the rocks in the direction of camp. Along with the setting sun, the stiff breeze was giving way to a cold wind.

Parker became suddenly aware of the rapidly dropping temperature. "I hope that wasn't our only match you used up there," he said, sitting down beside the small pile of wood Eric had prepared earlier.

Eric dropped the large bundle beside the wood. "So what if it was," he replied, adjusting a few smaller twigs at the base of the wood pile. "Matches aren't a necessity. Weren't you ever a boy scout?"

"In a manner of speaking," Parker said, grinning suggestively. He heard the strike of a match. "Cheater."

Eric laughed and held the match against a starter plug he had inserted into the wood. Within a few minutes the fire was burning brightly, casting its warm glow on the surrounding camp.

"Got a pocket knife?" Parker asked.

Eric reached into another pocket of his shorts and tossed a heavy pocket knife to Parker.

"Need I have asked?" Parker opened the knife and cut a small slit in the burlap covering of the bundle.

"Well?"

"As I thought," Parker replied. "Blocks of raw opium. Some heroin dealer is not very amused tonight." He handed the knife back to Eric.

"I'm impressed," Eric said, returning the knife to its cozy pocket. "This was some hunch you had, searching the base of the rock face."

"That's what great detective work is all about." Parker smirked. "Blind stumbling about." He felt the heat from the fire Eric had started. "That feels good."

"What do we do now?"

Parker yawned. "Get a good night's sleep," he said. "And then get this bundle of joy safely back to town and out of circulation."

"That works for me." Eric yawned in response.

"It's getting a little nippy up here." Parker said, hugging himself against the cold. "I left my electric blanket at home."

"You'll be plenty warm inside the tent." Eric poked at the fire with a small stick.

Parker glanced over at the small tent. "Looks like awful close quarters in there," he said. "I mean for two grown men and all."

"There's more room than you might think," Eric said. "Besides, we'll need things close in to help conserve body heat."

Parker liked that idea. "And me without my jammies," he said, brightening.

Eric shook his head and gave the growing fire a poke with a handy stick. "The rations are in your pack," he said. "Let's get the food going before the sun's all the way down."

"All right!" Parker clapped his hands together and rubbed them hungrily. "Got any marshmallows?"

Eric looked dumbfounded.

"We're not gonna roast marshmallows?" Parker's smile was teasingly innocent.

Eric reached across him and pulled a can out of Parker's pack. "Beans and franks." He let it drop in Parker's lap. "Knock yourself out."

Parker eyed the can. "No steak . . . no burgers...not even a hot dog?"

"They're in the can," Eric said, pointing.

"How do we get them out of the can?" Parker's stomach growled.

Eric retrieved the pocket knife from his shorts. He snapped open what looked like a hook with a knife point. "Here." He took Parker's hand and slapped the instrument into Parker's palm. "Open the can halfway and set it in the fire."

Parker studied the gadget in his hand. He held it at different angles about the can.

"Well?" Eric set the tin plates beside the fire, staring at Parker impatiently.

"Well." Parker pursed his lips. "I would be very interested to see how this thing works."

"Christ!" Eric grabbed the pocket knife with one hand and retrieved the can from Parker's lap with the other. "Don't you people take any survival courses in the Bureau anymore?" He stabbed the can with the point of the opener and rocked it about, rapidly opening the can.

"Sorry," Parker said. "My idea of camping is staying in a motel without snack machines."

"That's a bit unusual for a Texas boy." Eric laughed in spite of himself.

"I'm not your ordinary Texas boy." Parker poked a place for the can in the fire and waited for a response. None came.

Eric positioned the can and continued pulling eating utensils and supplies from Parker's backpack. The warmth from the small fire kept Parker near it almost as much as the heady aroma of food cooking out of doors.

The usual night sounds had begun their litany along with a few Parker could not identify. It had been a long time since he had sat by a camp fire and experienced the hypnotic surrealism firelight casts about the surrounding terrain.

"Hey, Mountain Man," Parker said, hearing something popping in the fire. "Those beans are starting to bubble."

Eric was busy laying out sleeping bags in the tent. Parker rummaged about in his pack for something to stir with and found a spoon. He stirred the contents of the can carefully, surprised at the heat generated. Suddenly he felt a presence behind him.

Before he could turn around a hand came around in front of his face holding a small squirmy snake and a loud voice yelled, "Gotcha!"

Instinctively Parker struck out with the edge of his hand, clipping his attacker's wrist and freeing the small reptile. In almost the same motion, he grasped the wrist and spun around on his buttocks, kicking out with his feet. The tall figure fell toward him. Parker shifted his weight, spinning the falling attacker so that he could secure the man in a strangle hold.

As the adrenaline cleared from Parker's vision he focused on the struggling figure he held securely in his lap. Eric struggled to speak but Parker's forearm was firmly wrapped around both his mouth and nose. When he realized who he had, Parker didn't know whether to be angry or embarrassed. For some reason, embarrassment seemed the best choice.

"Goddamn it, Eric!" Parker said, releasing his grip.

"Sorry, I didn't realize it was you." He still cradled Eric's head in his lap.

Eric did not move. "Damn that was fast," he said, taking a few gasping breaths.

Parker stared down at the surprised but beautiful face looking up at him. "Sorry, kid," he said. "Reflex I guess," he said.

Eric sat up slowly. He tested the hinge of his neck carefully. "For an old dude, you've got pretty damn good reflexes." He grinned, rubbing his neck.

"Are you okay?" Parker's hand still rested on the younger man's back.

"Nothing's broken, if that's what you mean."

"Sorry again," Parker tried to explain. "I'm a little jumpy. The last time I did a turn in the outdoors was the Travis River Murders two years ago. At least then I was in a small camper."

"I read about that. You worked that case?"

Parker patted Eric on the back before reaching to stir the beans and franks again. "I headed the special unit assigned to that investigation for a year and a half," he said.

"From what I remember that was some weird shit," Eric said.

"You got that right."

"You like that kind of work?" Eric asked.

"It's my specialty." Parker made a crazy face. "Serial killers. The kinkier the better."

"I'm starting to wonder about you." Eric reached into the fire with a pair of pliers and pulled their bubbling dinner out of the heat.

Parker laughed, rubbing his hands together in anticipation of dinner.

"How long have you been afraid of heights?" Eric asked without warning.

"What are you talking about?" Parker asked, his face darkening.

"Back there on the ledge." Eric looked at him for a moment. "The panic . . . I've seen it before."

Parker sat silently, scratching in the dirt. "Occupational hazard," he said finally. "I'll beat it."

"I've no doubt." Eric said, dropping the subject. He rubbed at his still aching shoulder. "Well, at least the snake got away unharmed."

"An FBI agent never harms the innocent," Parker said with a salute, laughing.

"Thanks a lot." Eric laughed too. He gave Parker a slap on the back. "Let's eat. I'm starved."

Eric meted out the rations of beans and franks onto the flimsy paper plates and added several rice cakes from a small plastic canister.

"Wow," Parker said without enthusiasm. "Beans, franks, and Styrofoam."

Eric handed Parker a plate. "I suppose you'd rather have a Twinkie or something comparable," he said, grimacing.

"I'll save that for desert," Parker replied. "How about some bread?"

"This is healthier."

"My system doesn't respond well to healthy stuff." Parker sniffed at one of the rice cakes. "What a horrible thing to do to rice."

Eric sighed heavily and reached around to Parker's back pack. He pulled out a small jar of peanut butter. "Here." He tossed the jar into Parker's lap. "Spread some of that on the rice cake."

"Now you're talking." Parker brightened.

"Consider that your dessert."

"But you said I could have a Twinkie," Parker said pouting.

Eric's mouth dropped open. "Get real," he said. "I didn't bring any Twinkies up here."

"You're such a goddamn tease," Parker said, trying not to look at the redhead.

"Shut up and eat," Eric said, repressing the smile pulling at the side of his mouth.

Parker took a tentative first bite and decided it was better than nothing. The two men finished off their meal in short order, and before long the paper plates were burning in the campfire, and the plastic spoons, can, and other refuse neatly gathered and stored away in a plastic bag in Parker's back pack.

Eric stretched out on the ground, hands behind his head, staring up into the clear night sky.

Parker followed his gaze. "I can't get over how bright it is up here at night," he said. "I've never seen so many stars."

"Let's just hope the weather holds." Eric closed his eyes and smiled wickedly. "Thunder storms can roll in rather unexpectedly, and rather violently."

Parker stared at Eric stretched out before him. He watched the shadow play from the flickering light of the dying campfire dance over the fair skin of the young man's muscular calves. The ranger's shirt tail had pulled out slightly from his shorts and Parker noted the soft line of reddish blond curls snaking in a line from under the belt buckle up over the belly button.

Unexpectedly Eric turned his head and caught Parker's eye.

"Fire's going out," Parker said, thinking quickly.

Eric inhaled deeply, sat up and stretched. "We'd best be turning in." He tossed dirt onto the glowing embers, and stirred it with a stick.

"This ought to be interesting," Parker mumbled, getting to his feet.

"What's that?" Eric asked.

"How are we and all this gear going to fit in that little tent?" Parker gestured to the back packs.

"Do you like a pillow when you sleep?"

Parker cocked his head. "Well, yes."

Eric pointed to Parker's back pack. "There's your pillow," he said.

"Of course." Somehow Parker wasn't surprised. He hoisted his back pack up to his shoulder and followed Eric to the small tent.

Eric sat down in the low door of the tent. He unlaced his hiking boots and pulled them off. "Keep your boots up by your head," he cautioned. "Wouldn't want any creepy crawlers making themselves at home in your shoes during the night." Eric disappeared into the tent.

Parker took a deep breath and crouched down to crawl into the tent. He stopped long enough to remove his own boots and dragged them and his back pack inside. Eric sat on the top of his sleeping bag unbuttoning his shirt. Parker positioned his shoes and pack and then began to unbutton his own shirt. He tried to ignore the urge to look at Eric for any longer than occasional glances. He always had a curiosity about redheads, and was pleased to note that all of Eric's visible body hair was the same reddish blonde. Parker hid his disappointment when he realized that the shirt was all that was going to come off. He glanced down at his own undershirt and solaced in the fact that Eric wasn't wearing one.

Eric lay back on his sleeping bag and looked over at Parker. "Let me know if you start to get cold and I'll fire up the heater," he said, pointing to a small metallic cylinder at his feet.

"It's a little chilly, but not uncomfortable," Parker said.

"Good. I hate the damn things," Eric said. "Never use them really. Battery powered, but they dry up the sinuses."

Parker stretched out on his own sleeping bag. "Do these things really keep you warm?" he asked, trying to keep the conversation going.

"Oh, yeah." Eric scratched at his chest hair. "And you'll be glad of that in another hour or so. Hear the wind coming up?"

Parker listened. Sure enough, the previous gentle breeze had stiffened up considerable. The small tent was beginning to shake slightly and the door flaps were rustling noisily. Eric spun around to zip up the opening.

"This is a pretty good little tent," Parker said. "I can't even feel a draft."

"It'll keep all our body heat inside," Eric said, returning to his comfortable pose.

Parker looked over at him. "Maybe we shouldn't have eaten beans," he said.

Eric groaned. "You'd better not even think of it." He laughed and kicked lightly at Parker's feet.

"Speaking of fishing . . ." Parker turned over on his side to face Eric.

"What?"

"What do you know about that Miss Hot Stuff DA?"

Parker asked. "What's her name ... Margaret something?"

"Curry," Eric said.

"Oh, yeah."

Eric shrugged and lay back on his sleeping bag. "Not a whole lot," he said. "The ranger station doesn't have much occasion to mix with Federal prosecutors."

"I thought she was a rather interesting sort."

"She's okay, I guess," Eric replied. "I don't go into town much."

Parker smiled inwardly and pressed on. "I would think a single, attractive and spirited woman like her would be in great demand around here."

Eric was silent a moment. "You interested in her?" he said, finally.

"In her?" Parker laughed. "No. But she did ruin my vacation."

"Unforgiving sort, aren't you?" Eric laughed.

Parker's internal gaydar was confused. He thought about Margaret's earlier ploy and decided to give her theories a test. "Let me ask you a question."

"Shoot," Eric replied.

"Do you like show tunes?"

"What?" Eric turned over to face Parker. "Show tunes?" He wrinkled his brow.

Parker laughed. "Forget it." He tried to think of a subtle way to see what kind of underwear Eric wore, jockey or briefs. He started to chuckle at the thought.

"What's so funny?" Eric asked.

"Just thinking about something that happened in town yesterday," Parker said. "It's nothing."

Eric shrugged and began to crawl into his sleeping bag. "We'd better get some sleep," he said. "Mornings come awfully early up here."

Parker sat up. "I gotta take a leak."

"What?"

"I gotta take a leak." Parker repeated with emphasis.

Eric rolled over. "Well, go take a leak," he said with a yawn. "What do you want me to do, hold it for you?"

Parker stared at Eric's back for a moment, smiling. He considered a hundred good responses, but he thought better of using any of them. He unzipped the tent flap and half crawled, half pulled himself out into the night air. He stood for a moment, again amazed at the illusion of light cast about the roughened landscape by the myriad of stars overhead. He tried to find a likely spot for his toiletry.

"Say, Ranger Red," Parker called back to the tent. "There aren't any trees close by." He hugged his bare skin, wishing he had put his shirt back on.

There was a rustling from in the tent. "Well, Agent Asshole," came the reply, "try a rock."

Parker crouched back down and thrust an arm through the tent flat to grab his shirt. For the sake of principle, he shot Eric the bird before pulling the shirt through the door. The only reaction he got from inside the tent was a snort. He pulled on the heavy flannel shirt, glad for some protection from the relentless wind. He moved a few paces from the tent before deciding, what the hell, unzipped his pants, and took aim at a small rock pile.

At first he thought it was the wind humming in the distance, but the sound was getting closer until he recognized a familiar throbbing rhythm to the sound. Parker listened carefully to the slow, increasing hum, gauging its distance and direction. There was plenty of moonlight to keep him out of trouble, and he figured he would confirm his suspicions first and then get Eric. Half empirically and half on a hunch, he started up the steep rocky hillside toward the area of the murder scene.

As Parker breached the hill's summit, the hum had become an ominous roar. He sprinted toward the rock cliff, looking about for some vantage point. The rock face was suddenly engulfed in an explosion of light. Parker froze inches from the focused spotlight's perimeter. He backed up quickly, scrambling into a grouping of medium-sized boulders out of the light's glare.

Shielding his eyes against the rising cloud of dust, Parker tried to look up for the source of the blinding light. The small helicopter was almost invisible behind the dust and light. Parker squinted to find some identifying mark, but visibility beyond the focused beam of light was next to impossible. The light slowly made its way across the base of the rock face, sweeping the ground in a circular motion.

He hugged the boulders about him, waiting and watching as the sweeping light beam moved methodically closer. When the beam swung away on its last pass before engulfing his hiding place, he darted out into the swirling dust toward the rock face itself. He stumbled blindly against the solid wall of rock, trying to stay ahead of the stalking spotlight.

Parker pulled the neck of his undershirt up over his nose to try and filter out the dust churned up by the chopper blades. He scrambled over the boulders toward the far end of the rock face where a rocky slope rose to a narrow ledge about fifteen feet from the base. He had almost forgotten the cold until he tried to pull himself up the slope and found his fingers stiff and numb. He tested each hand and foothold carefully, flexing his fingers before each grasp to try and increase the circulation and feeling.

Within minutes he had climbed above the swirling dust and out of the spotlight's search pattern. He reached the ledge with little difficulty and crawled snake-like out onto the solid rock, keeping his body close to the smooth surface. Once there, he realized the ledge was actually a separate up-shoot of granite parallel to the main rock face but not attached to it. Except for the steep sloping climb in front of him, there was a sheer drop on both sides of the narrow escarpment. It stretched out behind him another ten feet, but beyond that, seemed to disappear into the darkness.

Though the helicopter was moving closer to his position, the spotlight continued to be trained on the base of the rock face. Parker hugged the rock surface against the increasing funnel of wind generated by the chopper blades. The helicopter hovered less than twenty feet directly above him and Parker could feel himself sliding across the smooth rock, pushed along by the wind force. He slapped his hands over the surface of the ledge, desperately looking for a handhold.

The helicopter's engines roared suddenly as it turned a hundred and eighty degrees and veered away from the rock face. The wind force shifted hard and Parker tumbled across the rock. He felt his legs slip over the edge, and the rest of his body began to follow. Shouting an obscenity, Parker fell helplessly over the side of the cliff.

His body jolted suddenly and the neck of his shirt jerked up violently, almost choking him. The air suddenly stilled and the roar of the helicopter became a low drone in the distance. Parker flailed his arms about for something to grab, choking against the pressure of his shirt collar. The panic was instantaneous, the fear overwhelming.

"Hold still, goddamn it!" a voice called out from above him.

Parker realized someone had hold of him by the back of his short collar and stopped flailing instantly. He reached upward grabbing hold of the powerful arm that prevented his dropping to the rocks below. Slowly he was pulled up to the edge of the escarpment.

He braced his hands against the edge and at the same time found a crack in the rock face with his foot. In a tremendous effort, he pushed up with his foot and hands. That, combined with the muscular arm pulling him up hard by his undershirt, was enough to thrust him up over the edge. He rolled onto the ledge colliding violently with another body and rolling on top of it. His momentum was stopped by two sinewy arms gripping him about the waist.

Parker looked down into the wide, gold-flecked eyes looking up at him.

"You owe me, G-Man," the redhead said.

"Eric!" Parker's relief was overwhelming. He gripped the younger man's face in his hands.

"Who were you expecting?" Striking hazel eyes laughed up at Parker.

"Thanks, kid!" Parker panted.

Without thinking, Parker pulled the redhead to him, locking their lips together.

CHAPTER 4

"**You did what?**" Margaret's red lips parted in a shriek of delight. Hot coffee sloshed out of the mug she had been filling.

"I wasn't thinking." Parker sank back into the overstuffed sofa, pretending to study a garish print hanging over the fireplace of Margaret's condo. "I was caught up in the moment."

"I love it!" Margaret shrieked again.

Parker flinched. "I wish you wouldn't do that," he said.

"Is that what Eric said?" she asked, batting her blonde lashes at him.

Parker shot her the finger.

"Oooo, baby." She snuggled onto the sofa beside him and thrust the coffee mug into his hand. "Talk dirty to me."

Parker rolled his eyes for the hundredth time since he arrived. "Margaret, you're not helping."

She pushed away from him suddenly and took on a grave, professional demeanor. "You're right, dear. The

Love Doctor is in."

"Oh, shit."

"Now, now." she patted his thigh. "Talking about it will help. It'll give you perspective."

"There's nothing to talk about."

"Don't be evasive," Margaret said, shaking a finger in his face.

"It was just a kiss, Margaret." Parker shifted uneasily.

"Yes, but was that your first park ranger?"

"I never kiss and tell, Ma'am." Parker laughed, setting the hot coffee on the nearby brass and glass coffee table.

Margaret wrestled with his arm and grabbed his little finger menacingly. "Talk, damn you, Agent White!" she commanded.

Parker pulled her, still clinging to his little finger, onto his lap and wrapped both his arms securely about her.

"I've brought bigger men than you to their knees," Margaret said, giggling and trying to squirm free.

"So have I, honey," Parker responded. "So have I." He kissed her lightly on the cheek and brought his lips to her ear.

Laughing, she broke an arm free and wrapped it about his neck. "I won't brag if you won't," she said, adjusting her necklace.

"Deal," he said and gave her a squeeze.

"What did he say?" Margaret settled into his lap. "How did he react?"

"I'm not sure, really." Parker laid his head against hers.

"Not sure?" Margaret's nose wrinkled. "You were there, weren't you? Correct me if I'm wrong, but I was given to understand you were laying on top of that gorgeous man-god with your lips pressed to his." She bounced lightly in his lap. "It's a simple question. Did he smile? Did he vomit? Did he slip you the tongue . . . get a woody?"

"Margaret!"

"What the hell happened?" Her voice echoed off the stone fireplace.

"Well, nothing really," Parker said, not sure what she was wanting. "I rolled off, we climbed down the rock face, packed our gear, and hiked back to the road."

"Whoa there, Mister. Let me get this straight. He didn't say anything?"

"No."

"He didn't do anything out of the ordinary?"

"No."

"Nothing to let you know it was okay or not okay, accepted or rejected? Anything?"

Parker shook his head. "Not really," he said with a shrug.

Margaret hung her head in disbelief.

"I admit it's kind of weird," he began.

"What about you?" Margaret brightened suddenly. "Did you try and talk to him about it? Surely, you tried to talk to him about it. What did you say?"

"Nothing, really." Parker looked away.

"Nothing, really?"

"Well, everything kind of went into the twilight zone, or something," he said.

"Or something?"

"Well, damn, Margaret, that's what happened." Parker was tired of the conversation. "We said maybe ten words to each other from then on, and then only *I'll get this*, or *you carry that* . . . I mean . . . what do you want?"

Margaret jumped to her feet. She turned looking

down at him, shaking her head. "Men are so pitiful." She raised a hand to stop his reply. "Inexcusably, irrevocably, unbelievably pitiful."

Parker stared at her, not comprehending.

"You don't see anything wrong with this picture?" Margaret asked. She paced back and forth in front of him.

Parker shrugged and reached for his coffee.

"You're just going to let it go at that?" she asked, glaring at him.

The coffee had finally cooled off enough to take a sip. "Christ, Margaret," Parker said. "You know, I figured if he wanted to talk about it, he'd talk about it."

"Arrgh!" Margaret restrained the urge to hurl one of the oriental porcelains from her mantle at him. She paced, calming herself. "Okay, okay," she said, smoothing her hair. "This is stupidity under the bridge. Let's regroup." She plopped back down beside him.

"Margaret," Parker said, "I don't see the point—"

"The point, my fine fairy friend," she said, pulling his face towards her, "is that you're interested in this guy, right?"

"Well, I think that's a moot point since he doesn't seem to—"

She shook his head in her hands to shut him up. "For a gay man you're about as sensitive as a rock," she said. "You've been spending too much time over-compensating your masculine side to blend into that straight good-old-boy network at the agency."

Parker gave her a sarcastic smile and put his arm around her. "I guess that's the same reason you play the super bitch so well," he said.

"Chauvinist," Margaret said, feigning shock. "If I were a man you wouldn't say I was bitchy."

"I'm gay . . . of course I would."

She laughed and snuggled in his arm. "How do you know Eric's not interested in you?" she asked.

"Well, I think that's obvious don't you?"

"No."

"Wha—"

"Let's analyze it." Margaret took his hand. "Go back to the kiss. How long did it last?"

Parker's brow wrinkled. "Not long. No more than a few seconds, I'm sure."

"All right," Margaret said. "A few seconds. Who ended it?"

"What do you mean?" Parker asked.

"Who stopped the kiss?" Margaret said, exasperated. "Did he push you away, turn his head? What?"

Parker thought hard. "All I remember is that I just kissed him," he said. "I put my lips to his for a few seconds—"

"Hard?"

"I'd say so." Parker smiled slightly.

"Eyes closed?" she asked.

"Mine were . . . then it was over."

Margaret shifted excitedly. "Did you look into each other's eyes when it was over?" she asked.

Parker laughed.

"This is important," she persisted. "Did you have eye contact?"

"I don't remember."

Margaret sighed and rolled her eyes. "What was his expression?"

"I don't remember, Margaret."

"Try, damn it!"

"Well, as best I recall, his eyes were closed." Parker

searched his memory. "I pulled away, he sat up and started down the rock face . . . I followed."

"Excellent!"

"What?"

"He wants you," she said, nodding knowingly.

"What the hell are you talking about?" It was Parker's turn to stare in shock.

"Trust me on this one." Margaret nodded knowingly. "He's in the bag."

"You are so full of shit, Margaret." Parker pushed her away playfully.

"No, I'm serious." She slapped at his shoulder. "All the signs are there."

"Bullshit and bullshit!"

Margaret sighed heavily and leaned back into the sofa's embrace. "I can't believe it," she groaned. "The most beautiful, desirable, sexy hunk of a man in the Rockies . . . and you get him."

"I don't believe that for one minute." Parker laughed. "But if it's true, and you're jealous, then I'm happy."

"Don't be too proud yet, miss thing." Margaret smiled knowingly. "You may have hooked the biggest fish, but you haven't got him in the boat yet."

"You doubt me?" Parker asked, feigning insult.

"Hell, you haven't even talked to him about your feelings. It's obvious that without Matchmaker Margaret's help you won't even get to first base."

"All these sports analogies." Parker flashed her a devilish smile. "Are you sure you're not a latent lesbian?"

"Such a pig!" Margaret elbowed him in the stomach. "You're one of those woman-haters aren't you?"

"Oh, I love them an awful lot." He wrapped his arm around her and bussed her cheek. "I just don't . . . shall I say . . . *love* them."

"Pity." She took on a Mae West attitude. "You don't know what you're missing."

"Maybe," he responded, taking up his coffee mug for another sip. "But I know what I want."

Margaret turned to stretch out on the sofa, resting her head on Parker's lap. "He *is* gorgeous," she said with conviction.

"It's those hazel eyes."

"Ooooo," Margaret cooed. "So romantic. I thought all men ever noticed was a nice piece of ass."

"He doesn't lack in that department either," Parker said, smiling at the ceiling.

"What do you really like about Eric?" Margaret clasped her hands in delight. "I mean, what is the real basis of your attraction?"

"Hello?" He rapped his knuckles lightly against her temple. "Anyone home?"

"You know what I mean." She brushed his hand away. "Men with muscles, tight asses, and chiseled cheek bones are a dime a dozen in any gym. Why Eric?"

Parker rolled his eyes.

"Now be serious," she said. "This is for your benefit, you know." Margaret took his hand. "Let's talk it out."

"I'm not one to over-analyze a relationship."

"Aren't we jumping the gun a bit?" Margaret asked. "What relationship?"

"You have a point." Parker cocked his head and smiled.

"That's more like it." Margaret settled her head comfortably on Parker's lap. "Now, what do you find most appealing about the man?"

Parker smiled, lacing his finger behind his neck and

stretching. "Well, of course," he said, "the first phero-mone, if you will, is the physical."

"Of course." Margaret nodded.

"I mean, a guy'd have to be blind to notice just the eyes—"

"When there's that crotch."

"Precisely," he agreed.

They smiled at each other.

"He's a total package," Parker continued.

"Total perfection."

"Absolutely."

They laughed together.

"And beyond the physical?" Margaret prodded.

"I'm not through with the physical yet."

"By all means, let's continue with the physical," Margaret said with a giggle.

"That smile of his is devastating."

"Totally." Margaret sighed.

"He moves like gravity is an after thought . . . fluid."

"Sensual." Margaret bit her lip.

"Right."

"Damn, right!"

They hugged, laughing. Margaret grabbed an accent pillow and plopped it in Parker's lap before resting her head again.

"Is my lap getting uncomfortable?" Parker asked in apparent innocence.

"It's getting a little lumpy," Margaret replied batting her eyelashes up at him.

"Maybe we ought to move off the physical now."

"Either that, or we can take a cold shower together."

Parker gave her hair a playful tug. "Where was I?" he began.

"Getting off . . . the physical, that is." Margaret giggled like a little girl.

"Oh, yes." Parker stretched back again. "I'm very attracted by his complete independence, but . . . I don't know . . . there's also a sense of compelling vulnerability about him."

"Oh, I like that. Please explain," Margaret said.

Parker thought a moment. "It's like there's some vibrant force of potential energy about him."

"His aura."

"Whatever." Parker smiled and shrugged. "It just seems as though he wants to be open, accessible, and connected, but for some reason steps back from the brink. There's a . . . a palpable tension . . . no, that's the wrong word. It's like he's caught between resistance and attraction, and you feel like you want to rush in and rescue him."

"Well put," Margaret said.

"It's hard to explain."

Margaret reached up to pat his cheek. "That's a pretty good analysis for someone who doesn't analyze relationships."

"What relationship?" he asked, mimicking her earlier sarcasm.

"The one I'm going to help you get," she said with determination.

Parker laughed. "Why, Miss Margaret," he drawled. "You are the sweetest little thing."

"Now, what else?" She fidgeted impatiently. "He's a vulnerable Viking god. What else attracts you to him?"

"Margaret?"

"Yes, dear?"

"Shut up." Parker looked at the ceiling and smiled.

"Okay." Margaret snuggled. "We'll continue this when you have a little more first hand experience with the subject."

"Christ!"

Margaret patted his shoulder. "Now, now, let's change the subject," she said. "If we can't talk about sex, then murder's the next best thing."

"You kinky, little vixen." Parker raised an eyebrow at her.

"Now, we have a ten o'clock meeting in the morning with everyone. It ought to be rather animated. You know, we've never had that large a quantity of drugs found up here before."

"I think that bundle was one part of an even larger drop," Parker said, relieved to talk about business.

"Larger?" Margaret's eyes widened. "How much larger?"

"It's only an assumption mind you," Parker continued. "Those bundles are standard fare in the opium trade. Helicopter drops usually run from four to eight bundles because of weight and expense."

"I don't understand."

"It's not considered worth the expense and risk to drop just one bundle," he said. "One little eight-kilo bundle can be handled better, less dramatically than a plane ride."

"That makes sense," Margaret said. She whistled. "So we're talking about thirty to sixty kilos of raw opium."

"Probably."

"That's a lot of money."

"Big business at its best," said Parker.

"Why here?" Margaret asked. "The top of Rocky Mountain National Park isn't exactly the most accessible spot."

"Precisely," Robert said. "But it's a good midway point between Mexico and Canada; a semi-wilderness spot, trafficked only by a few people, hidden from daily view, but accessible by various trails and close to a city on regular transportation routes."

"You mean they funnel these shipments through Estes Park?" Margaret's brow furrowed.

"More likely Denver. It's only an hour away."

"It still doesn't make sense," Margaret persisted. "Risking that large a drug shipment at a place where you never know when someone may be camping out. Rifle blasts and murder don't exactly keep things a secret."

"Now that you mention it, that is an interesting point," Parker said. "You see, Eric said that camping or any access to that area is obtainable only by permit from the Park Service. You have to be a registered guest in the Park and fill out all sorts of paper work."

Margaret sat up, looking at him intently. "You think someone in the ranger station, an insider, was keeping the bad guys informed?" she asked.

"It's a possibility," he said.

"Except this particular incident kind of blows that theory out of the water."

"Perhaps." Parker sat silently, staring into the fire.

Margaret kept looking at him waiting. "Perhaps what?" She gave his shoulder a push. "What are you thinking?"

"I've left out a little tidbit of info," he said, smiling.

"Spill it!" Margaret took his face in her hands. "Out with it, Agent White. Talk!"

Parker laughed. "What, no threat of torture?"

"First, I'll rape you," she said, pinching his cheeks.

"No, no! Not that!" he protested dramatically.

"Such a clown." Margaret rolled her eyes.

"No big deal," Parker said, leaning back into the sofa. "Our victim couple had no permit to camp in the park."

"Ah." Margaret nodded her head. "Breaking the law has its consequences."

"You're rather scary for a mountain top DA," Parker said.

"You ain't seen nothing yet." Margaret looked at her watch. "Any minute now."

"Any minute now, what?" Parker eyed her suspiciously.

"Just remember," she said. "I am your fairy godmother."

"What are you up to?"

Margaret began to giggle.

"Margaret!" Parker pulled her onto his lap and began to tickle her about the waist. "I don't like secrets."

Before Margaret's laughter became a scream, they were interrupted by a knock at the door. Parker started.

"Who are you expecting?" he asked.

Margaret jumped off his lap and dove for the door before he could grab her.

"Margaret?" he asked, again.

She stood, smoothing out her clothing. "Now behave yourself, Agent White. You ... I mean we have company."

Eric sat on his bicycle under the street light, staring blankly at the ground. He preferred to get about on his mountain bike. Riding in the open air helped him think.

He threw his head back. Why wasn't it helping now? He unsnapped the chin strap and lifted his helmet off, hanging it as an afterthought over the handle bar. The cool night breeze rippled through his ginger locks and, in the absence of the physical exertion of peddling, Eric became aware for the first time since leaving his cabin of the cold. He brushed his hand over the goose bumps trying to pop up on his bare thighs. The other rangers loved to make fun of his penchant for cycling around in skin tight spandex shorts and shirt that were the uniform of really serious cyclists. He just liked the freedom of movement it afforded him.

Even the long ride from his cabin door to the edge of Estes Park had not helped clear his mind from the incident earlier in the day. It was all he had been able to think about. After an almost sleepless night of worry and angry self-recrimination, he had been able to get very little of his work done and the ensuing paranoia had restricted him to the most solitary tasks, which in turn, disabled his mind from giving the previous day's events a rest.

He hammered the bike's handle bar once more. What was that FBI guy's game? What was he after? Eric couldn't shake the feeling that he was being made fun of—being toyed with. The anger overtook him once more. Anger at himself for not putting up a bigger protest—he should've punched the older man, told him to back off—fuck off! But it had all been so unexpected. Eric shook his head. He wasn't prepared for the kiss. It was some sort of setup. What was the FBI agent suspicioning? What was he trying to prove?

Eric looked up at the townhouse he had been summoned to. Now the DA wanted to see him. She made him more uncomfortable than anyone he had ever met. It was the way she looked at him—teased him. Eric filled his lungs with the cool night air. She suspected something. But how? He affixed the bar lock to his bikes wheel and spokes, taking his time, stalling. He feared being alone with this woman. What did she want to see him for?

"Fuck!" he muttered to himself, trying to accept the inevitable. He had tried to make excuses, but the lady DA had made it clear that this was official business. She had given him the impression that he didn't have a choice.

He started up the walkway feeling as if, for some reason, he was walking the last mile to some sort of execution. He tried to laugh at the idea. He wasn't physically afraid of her. That was silly. But he was afraid and couldn't figure out why—for what reason? He shut his eyes for a moment, took another deep breath, and knocked on the door.

Margaret opened the door quickly before Parker could muster any more comment. "Eric Borenson." She smiled broadly, ignoring the sudden intake of air from behind her on the sofa. "Come in. What a surprise."

Eric stepped hesitantly into the doorway. "But," he said, tentatively. "You did ask me to stop by after work, didn't you?"

Margaret took his arm and pulled him into the room. "Who cares what the reason was." She could sense Parker glaring at her. "It's so nice to see you under any circumstances."

Eric stopped at the sight of Parker on the sofa.

"You know Agent White, don't you, Eric?" She felt

Eric's arm tense.

Eric cleared his throat and nodded in Parker's direction.

Parker smiled death at Margaret. "Margaret," he said, narrowing his eyes at her. "You didn't tell me Eric was coming over."

"Eric, Parker, and Margaret." Margaret gushed. "All on a first name basis now. We're going to be such good friends."

"Margaret," Parker began.

She interrupted. "Can I get you something to drink, Eric?"

"I don't want to interrupt you," Eric said, shrugging. "I just stopped by to find out what you wanted to tell me about the murders. I can come back tomorrow if—"

"Don't be ridiculous." She pulled him toward the sofa. "Come in and sit down. Parker and I were just discussing the possibilities and direction of the investigation, weren't we Parker, dear."

Parker stared at her silently.

"Well now, Eric." Margaret all but pushed him on the sofa by Parker. "Make yourself at home. I'll make you a hot toddy."

"Nothing for me, thank you." Eric scooted to the opposite end of the sofa from Parker. "I can't stay long. I've got—"

"Nonsense." Margaret plopped onto the sofa between them. She looked from one to the other. "Parker was just telling me about his day." She looked at him waiting. "Weren't you, dear?"

"There's no need to bore Ranger Borenson—"

"Eric," she interrupted, smiling.

"Eric . . . with our private," he leaned on that word,

"conversations."

"Don't be silly, Parker, dear." She patted his cheek for emphasis. "We're all going to be working closely together on this case, especially the two of you. We need to clear all barriers to effective communication."

"Says who?" Parker patted her cheek back, a little harder.

Margaret threw a smile in Eric's direction. "FBI men are so stern," she said with a yawn.

"I should really go." Eric shifted uncomfortably.

"Parker was just telling me about his experiences in the Bureau," Margaret said, ignoring him.

Parker started to rise, but Margaret jumped over into his lap, stopping him. "Did you know Parker was the very first openly gay man to be accepted to the Bureau?" she asked.

Eric's eyes widened.

"And it was about time, too," Margaret continued. She elbowed Parker. "We can do anything a man can do, can't we, honey."

Parker buried his head on her shoulder, not knowing whether to laugh or bite her on the neck.

Margaret gave Eric an exasperated look. "Don't you ever say anything, dear?"

Parker clamped a hand over her mouth. "Maybe he can't get a word in edgewise . . . *dear*," he said, pulling his hand away before she could bite. "Margaret, make some fresh coffee, please."

"But I—"

He stopped her with a look. "Now please, Margaret."

Reluctantly she got up and started for the kitchen. "I think maybe this time you ought to have decaf," she said.

He threw an accent pillow at her.

Parker sat silently for a few minutes watching Margaret in the kitchen. Finally, with a deep breath, he turned his attention to Eric. "All right, Borenson," Parker began. "Let's clear the crap. One thing's for certain, we do have to work together on this case. I, perhaps, acted a little impulsively this afternoon. I apologize. It won't happen again. Now, if you have a problem here, I wish you'd tell me now."

Eric swallowed. "Dude, I didn't know you were gay," he said.

Parker sat forward defensively. "Yeah, I'm gay. A lot of people are," he said.

"I mean," Eric stammered, "I wish you'd told me."

"Well, I left my pink triangle at home. Sorry."

"What are you getting so pissed about?" Eric straightened.

Parker sat back in the sofa shaking his head.

"I mean," Eric continued, "you just up and did that to me out of the blue."

"Did what?" Margaret stuck her head in from the kitchen.

"Goddamn it, Margaret." Parker grabbed for another pillow.

"Okay, okay!" She ducked back into the kitchen.

Parker turned back to Eric. He took a deep breath. "It's called a kiss," he said evenly.

"Whatever." Eric looked away. "You just should have told me."

Margaret barreled out of the kitchen carrying a tray of coffee cups. "You know, for a detective you're not worth a damn," she said, dropping the tray onto the coffee table in front of Parker.

"I thought, I told you—" Parker began.

She showed him a fist. "No man tells me what to do."

"Now I'm a man."

"No, you're a bitch." She plopped back into his lap. "Allow me to clarify the situation for both of you." She threw her hair back. "Men are such asses," she said to herself.

"You're giving me a sexual identity crisis," Parker said, chuckling.

"Mother will make things better." She kissed his nose. "Now, doofus. Pay attention." She looked at Eric. "You too, beautiful."

Eric looked up, surprised.

"Now," Margaret continued. "I'm struck by the fact that Eric is not so much upset that you kissed him—"

"You told her that?" Eric started.

"Of course, he told me," Margaret said, patting him on the knee. "We tell each other everything, don't we, baby."

"Unwillingly," Parker responded.

Margaret ignored him. "As I was saying," she continued. "He's not so upset that you kissed him as he is that you didn't tell him you were gay."

Parker frowned at her. "So?"

"God, you're dense." She crawled across the sofa and settled in Eric's lap. "Let me try this side of the room."

Eric froze. He looked for a place to put his hands.

"Get used to it, Big Red. I'm not going anywhere." Margaret grabbed his hands and wrapped them about her waist.

He smiled weakly.

"Now." Margaret looked Eric in the eyes. "Eric, why did it upset you that Parker didn't tell you he was gay?"

Eric shrugged. "I thought he was just messing with

my head," he said.

Margaret stared at him. She patted his cheek and looked at Parker. "He's so young." She turned back to Eric. "What do you mean, messing with your head?"

"You know." Afraid to move his hands, Eric shook a lock of wavy red hair from his face. "Making fun of me."

"Making fun of you." Margaret pursed her lips. "Hmmm. So you thought the macho FBI man was making fun of you, the gay forest ranger."

Eric bit his lip. Margaret crawled back across the sofa to Parker's lap.

"You're worse than my cat," Parker said wrapping his arms about her.

"Parker," Margaret said, snuggling against him. "I'd like to introduce my friend Eric, the gay park ranger. Eric, I'd like you to meet my friend, Parker, the gay G-Man." She got up from Parker's lap. "And now, I deserve a piece of chocolate ripple cheese cake." She headed for the kitchen.

Eric and Parker sat silently looking at the logs burning in the fireplace.

Parker scratched the back of his head. "Apparently," he said, "women are supposed to be much better communicators than men."

"If you mean they do a lot more talking, yeah." Eric replied.

"I heard that," Margaret called out from the kitchen.

"Mind your own business," Parker hollered back. He smiled at Eric. "We can talk about all this later."

"Yeah." Eric got up from the sofa. "I've really got to get home."

"Yeah, it's getting late." Parker got up too. "Back to business. Look, Eric, if it's okay, I'd like to get a look at the other areas where you said this funny business has been going on."

"Those are all up in the high tundra," Eric said. "We'll need to get an early start in the morning."

"I'll be at the ranger station at seven."

"What's this?" Margaret came out of the kitchen. "Leaving already?"

"Sorry, Ms. Curry, I have an early day tomorrow." Eric started for the door.

Parker opened the door. "See you in the morning," he said.

Eric smiled shyly.

Before he could get out the door, Margaret took his hand in hers. "Don't be such a stranger in the future," she said.

"Yes, ma'am." Eric nodded.

"And Eric, dear."

"Ma'am?" he asked.

"If you call me *Ms. Curry* or *ma'am* one more time I'll rip every freckle off that pretty face of yours."

"Yes, ma' ..." He caught himself and smiled. "Margaret."

"That's better."

Parker shut the door behind him. Margaret stood staring at him, tapping her foot.

"What?" Parker asked.

"What do you mean, *what?*" She threw her hands up. "You just let him leave."

"I'll see him again tomorrow . . . in private."

"Now I'm hurt." Margaret's lips drew into a pout.

"No you're not." Parker grabbed her around the waist and lifted her up to face him. "You've been a bad girl."

She curled her arms around his neck. "So spank me."

Parker dropped her back onto the sofa with a groan. He toyed with the buckle of his belt, but thought better of it.

CHAPTER 5

Bright sunlight had just begun to filter through the canopy of pine needles and dapple the dew-laden forest floor with sequined flashes of gold. Every species of bird was represented in the antiphonal morning song that trilled from tree to tree as chipmunks scurried through the underbrush tidying up their respective lawns. The unfamiliar crunch of approaching footsteps in the carpet of pine straw sent the small creatures scrambling back into their dens, annoyed at the disturbance to the beginning of their workday.

Parker breathed in the crisp morning air. He felt strong, relieved that he was finally adjusting to the thinner air. The backpack was not nearly as heavy as before. "It's beautiful up here in the morning," he called out.

Eric halted his lead for a moment to appreciate the vista that surrounded them. "It's beautiful up here any-time," he replied.

Parker laughed, adjusting his backpack. "I can't help but recall that the last time I was trudging around on tundra," he said, "it almost got me shot."

"Oh, I wouldn't have shot you."

"No?"

"Winged you maybe," Eric said.

"Thanks a lot." Parker kicked a rock at him.

"Besides," Eric continued. "As long as we stick to established trails, we won't cause any undue damage to the ecosystem up here."

"I'll remember that."

Eric pointed a finger at a huge slab of granite jutting up from the open space a few hundred yards higher. "Up there is the place that first got my suspicions going," he said.

"Good." Parker followed him up to the site. "I could use a break from carrying this pack."

Both men let their backpacks slip to the ground. Parker found a good rock to sit on while Eric sat down on the stiff moss that seemed to blanket the landscape.

"I hope you recovered well from the Margaret experience," Parker said, fumbling with a pocket on his back pack.

"She's a neat lady. I like her," Eric said somewhat sheepishly.

"So do I, against my better judgment."

Eric laughed. "Why do you say that?" he asked.

"She upsets my equilibrium." Parker pulled a small package from his backpack.

"What's that?" Eric asked.

"Twinkies. Want one?"

"I can't believe you!" Eric expelled an exasperated groan. "You're actually gonna eat that crap?"

"I happen to like this crap," Parker said. "I got through six years of college on this crap and diet soda." He shoved a whole Twinkie into his mouth.

Eric shook his head.

"Look." Parker said, thinking about Margaret's advice from the night before. "If you don't mind I'd like to say something more about the other day."

Eric looked at him.

"I shouldn't have taken advantage of the situation the way I did," Parker said. "At least without having found out where you stood. In my defense though, I was a little . . . caught up in the situation, so to speak."

"You mean, scared shitless?" Eric shrugged and smiled. "It's okay. I might not have told you anything about myself anyway."

Parker studied him a moment. "You're not still hiding in the closet, are you?" he asked.

"I'm not walking around waving a rainbow flag if that's what you're asking." Eric stretched his muscular legs out. "It may be okay in the FBI, but things are a little different in the forestry service."

"Oh, really."

Eric looked at his shoes sheepishly. "Okay, okay," he said. "Maybe things aren't so different. Maybe it's just easier to keep quiet about it."

"Believe me." Parker smiled at him. "I can understand that."

"Besides," Eric continued, "I don't mind being alone up here."

"Bullshit!"

"Okay." Eric tried to smile. "You get used to it up here."

"Do you mind a few personal questions?"

Eric hesitated. "I guess not," he responded.

"You don't sound too sure," Parker said.

Eric tried to laugh. "I'm just not . . . I don't talk much

about being gay." He waved at the empty expanse. "Not much opportunity for it."

"Opportunities are made." Parker studied the almost radiant sheen of unpolluted sunlight reflecting off of the younger man's legs.

"Aren't you the wise old man of the mountain this morning," Eric said.

"Old enough to know who I am, what I am." Parker laughed. "And old enough to like most of what I know."

"I know what I am," Eric said defiantly.

"What about the *like* part?"

"I'm not into self-hatred," Eric said with a shrug.

"That's a start." Parker smiled at him. "Sure you don't want one of these?" He held out the last Twinkie to Eric.

"How can you eat that and like yourself?" Eric wrinkled his nose.

"Don't knock it till you've tried it," Parker answered with a wink. He bit into the pastry with added relish. "Ever been in a relationship before?"

"I tried." Eric stretched both his legs out. "A couple of times in college. Nothing that lasted long enough to constitute a relationship though . . . if you want to get technical."

"Been there, done that."

"I just bet you have," Eric said.

Parker choked on the Twinkie. "When you're young it's all practice," he said, recovering. "Experimentation . . . a learning experience."

"And when you're old?" Eric pulled a piece of leathery-looking meat from a Ziploc bag.

Parker gave him the finger. "I'll let you know when I get there," he said.

Eric chuckled and took a bite of his snack.

"What's that stuff?" Parker licked a little cream filling from the side of his mouth.

"Turkey jerky."

"Beg your pardon?"

"You heard me." Eric offered the small plastic bag. "Want some?"

"I'll pass," Parker said, eyeing the bag as if it were so much garbage.

Eric shrugged and took another bite.

"What do you look for in a relationship?" Parker asked.

Eric shoved the plastic bag back into his backpack and stood. "Are we going to sit here and play twenty questions all day or are we going to check out these sites?" he asked.

Parker cocked his head to one side. "Oh, I think there's time for a little of both." He wiped his hands on his shorts. "Lead on, McDuff."

They left their packs and climbed the path the rest of the way to the granite outcropping.

Parker studied the site for anything unusual. "What happened up here?" he asked.

"This was the first of three high range areas that I discovered were being illegally accessed." Eric pointed along the ground. "There are a series of trails that span the tundra areas and which are supposed to be accessible only by the rangers. During the spring and summer months when these areas are reachable we try to keep track of vegetation, glacial retreats, and wildlife."

"Wildlife?" Parker glanced behind him.

"We have several flocks of bighorn sheep as well as herds of elk that sometime venture up into the tundra during these months. And more rarely, even an occasional grizzly."

"As in *bear?*"

"You never know." Eric patted the rifle slung over his shoulder.

"Great." Parker looked about the base of the outcropping. "What kind of disturbance did you find?"

Eric's face darkened. "Some bunch of bastards," he said. "I'd say three or four . . . trampled all over the place up here." He squatted on the ground and pointed out several spots along the ground. "You wouldn't believe the amount of footprints. Goddamn senseless destruction!"

"Whoa there." Parker gave the ranger's shoulder a squeeze. "Plants grow back."

"Yeah, in about a hundred years."

"What?"

"This isn't your normal garden variety vegetation," Eric explained. "Tundra grows only at these altitudes. It can take scores of years for these mosses and lichens to establish. It only takes one careless footstep to kill it."

"Shit!" Parker looked at the small, hardy vegetation covering the ground around him. "No wonder you looked like the avenging angel when you caught me off the roadway the other day."

"Well, anyway," Eric said, standing. "You could tell there was a lot of activity that went on here. At least the scum used the trail to get up here."

"You have to admit this could have just been a group of mischievous hikers and nothing more."

"If this had been the only incident, maybe," Eric said, shaking his head. "And that's what I thought at first." He pointed out over the expanse. "But then, I came upon two other similar sites . . . one about a mile north, and another a half mile east of that. It really pissed me off.

Looked like some bunch of assholes were really having a party all over the high range."

"But what made you think it was someone other than illegal hikers?" asked Parker.

"I upped my patrols to these areas," Eric said. "The disturbances happened on more than one occasion, but always at one of these three sites. People would come up here, forage around, and then leave."

"No evidence at the scene?"

"An occasional cigarette butt." Eric wrinkled his nose.

"Always trust a smoker to leave evidence behind."

Eric nodded. "One of them took a crap at site two."

"Don't you just love the criminal mind?"

"Which reminds me," Eric said, turning. "What did you do with that Twinkie wrapper?"

"All present and accounted for, sir!" Parker reached in the pocket of his shorts and pulled out the remains.

"Three brownie points for you," Eric said with a smirk.

"What's my reward?" Parker asked with an expectant smile.

Eric snorted and turned to head back for their gear. "I'll just walk a little slower for you from here on," he said.

"Gee, thanks." Parker followed. "And swing that pretty ass a little more for me."

"Quit looking at my ass." Eric shot him the bird without looking back.

"I'm only human, kid."

Eric reached for the backpacks and deftly swung his up onto his shoulders. "Besides," he said. "You've got everyone thinking you're another notch in Ms. Curry's bed post."

"Margaret likes your ass too," Parker said in his best Groucho Marx impression. He grabbed up his pack.

"I'm glad she did what she did last night," Eric said.

"Don't say anything you'll regret later."

Eric laughed. "No, I mean . . . now that she knows my story." He stretched out full in the morning light much to Parker's delight. "She used to make me real nervous."

"Said the rabbit about the hungry tigress."

"Not that way," Eric's face flushed. "She just asks a lot of questions. And she *is* the DA."

"You're blushing."

"No I'm not."

Parker reached out and touched the younger man's reddened cheek. "Looks like blushing from here," he said.

"Fuck you, man." Eric pulled his face away, trying not to laugh.

"Damn," Parker said, "I thought you'd never ask." He thought the younger man's face reddened even more, if that was possible.

"You don't ever let up, do you." Eric gave Parker's shoulder a playful punch. "Keep it up and we'll see how fast you can hike a mile."

"Before or after we fuck."

"You're driving me fucking crazy." Eric threw his hands up and started up the almost invisible path that wound around the granite outcropping.

Parker broke into a trot to catch up with him. "Don't you like sex?" he asked.

Eric put his hands to his head and screamed into the stiff breeze.

"All right!" Parker closed in on him. "I like a man who's noisy."

"You'd better back off, old man." Eric scrambled up a short slope, laughing.

Parker made a grab for Eric's legs and got a cloud of dirt kicked down on him for his efforts. He pulled himself up the slope.

"You're dead meat, kid," he said, spitting dirt out of his mouth.

Eric backed away from the slope. "Come on, Methuselah." He gestured with both hands for Parker to come. "Give it your best shot."

Parker stood at the top of the slope panting and laughing.

"Let's face it." Eric put his hands on his hips, mocking. "I'm younger and faster."

Parker lunged after him. Eric spun on his heels and started to break away into a run. With one fluid motion, Parker let his backpack slip from his shoulders into his hand. He flung the pack at the back of Eric's knees. Eric's legs collapsed beneath him and he tumbled over onto the path.

Parker leapt on top of Eric, pinning him to the ground. "Face it, kid," he said with a Cheshire cat grin. "I'm older and craftier."

Eric recovered his composure quickly. "You're also fatter," he said with a moan. "Get off me!"

"Fat!" Parker struggled to keep Eric pinned to the ground. "Why you little shit. You'll pay for that one." He felt the raw muscle under him flex and wondered if he could keep his hold.

"Get your fat Twinkie butt off me!" Eric looked Parker in the eyes.

"Maybe you prefer to be on top," Parker said with a triumphant smile.

Eric thrust his hips upward, trying to put Parker off balance. Parker countered by sliding his rear down over Eric's groin. The feel of Eric's hard body grinding against his buttocks had a different hardening effect on Parker. He thought his erection would burst through the zipper of his shorts with every move Eric made beneath him.

Eric's struggle ended abruptly. Parker felt the reason rising up beneath him. He looked down with unmasked admiration at the impressive evidence of Eric's erection and then at Eric's face, flushed with embarrassment.

Parker bobbed his eyebrows at Eric. "That's why I quit the wrestling team in junior high," he said. "This always seemed to happen."

"This is embarrassing," Eric managed to say.

"Embarrassing?" Parker responded with a smile. "This isn't embarrassing. Try getting a hard-on in a spandex jumpsuit. Now that's embarrassing." He sat up, releasing his hold on Eric's arms. "But if I could have put on a more impressive display like this . . ." He rested a hand on Eric's groin and gave the engorged flesh a squeeze through the cotton shorts. ". . . I might not have minded so much."

Eric's whole body stiffened at Parker's touch. He sat up suddenly, nose-to-nose with Parker who still sat astride him. "That wasn't fair," he said.

"All's fair in love and war." Parker smiled down at the offending hand.

"And that is trite," Eric said with a smirk.

"Whatever works." Parker found himself staring at the young ranger's face. He'd certainly seen beautiful men before, but this was different—scent, heat, strength, a mega-dose of testosterone.

"What?" Eric asked. "Do I have a zit on the end of

my nose, or something?" He ran a hand over his nose self-consciously.

"Hardly," Parker said, his voice low and husky. He reached up to brush a smudge of dust from Eric's forehead. "I'd kill to kiss you right now," he said. The sexual tension was excruciating.

Eric lay back on the ground, hands behind his head. Unable to look up at Parker, he stared into the sky instead. He smiled to himself. "Well, at least you have the decency to ask this time."

"What harm would a little kiss do?" Parker leaned over Eric, looking down into his face.

Eric continued to stare up at the sky noncommittal. "Boy," he said, thinking. "I could make a million on a sexual harassment suit."

"Let's go for ten million." Parker smiled down at him.

"You're too old for me." Eric wrinkled his nose again.

"Asshole!" Parker dug his fingers into Eric's sides.

"Not fair!" Eric writhed in hysterical agony. "Not fair!" He shouted, gasping for air between paroxysms of laughter.

"You're ticklish," Parker said, continuing his relentless torture.

"No I'm not," Eric managed, grabbing for Parker's hands.

"Now I know your weakness." He fended off Eric's grasp and began searching for other ticklish spots. "Say uncle," he said, finding no end to sensitive places.

"Eat shit and die!" With strength born out of desperation, Eric managed to push Parker off balance and rolled him over to gain the upper hand.

Laughing, the two men wrestled for control, tumbling

about on the pebble strewn path.

"Well, isn't this a cozy sight!" The unexpected voice froze Eric and Parker in their play. "I hope I'm not interrupting your fun," rasped the voice, taking on a sarcastic edge all too familiar to Parker.

Parker stood quickly, facing the short, thick-set man. He eyed the khaki uniform. "You need something, ranger," he asked, brushing the dust off his pants. "Or are you just out for a stroll?"

"Bonner!" Eric recognized the intruder. "What the hell are you doing up here?"

The other ranger smiled nastily. "You're not the only ranger in the park you know, boy." He ran stubby fingers through his oily, dark hair. "I guess the rumors are true."

Parker moved in menacingly, pulling his full height above the shorter man. "And what rumors would those be?" he asked. "Bonner is it?"

Bonner shifted uncomfortably. "It ain't no secret." His eyes would not meet Parker's.

"Oh, that rumor." Parker stared down at him. "But I'd hardly call it a rumor."

"Yeah, whatever." Bonner's confidence returned. "Now I guess we got us one in the Park Service." He sneered in Eric's direction. Eric looked like an extension of the granite outcropping.

Parker stepped in front of Bonner's sight line. "Oh, I know the Park Service very well," he said, meaningfully. "You have a whole lot more than just one of . . . those."

Bonner eyed him skeptically.

"Why," Parker continued, "I've met several old friends right here in Estes Park."

Eric stepped in. "I asked you a question, Bonner," he said. "What are you doing up here? You're assigned to the camp grounds."

"I don't take orders from you." Bonner stood like a bantam rooster ready for a cockfight.

Parker raised an eyebrow at Bonner. "Now I'm asking," he said, scraping the path with his boot. "As part of a federal investigation that I just happen to be in charge of."

"Fuck your investigation!" Bonner waved a dismissive hand.

"Well, good buddy, I'll tell you." Parker said, matter-of-fact. "That's not a very smart answer. Unless you're married to the Secretary of the Interior's daughter, I'd be a little more responsive. I know Secretary Kemp well . . . real well. And your little career's gonna eat shit if you don't get real cooperative, real fast."

Bonner gritted his teeth, considering the threat. "I could ask you the same question." His eyes darted about. "This area is off limits."

"There is no federal property off limits to me," Parker said. His gaze hardened. "And what I'm doing up here is none of your business."

"I'm just doing my job." Bonner checked his watch. "And I've got to get back to it."

"Spare me a moment." Parker's voice betrayed his impatience. "Exactly what is it about your job that brings you up here?"

Bonner shrugged. "A couple of times a month I come up to get water samples from the base of the glacier on the east ridge," he said. "He unzipped his fanny pack and pulled out a plastic sample vial, waving it agitatedly in Parker's face. "For the guys at the University."

Eric snorted. "You're a little off track then if that's where you were headed," he said.

"That so?" Parker gave Bonner a hard look.

"Look, I heard a noise in this direction." Bonner sneered at them. "You two were having a good old time. For all I knew a bunch of kids were up here having an orgy or something." He checked his watch again. "If I don't get these samples it'll be a while before I can get back up here."

Eric started to speak, but Parker raised a hand. "Well, Bonner?" he said. "Don't let us keep you from your duties."

Bonner spun around on the path. "Fucking queers," he mumbled. Scurrying around the boulders, he disappeared over a ridge.

"You certainly made him nervous," Eric said, brushing some moss off his shorts.

"Me?"

"He couldn't get away from here fast enough."

Parker smiled. "Oh, I didn't have anything to do with that," he said. "I think Ranger Pig has another agenda."

Eric's orange brows went up.

"Elementary, my dear." Parker patted Eric on the cheek. "Now, where did I put that scanner?" He knelt by his backpack, rummaging through its contents. "Ha!" He extracted the hand-held, shortwave receiver, triumphantly holding it up to Eric's puzzled face.

"What good's a police scanner going to do you up here?" Eric asked.

"Nothing as specialized as that," Parker said, switching the device on. He made a few adjustments. "We'll let it scan and see what we pick up."

Liquid display crystals flickered across the face of the small scanner as it searched the air for invisible signals. It crackled and hissed before locking in on something.

"Ah!" Parker said with a smile. He adjusted the volume.

"What was that?" Eric leaned an ear in closer.

"Shhh," Parker admonished.

The scanner came alive and Eric heard an unmistakable voice. "Abort. Abort," the voice said urgently. "High Range calling Climber. Abort. Repeat. Abort."

"Goddamn!" Eric muttered. "Bonner!"

"A clue, Ranger Hunk." Parker batted his eyelashes at the younger man. "The game is a-foot."

"What now?" Eric grabbed up his pack excitedly.

Parker stepped directly in front of Eric, almost nose to nose. "You still owe me a kiss," he said, bobbing his eyebrows.

"Shit!" Eric managed before Parker locked lips with him.

CHAPTER 6

"**So, they have a man on the inside.**" Margaret stretched out on the white cotton bedspread that was draped neatly over the full-size bed in Parker's motel room. "I'm hungry." Her shoes fell to the floor. "Bonner. That snake!"

Parker sat at the small table by the picture window, typing furiously on his laptop. He cast a bemused glance at Margaret's posturing on the bed. "I need to get this report faxed to the Bureau," he said. "We need some background checks on ranger personnel around here."

Eric stopped his pacing and sat on the end of the bed. "I can't believe anyone else at the Station could be involved in this," he said.

Margaret sat up slightly, staring intently at Eric. "Is that a hickey I see?" She pointed a stockinged big toe at him.

Eric's hand went up to his neck.

"Yes, it is!" Margaret screeched, scooting over the bedspread for a closer inspection. "That's a damn hickey."

"Leave the boy alone, Margaret," Parker droned without looking up from his computer.

"I . . . I think that's where a tree branch poked me," Eric said, rubbing the spot.

"Liar!" Margaret draped herself over his shoulders. "You've been necking with Parker."

"No, really." Eric reddened and grinned at the floor. "When we were on the ground—"

"On the ground?" Margaret squeezed his shoulder.

"I mean," Eric tried to continue. "I got scraped by a rock or something."

Margaret zeroed in like a bird of prey. "What were you two doing on the ground?" She pretended to gasp. "Oh, my God. You were screwing in the heather."

"No, no." Eric almost choked. "We were just messing around."

"Oooo!"

"Margaret!" Parker called out.

"I mean we were just wrestling." Eric rolled his eyes back, exasperated. "God, in a minute you'll have me confessing to the murders."

"Oh, you boys are hot." Margaret rested her chin on Eric's shoulders. "Doing it out of doors. Ummmm!"

"Parker?" Eric pleaded.

"It was just a kiss, Margaret," Parker muttered, not missing a beat on the computer keyboard.

"Was he as good as he looks, Eric?" She smacked her lips.

"I was better." Parker slapped at the enter key. "There. Report emailed."

Margaret reached a hand out to Parker. "Kiss him for me, Hot Lips."

Eric laughed, trying to push her away.

"Come on, Parker." She slapped at Eric's protesting hands and solidified her position at his back. "Give him a good one. I want to watch."

"Why Margaret?" Parker shook his head at her. "Voyeurism?"

"Don't be such a wuss," she said. "There's a lesbian scene in every porno film. Men love it. I want equal time."

"Don't listen to her Parker." Eric chuckled nervously.

Parker smiled down at Eric. For a moment, he considered Margaret's challenge. His eyes caressed the shape of Eric's jaw to the sensuous mounds of salmon that were his lips.

"Now really, Margaret." Parker diverted his gaze to Margaret, but the stirring in his groin betrayed his true desires. "Ranger Borenson and I are professionals in the midst of a murder investigation."

"Do tell." Margaret's face contorted into a sarcastic parody of attentive interest.

"Let's all try and keep our minds focused on the problems at hand," said Parker.

"Like that erection?" Margaret raised an eyebrow in the direction of Parker's groin.

"Margaret!"

"Sorry." Margaret smiled innocently at him. "I'm just trying to move things along."

Eric sat silent, hands over his face.

Parker noted an unmistakable quivering about the redhead's shoulders. "What the hell are you laughing at?" He gave the back of Eric's head a light slap.

"I'm not laughing." Eric uncovered his crimson features.

The phone on the bedside table rang out in

interruption.

"I'll deal with you later." Parker said and reached for the phone.

Margaret seized the opportunity and tapped Eric's knee for attention. "Eric," she said. "I don't really mean to embarrass you."

"Oh, yeah?" Eric smiled at the floor.

She put an arm around his waist. "I get the feeling a lot of this bawdy banter makes you uncomfortable."

"No, I don't mind . . . really."

"Good, then let's have some serious girl talk."

"What?" Eric gave her a puzzled smile.

Margaret sighed, pushing a strawberry colored tress behind his ear. "You are so beautiful," she said.

Eric blushed again.

"But, it's obvious you don't get out much," she added.

"Well," Eric said, "I'm not exactly a social butterfly, if that's what you mean."

"I'll say." Margaret laughed.

"I like being alone," Eric protested.

"So do I," Margaret said. "To a point." She squeezed his rippling bicep. "But I...," she said winking, "and certainly young men like you, with this much hormonal overkill, must have . . . needs." Her voice lowered to a sultry pitch. "Strong needs."

"I hike a lot." Eric raised his eyebrows and smiled.

They laughed together.

"Parker's a good guy," Margaret said.

Eric rolled his eyes.

"You know I'm right." Margaret rubbed his back. "I think he's head over heels for you."

Eric shrugged again. "He'll be back east when this

investigation's over," he said.

"Ah." Margaret pursed her lips.

"Ah, what?" Eric looked at her.

"I was wondering what excuse you would come up with to keep from getting involved."

"I think it's more of a reason than an excuse, don't you?" Eric said.

Margaret shook her head and sighed. "It's just an excuse," she said. "You're scared of who you are . . . what you imagine you'll have to cope with from the straight world. You're settling for some delusion of fitting into the mainstream while, in truth, you're just hiding out."

Eric just looked at her.

"Parker could be the best thing that ever happened to you," she said, taking his hand.

"I don't want a little two-week affair," Eric said. "Thank you very much."

"Two weeks is better than nothing," She hugged his waist. "If you want more, then go for it. Put on your gloves and come out swinging for the gold. I'm in your corner."

Eric smiled and touched his forehead to hers.

"Aren't you two getting cozy?" Parker pushed on the bed, bouncing Eric and Margaret about.

"He's too good for you." Margaret kicked at Parker. "I've decided Eric needs a real woman."

Parker pulled her up into his arms. "Honey, what he needs, you ain't got," he said, rubbing his nose against hers.

"Don't be silly, dear." She wrapped her arms about his neck. "I can buy one of those in any novelty store."

"Good grief!" Eric stood with hands on hips. "Then, I think *both* of you should go shopping."

The two looked at Eric from their embrace.

"Do you think he'll fit in my basket?" Parker asked.

"I don't know, sweetie. He's an awful big one." Margaret winked at Eric.

Eric smiled in spite of himself. "Now I know what a rump roast feels like," he said.

Margaret and Parker both started to respond.

"Never mind." Eric raised a hand. "No rump references, please."

Margaret and Parker batted their lashes at him innocently.

"What was the call about?" Eric asked.

"That was your Superintendent." Parker released his hold on Margaret. "Bledsoe, is it?"

"Superintendent Bledsoe?" Eric's face fell. "What did he want?"

"He'd like to see you . . . immediately."

"Shit!" Eric rubbed his temples.

"I guess Bonner's been running off at the mouth since our little encounter up in the Park," Parker said. He could see the anxiety in Eric's face. "Don't let this get to you, Eric." He reached a hand out to Eric's shoulder.

"Easy for you to say," Eric said, recoiling. "If I don't get canned, I guess I'll be scrubbing out the toilets in the campgrounds for the next thirty years." He slumped onto the bed holding his head.

Parker caught Margaret's eye. She stepped back quietly, motioning with her head for him to go to Eric. He shrugged and she aimed a lethal look at him, jabbing a finger in Eric's direction for emphasis. Parker sighed and sat on the bed next to Eric.

"Don't say anything," Eric said. He straightened and took in a deep breath. "I'm not blaming you for this."

"That's good news," Parker responded lightly.

"Nothing ever lasts." Eric looked at the floor, resigned.

"Come on, Eric, get real." Parker looked at him sternly. "This isn't a soap opera, it's real life. You're not going to lose your job and there aren't going to be any back door recriminations from the good-old-boy Superintendent."

"You're right," Eric said, almost laughing. "This is real life . . . not that fantasy world in Washington where you come from. Political correctness hasn't climbed this high."

"Eric," Margaret intervened. "You're not alone up here anymore." She knelt in front of him with arms folded over his knees. "Listen to Parker. He knows how to handle this. I've been to Washington and I can tell you it's not such a fantasy land. Parker's taken a lot of crap to be who he is and to get where he is. For that matter, so have I. I've had to rack a few good-old-boy nuts in my day, too."

"I just bet you have," Parker said, rolling his eyes.

"I feel like I've been hit by a Mack truck." Eric's shoulders slumped further.

"That's just the weight of a closet door trying to creak shut again." Parker put an arm around him. "If you'd like some help, we could kick it off the hinges."

"You both must think I'm a real fuck-up." Eric managed a smile.

"No we don't." Parker took his hand and leaned around to face him. "I've been in your shoes before and, if you'll trust me, I can help you through this." He straightened. "Besides, I owe you. You've saved my keister twice already."

"And if it counts for anything," Margaret interjected, "you've got the best and most influential federal prosecutor in the Rocky Mountains on your side. If anyone fucks with you, this blonde will have their balls for lunch."

"There's just entirely too much talk about sex around here." Eric's demeanor brightened considerably.

"Damn right!" Margaret slapped his knees. "Enough talk. Let's have some action."

"Great." Parker winced. "Now Margaret's got a hard-on."

"You wish." Margaret stood and adjusted her skirt.

"Well," Eric said up pushing off the bed. "No sense delaying the inevitable."

"That's the spirit," Margaret said, slapping him on the back. "Let's go."

Eric shook his head. "You two stay here and chill a while," he said. "I'll be back as soon as the wounds stop flowing."

"Bullshit!" Parker said emphatically.

"Double bullshit!" Margaret took Eric's arm. "We're going with you."

"All for one and one for all." Parker wrapped an arm around Eric's shoulder.

"This is sick." Eric looked from one to the other and laughed.

"No, no, darling," Margaret said. "This is a power play."

"I'm federal law enforcement," Parker said with a dramatic flair.

"I'm the right hand of the law and he's the left," Margaret added with a wink.

Parker butted his head against Eric's. "Now," he said.

"Let's go see your confused little supervisor and give him a good double-fisting!"

"We'll offer him the benefit of our years of experience, guidance, and legal expertise." Margaret pulled the door open for them.

"And if that doesn't work?" Eric paused at the door.

"Then," Parker said, baring his teeth, "we'll threaten and scare the be-Jesus out of him."

They laughed together and headed out the door onto the covered walkway that opened onto the motel parking lot.

"Let's take your Range Rover," Margaret said. "It's roomier than my little Beemer." She carefully stepped through the scrawny little hedge of hawthorn between the walk and the parking lot.

Parker unlocked the car door and they all climbed in. Margaret settled in the back, sitting forward in the center of the seat so as to be directly between the two men.

"Let's see what this baby will do," Margaret said, grabbing on to the backs of their seats.

"Margaret." Parker started the engine. "Don't you have any work to do at the office? We don't want to keep you from your appointed duties." He smiled cattily at her in the rear-view mirror and shifted into reverse.

"No, it's Tuesday," she replied, equally snide. "All I do on Fridays is catch up on paperwork and I can do that later."

Parker pulled out of the parking lot onto the two lane street. "Pity," he said under his breath.

"I heard that," Margaret said into his ear. "And you'll pay for it."

Parker only smiled.

"Really, you two should let me deal with this," Eric

interjected. "I know you both have more important things to do than baby-sit me."

Parker negotiated the tight, hilly curve before coming to a stop at a red light. He turned to Eric. "No more arguments," he said. "We're going to help you straighten this out." He looked into Eric's bright hazel eyes and saw the nervousness there . . . a familiar insecurity. He put a reassuring hand on Eric's thigh and squeezed. "Everything is going to be fine. You'll see."

The traffic light changed.

"Seriously, Eric," Margaret said, leaning forward. "We're not going for the purpose of making more trouble for you. This will be straightened out." She nuzzled his cheek. "I won't have you being afraid of being yourself anymore."

They rode in silence for a few minutes.

"I'm not afraid of being myself," Eric said, quietly. "This is pretty much me. I'm just worried about losing a job I love, or at the least, have a job I love made too unbearable to continue."

"Ain't gonna happen, friend." Margaret threw her arms about his neck.

"At least not that dramatically," Parker said. "There will, of course, be the occasional asshole to deal with." He pulled into the ranger station compound. "Speaking of which—"

"Damn!" Eric stretched his arms against his knees. "Oh well. Here goes."

They climbed out of the Range Rover and headed into the ranger station with Eric in the lead.

Margaret paused momentarily at the door and opened another button of her blouse. She caught Parker's quizzical gaze and smiled. "Just putting the finishing touches on my war paint," she said with a smile.

"I love a woman who fights dirty," Parker said, opening the door for her.

Margaret threw her head back and gave her hair a fluff. "I fight to win," she said, "period!" She took Parker's arm and made her entrance with him in tow.

They walked into an open, rustic great room with rough-hewn log walls bordered by display cases, stuffed birds and animals, and slotted stands of brochures and tourist information. Eric approached the long counter staffed by a single female in uniform. Margaret and Parker caught up to him.

"Hi, Alice," Eric said with a deep breath.

"Eric." The brunette looked at him sadly. "The Superintendent said to send you right in the moment you got here."

"Thanks, Alice," he said, nodding. He turned to Parker and Margaret. "It's down the hall." He pointed to a narrow corridor behind the counter. "Right," he muttered and headed around the counter.

Margaret took Parker's arm. "This is all your fault, you know," she said, pulling him along.

"My fault?"

"Just couldn't keep your hands off the natives."

Eric stopped at one of the doors. He glanced back at Margaret and Parker. "You two really don't have to come in," he said, rapping on the door lightly.

Parker gave him a wink and reached up to squeeze Eric's shoulder.

"Stand by your man," Margaret whispered. "That's my motto."

"In!" The door shook from the volume of the gravelly voice inside.

Eric turned the knob slowly and took another deep breath. He opened the door slightly. "It's Borenson, Superintendent," he called out respectfully. "You wanted to see me?" He stepped into the room followed closely by Margaret and Parker.

The hulking man behind the desk took off his reading glasses and glared up at the intruders. He stood sharply at the sight of Margaret and smoothed his impeccably starched uniform. "Borenson, I wanted to see you in private," he barked imperiously.

"Yes, sir." Eric forced a smile. "You remember Ms. Curry."

"I know the District Attorney," the Superintendent said. He gave her a steely glance before focusing his attention on her last opened button.

"Hi, Dan." She smiled demurely. "You're looking fit."

The Superintendent muttered something akin to "harrumph!"

"And I don't believe you've met Special Agent Parker White." Eric motioned to Parker. "He's heading the investigation for the FBI into the murder of those two climbers up by Bear Lake."

The Superintendent eyed Parker with particular distaste.

Parker freed himself from Margaret and stepped forward. "A pleasure, Superintendent Bledsoe," he said, extending his hand.

"Agent White." Bledsoe took his hand hesitantly.

Parker decided a little off-balancing was in order. "We missed you at the briefing the other day," he said.

Bledsoe waved a hand as if in dismissal. "I also run a rather large Federal operation here as you can see, Agent White."

"But still," Parker said. "It is a murder investigation. I would have thought this would be a high priority item for you. I didn't think murder was that frequent an occurrence in the Park."

"I can assure you, Agent White that these murders are accorded plenty of priority by this office." The Superintendent's jaw set. "I believe I had a representative at that briefing . . . one you've apparently gotten to know pretty well."

Eric stiffened perceptibly.

Parker only smiled. "If you're referring to Ranger Borenson," he said, "yes, I have the privilege of working closely with him." He bowed toward Margaret. "As well as Ms. Curry."

"We make a great team," Margaret interjected. She lowered herself into a side chair, crossing her legs and adjusting the view of her thigh. "Very dedicated."

Parker also pulled up a chair and motioned for Eric to do the same. "I hope you don't mind the DA and I taking the initiative to tag along for this meeting," he continued. "We assumed it would be a briefing on the investigation, and I did have a few questions for you."

"I do mind." Superintendent Bledsoe glared down at him from behind his desk. "This meeting is none of your business. It is an administrative matter and has nothing to do with your investigation."

"I appreciate that Superintendent." Parker leaned back comfortably. "But when I head a murder investigation, I consider everything that affects my team to be my business."

"One for all and all for one." Margaret batted her lashes.

Parker resisted the urge to kick her. "Working on my

team," he continued, "can sometimes create problems for my people with their regular jobs and I like to be the one to smooth that over when necessary."

"I assure you, Agent White," Bledsoe began, "that you have no—"

"I remember one case in particular," Parker interrupted. "A white supremacist militia group in Idaho. We were working some surveillance when a local sheriff's deputy who was on my team ... pretty sharp kid ... began to get some major flack from his boss and fellow deputies. You know the drill ... docked pay, missing equipment, a few hazing incidents, threats ... the works. I had to come down pretty hard there with a little intimidation of my own. Turns out the sheriff was a veritable pipeline of arms and info to the militia ... the head bigot so to speak." Parker paused for effect. "He's currently doing time for obstructing a federal investigation."

The two men stared at each other while Margaret and Eric squirmed.

"I'm sure you have many amusing stories to tell us, Agent White," the Superintendent said, regaining his seat. "But that doesn't change the fact that this meeting does not concern you or your investigation. I'll appreciate your waiting out in the lobby while I deal with Ranger Borenson in private."

"With all due respect Superintendent, and with Ranger Borenson's permission," Parker said, leaving no room for debate, "I think I'll sit in on this and be the judge of its relevance myself."

"Borenson?" The Superintendent glared up at Eric.

Eric steeled himself. "I don't mind them sitting in, sir," he said.

Superintendent Bledsoe patted the desk with his fist. "Have it your way then." He pulled a sheet from a stack of papers. "I have received a rather serious complaint here that calls into question both your professionalism and your ability to act effectively in the ranger service as a whole."

"I can't imagine what that could be, sir." Eric tried to look naive. "I've been with the service now for some five years, three here at Rocky Mountain. I've received numerous commendations, several pay upgrades, and no negative evaluations in that whole time."

"That's all very well and good, ranger." Bledsoe tapped on the paper. "And I would hate to see it all thrown away because you've decided to act on some suppressed perversion."

"Perversion." Parker's eyebrows shot up in amused interest. "Now, this is getting good."

"I don't know what you're talking about, sir," Eric interjected over Parker's comment.

Bledsoe hammered a fist down onto the desk. "I'm talking about sodomy, boy, and you damn well know it!" he bellowed. "Faggots screwing around in my Park!" He shook the paper at Eric. "I'm not going to have this kind of crap going on under my nose, threatening the good name of the Park, not to mention the ranger service."

"Sir," Eric Began, "I—"

"I'm not finished." Bledsoe slammed the paper down onto the desk. "I am pissed as hell, even to think that some queer has been hiding behind a ranger uniform, in my employ, trying to fool everyone—"

"We prefer the term *gay*, Superintendent," Parker said quietly.

"What?" Bledsoe blustered.

"Gay." Parker continued. "*Faggot* is considered a derogatory term coming from straights. We feel about it the way black people feel about the N word."

Bledsoe's face bloated a steamy red. "I don't give a goddamn what—"

"And if you're addressing me, Superintendent." Parker stood suddenly and leaned across the desk menacingly. "I'd suggest you lower your voice and change your tone, or I'll make you regret it in more ways than you can count."

"Gentlemen, gentlemen." Margaret clapped her hands for attention. "Let's give it a little rest." She pulled Parker away from the desk by his belt. "Dan, I've never seen you so out of control."

"Now damn it, Margaret!" Bledsoe straightened his tie. "This is serious business."

"Yes, yes, I can see that," she said. "But you're not giving Ranger Borenson a chance to respond to your allegations or anything." She jerked on Parker's belt so he would sit back down.

Bledsoe took a deep breath and rubbed his temples. "Okay. You're right," he said. "I'm sure there's a reasonable explanation." He motioned to Eric. "All right, Borenson. I may be jumping the gun here. But you can appreciate that this is serious stuff. You have the floor."

Eric wiped his mouth and gave Margaret a pleading look. She only smiled and nodded at him. "Before I can provide any explanations," Eric said, taking a deep breath, "I need to know some details of the alleged complaint."

"What details?" Bledsoe eyed him suspiciously.

"Well, sir, the date, time, and place of the alleged incident and what exactly was supposed to have happened. I'm kind of in the dark here."

"We've been through that once, haven't we?" Bledsoe blinked at him.

"No, Sir." Eric shook his head. "I think you were too upset."

"Yes, well." Bledsoe cleared his throat and smoothed the complaint form in front of him. "Yesterday evening, eleven-fifty a.m., up by Boulder Overlook. You were observed to be rolling about on the ground, in the . . . embrace, if you will, of Agent White." He glared in Parker's direction.

Parker smiled innocently at him.

"I see," Eric responded thoughtfully.

"Well?" Bledsoe prodded.

"Sir?"

"You hopefully have an explanation for this?"

"No, Sir." Eric shook his head.

"What the hell do you mean, *no sir*," Bledsoe's voice rumbled ominously.

Parker and Margaret exchanged glances.

"What I mean, sir," Eric continued, "is that I don't think any explanation is in order."

"Well, boy, I'd suggest you think again." Bledsoe's face hardened.

"What I mean to say, sir," Eric continued, "is that I'm off on Mondays. I was helping Agent White on my off time. I don't believe I need to account to you or anyone else about what I do on my off time. I also don't think my personal life is any concern of this department."

"Bravo!" Parker said under his breath and he gave Margaret another nod.

"Doesn't have anything to do with this department?" Bledsoe almost shouted.

"No, Sir." Eric responded evenly. "I do my job very

well. My record proves that. So long as my personal life does not affect my job performance, then it isn't a subject for discussion."

Bledsoe sat back in his chair dumbfounded. "You've made a serious mistake, here, Borenson," he said, recovering quickly. "Having your kind working here is going to cause too many problems. If you had been honest in the beginning, I could have avoided—"

"I haven't been dishonest, Superintendent," Eric cut in. "I have told no lies. I have not attempted to hide anything. I have falsified no documents, nor have I evaded any question."

"I call pretending to be something you're not—"

"I haven't pretended anything," Eric replied hotly. "I'm not acting, looking, thinking or working any differently now than when I started. The only thing different here is what you think of me as a person, which frankly I don't give a damn about."

Bledsoe sat up sharply.

Eric pointed a finger at the Superintendent. "The only thing dishonest here," he continued, "is the sudden change in your assessment of my character based on a trumped up complaint by some shady piece of trash like Bonner."

Bledsoe stood suddenly, slamming his hands onto the desk. "At least Bonner's a real man and not some—"

"That's enough!" Margaret pushed in between them. She turned on Bledsoe coldly. "You can stop right there, Dan, before you say anything more to embarrass yourself and this department and endanger your career."

Bledsoe looked at her in disbelief.

"You boys go on outside for a while," she said, giving Eric and Parker a look that brooked no argument. "This is a job for a government lawyer and things could get a little nasty." She gave Eric a push and a wink. "Go along now. Everything will be fine."

"Come on, Red," Parker said, taking Eric's arm and pulling him toward the door. "You can show me the stuffed squirrels." He jerked Eric on out the door and shut it behind them.

"Parker, I think we should stay in there," Eric protested. "My job's on the line."

"Your job is safely in the hands of Wonder Woman," Parker responded. "Let her saw at the superintendent's testicles a while in there, and I think he'll come to his senses."

"You don't know Superintendent Bledsoe," Eric said, shaking his head.

"You don't know Margaret."

"And you do?" Eric asked.

"She's a lady lawyer," Parker said. "They have a particular craving for sweet meats. Bledsoe's just a son-of-a-bitch. I'd rather face him than her in a fight any day."

"I hope your right." Eric tried to look hopeful.

"Trust my gay-man's intuition," Parker said with a wink. "When she's through with him, you'll probably have a promotion."

"You're making my life hell." Eric made a visible effort to relax and tried to smile.

Parker bobbed his eyebrows at him. "Let me kiss it and make it better." He was rewarded with a small laugh from Eric.

They heard the door to Bledsoe's office open and both turned expectantly. Margaret stood framed in the door fluffing her long blonde hair before taking notice of them with a satisfied smile.

"Now, Dan," Margaret said turning back into the office, "you be sure and do that for me, and this whole situation will blow over. No sense making trouble for yourself this close to retirement." Margaret gave a little wave into the office and pulled the door to.

She looked at Parker and Eric. "There are my two favorite men." She sashayed across the floor to them. "All done."

Eric started to speak.

"Let's go get a bite to eat," Margaret interrupted, taking his arm. "I'll tell you all about it then. Right now I'm hungry."

Parker leaned close to Eric's ear. "So am I," he whispered huskily.

Eric pulled away from both of them with a laugh. "You can both eat shit and die," he said standing with hands on hips.

"He's beautiful when he's angry," Margaret said with a sigh.

"Gorgeous," Parker assented.

"What are we going to do with him?" She shook her head at Eric.

"I have a few ideas." Parker licked his lips.

"Oh, dear." Margaret hugged herself with delight. "We'll talk about that first over the salad."

They headed out the front door leaving Eric standing in the middle of the great room.

"Hey!" Eric dropped his hands. "Wait up." He ran after them.

CHAPTER 7

"Mother of God!" Parker almost shouted. He braced himself for the next hairpin curve. "I thought you said driving would help you relax."

"It does," Eric said.

"Keep your eyes on the damn road, thank you." Parker closed his eyes for the next turn. "I'd hate to be your insurance company."

"I'll slow down if it'll make you feel better." Eric backed off the accelerator slightly. "You must be lousy in a high speed chase."

"It's not the speed that bothers me." Parker tried to look out the window.

Eric thought a moment. He turned to Parker again. "Still fighting that heights thing, are you?" he asked.

"Eyes on the road!" Parker held tightly to the edge of his seat. "I'm not *afraid* of heights. I'm just a little unsettled careening around ninety degree turns on a mountain dirt road with nothing but granite walls on one side and sheer drop-off on the other."

"You're afraid of heights."

"I'm not afraid!"

Eric steered close to the road edge, barely pulling away before the tires slipped over the side.

"Goddamn it!" Parker grabbed for the door handle with one hand and Eric's arm with the other.

"Sorry," Eric said genuinely. He slowed the Range Rover considerably and held it close to the center of the small roadway.

Parker took deep breaths, inwardly cursing himself. He loosened his grip on Eric's arm and willed himself to calm down.

Eric eased the auto around another sharp curve. "Remember? I had it figured it out from your reactions on the hike up above Bear Lake the other day." He nudged Parker's thigh with the edge of his hand. "These cliffs would bother anyone. It's nothing to be ashamed of."

"Who said anything about being ashamed?" Parker said evenly.

"Is my driving more to your liking now?" Eric flashed Parker a broad grin.

"Much." Parker could not deny his relief at Eric's change in speed and driving care. "Thanks."

"Don't mention it."

Parker relaxed visibly. "Where have we been heading in such an all-fired hurry?" he asked.

"You'll see soon enough."

Parker accepted that for the moment. "As long as I don't have to climb anything," he said. "Or swing from anything, or hang from anything, that's fine with me."

"I didn't think you would be the one to limit our possibilities so," Eric said, laughing.

Parker leered at him. "As long as it's indoors, these

restrictions do not apply," he said.

Eric laughed again and turned off onto a gravely dirt road that climbed upward through a grove of aspen.

"I really do like it when you laugh." Parker reached an arm around Eric and squeezed his shoulder.

"I'd be more interested in the things about me you don't like," Eric responded.

"Haven't found any," Parker replied. "Yet."

"I'll see what I can do about that," Eric replied.

"This is good," Parker said, nodding. He scooted a little closer to Eric. "You haven't broken out into a nervous sweat or anything."

"I'm not afraid of you." Eric shot him a sidelong glance and smiled.

"Good. I was beginning to wonder."

Eric turned his head sharply and gave Parker's hand a playful bite.

Parker howled dramatically and leaned around into Eric's line of vision. "I can bite too, you know." He cast a suggestive glance downward.

"Wouldn't be a wise move while I'm driving up here." Eric jerked at the wheel of the Range Rover, jolting Parker back into his seat.

"Okay, okay!" Parker cried out. "I'll be good."

"That's more like it," Eric said, downshifting into a sharp, upward turn.

Parker looked at the younger man's face, tracing the long, chiseled lines of Eric's jaw. He let his eyes wander down the muscular, freckled arms to the long, powerful fingers that worked the steering wheel so expertly.

"Stop staring at me," Eric finally said.

"I'm merely appreciating," Parker said, continuing his gaze.

"You're ogling."

"Ogling," Parker said thoughtfully. "I like that word."

"It's a little bumpy," Eric said, slowing the Range Rover, "and a whole lot steeper from here on."

"Here on, where?"

"Almost there," Eric said. "Keep your hat on."

Parker tried to relax. "When you said we were going to dinner, I pictured a quaint little downtown restaurant, a little ambience, a good wine list, you know?"

"There will be plenty of ambience," Eric said, "and I doubt that you'll find much to complain about with the wine list."

"But not downtown?"

"Not downtown."

Parker turned in his seat and laid his head to the side on the headrest, studying Eric. "I hope we're not going up on a glacier for a picnic," he said, fishing.

"No," was all Eric would say.

"Some little romantic spot," Parker said. "Something private."

Eric should his head and rolled his eyes. "You have only one thing on the brain, don't you?"

"I'm just curious," Parker protested. "You're being awfully mysterious."

"Curious!" Eric laughed. "You're cross-examining me like I *am* some sort of murder suspect."

"That's it!" Parker said with feigned excitement. "I can see it now. You've murdered, conspired, and now you're luring me to some remote mountain site to murder me and dismember my body for the wolves to dispose of. If you'd only succeeded with Margaret, you'd be well on your way to mass-murderer status."

"Don't be mean to Margaret," Eric said, turning the

Range Rover a little too sharply for emphasis.

"Shit!" Parker said, grabbing the sides of his seat for support. He reached over to punch Eric on the arm. "There's no need for further violence. I could probably get you off for doing in Margaret."

"Just for that," Eric said, "We're going to spend the rest of the evening going over all the evidence related to the murders up on Climber's Ridge. You'll be lucky to get a bag of trail mix for supper."

"I'm onto you," Parker said. "Excellent ploy . . . playing on my weaknesses. You are a worthy adversary for one such as I."

"One such as you?" Eric's laugh overshadowed the roar of the vehicle's engine. He flashed Parker a smile. "Yes, I know what your weakness is and, for right now anyway, you're gonna have to . . . play on it yourself." Eric's eyes seemed to sparkle in the slowly descending twilight.

Parker sat quietly, his head still propped sideways on the headrest. The moment almost astounded him. As he watched Eric, he tried to convince himself that his was a simple physical attraction. The younger man was, indeed, strikingly beautiful, muscular, intelligent, and seductive. But, Parker was becoming increasingly aware that his feelings toward Eric were something more. This was someone he wanted to be with. Someone whose very presence seemed to fill that nebulous void that Parker thought was only loneliness. That realization and the feelings it invoked, thrilled him more than he could make sense of, and also frightened him to some degree. He reached out to caress a wayward tress of red hair from off Eric's ear, letting his fingers slowly trace the line of the man's strong jaw.

The younger man's features softened in response. "You're staring again," Eric said softly, not really protesting.

For some reason, Parker found he couldn't respond. A depth of feeling had so overtaken him, that he was afraid to open his mouth.

"And your being awfully quiet," Eric said. "You're not falling asleep over there are you?"

Parker drew in a deep breath. "I don't know what I'm doing," he finally managed to say. "I guess I'm trying to figure out why I can't seem to take my eyes off you."

"Stop doing that," Eric said without meaning it.

"Doing what?"

"You're making it hard for me to concentrate on my driving."

Parker reached over to massage the back of Eric's neck. "Then pull over and we'll . . . we'll just take a little break."

"Keep your shirt on," Eric said down shifting the transmission. "Only a little farther." He turned sharply off the road into the trees. "Better hold on."

Parker felt the first jolt as gravel began to give way to small boulders. Gravity pulled his weight back into the seat as the powerful engine pushed the auto into a steep incline.

"Have I mentioned that I can't stand heights?" Parker asked, pressing closer to Eric's shoulder.

Eric gave him a reassuring smile. "You'll be on solid ground the whole way." He pulled the wheel sharply as the terrain suddenly leveled off a little. He slowed the vehicle beside a stand of small, thin aspen and came to a stop. "Everyone out," he said, swinging the driver's side door open.

"Why are we stopping here?" Parker asked. He reached tentatively for the door handle.

"Come on." Eric pulled a bulky sack out of the back seat. "Don't dawdle."

"I'm not going to go off trekking in the woods with you again," Parker said, climbing out the passenger side.

"No spirit of adventure," Eric called back, starting for the aspens.

"No death wish!" Parker answered. He caught up to Eric. "I thought we were going to your place?"

"We are." Eric maneuvered his load through a break in the grove. He nodded for Parker to follow.

Parker ducked through the grove of aspen to find himself standing at the back of a rock garden stretching along a short path upwards. He squinted in the moonlight to make out a small cabin nestled at the foot of a stand of pine. The cabin was an indistinct shadow in the moonlight and seemed to blend into the surrounding dark shapes of trees and boulders.

"Like it?" Eric asked. He studied Parker's reactions closely.

"Does it have indoor plumbing?" Parker asked.

"Of course." Eric's disappointment was evident.

"I'm only kidding." Parker threw an arm around Eric's shoulder. "Lead on, mountain boy. I sense the prospect of a cozy fire."

"It's not *Architectural Digest*, but it's home," Eric said, starting up the path.

They climbed the path together to the covered porch that spanned the front of the small cabin. Parker eyed the dark stained log beams that comprised the exterior walls.

"Don't be too impressed," Eric said, unlocking the door. "I built it from a kit."

"By yourself?" Parker looked impressed anyway.

"Well, not entirely." Eric reached inside for the light switch. "I did have to have a couple of the guys help set the roof trusses."

The cabin's interior was bathed in the warm glow of indirect lighting that spilled upward into the vaulted ceiling. The cabin proper was a fully open great room with only a small portion of the rear wall partitioned off into what appeared to be a bathroom. A stairway rose up to a loft area that Parker hoped was the bedroom.

Eric stepped up onto a platform that separated the small, but well-appointed kitchen and dining area from the main living space. He set his load on the granite counter top and began pulling leafy vegetables and pasta from the sack. "Make yourself comfortable," he said and hoisted a large pot from under the counter.

"Where's the bar?" Parker shed his coat. "I'll make us a drink." He hung it on a hook by the door. "Never mind," he said before Eric could answer. "I think I've spotted it."

He angled around an over-stuffed love seat toward an antique radio cabinet topped with an assortment of lead crystal decanters. He opened the small double doors and peered inside. Perched in the front was an unopened bottle of single malt scotch. He extracted it triumphantly. "Ah, me laddie," he called out in his best brogue. "Now I know it's love."

Eric laughed and threw a handful of spice into the pot. "I don't ever drink the stuff," he said.

"Infidel!" Parker hollered, clasping the bottle to his heart.

"Sorry," Eric answered. "Just an occasional glass of Merlot for me."

"Oh well. More for me." Parker pulled the cap off and poured a generous portion into a cut crystal glass. He cast a glance at Eric who was busy chopping at several celery stalks. Smiling to himself, he poured a small sampling into another glass. "What's happening in that pot over there anyway?" he asked, walking carefully to the kitchen balancing both tumblers of precious liquid. "I have a particular bias for Italian." He held the glass out to Eric.

"You just don't take no for an answer, do you?" Eric said, rolling his eyes.

"One of my current missions in life is to get you to try more new things." Parker donned his best leering expression and urged the glass at Eric. "Just a sip, now. How can you have a great bottle of scotch like this and not drink it?"

"To be honest, I saw the bottle you had in the motel room." Eric took the glass reluctantly. "I picked some up at the liquor store in case you wanted a drink."

"Why you young snake charmer you."

"Snake charmer, hell!" Eric said. "That stuff costs a mint."

"And worth every drop." Parker took a sip and smacked his lips. "One of life's finer things."

"Well," Eric said, sniffing the contents of the glass and frowning. "As much as I paid for it, I guess I should sample it."

"Now you're talking," Parker replied. "The scientific method is always the best approach."

Eric took a tentative sip.

"Don't swallow it yet," Parker cautioned. "Let it envelope your tongue for a second, then just let it fall down your throat."

Eric's eyes began to water and he swallowed hard. "Jez!" he managed, coughing. "That is nasty." He tried to catch his breath.

"Don't rush to judgment on the first taste." Parker patted him on the back. "A good scotch is an acquired taste."

"Why?" Eric grimaced and set the glass down.

"Why what?"

"Why," Eric sputtered, "would you want to acquire a taste for something that tastes like dirty kerosene."

"Philistine!" Parker shouted. He took a bracing swig from his glass.

Eric pulled a small bottled water out of the fridge. "I'll stick to nature's own, thank you very much," he said.

"Oh well." Parker poured the contents of Eric's glass into his own. "Waste not, want not." He eyed the contents of the simmering pot on the stove. "All right. I give up. Where are the meatballs?"

"There aren't any." Eric gave the contents a stir. "You're eating vegetarian tonight."

Parker wrinkled his nose and sipped his drink. "Of course," he said, "you know Hoover concluded that vegetarianism was just another front for the Communist conspiracy."

"Well," Eric said, smoothing his hair. "Never doubt the word of a man with such fine taste in dresses."

"Now don't go besmirching the good name of the Bureau just because our founding director occasionally liked to don a frilly frock."

"I have nothing but respect for the FBI." Eric's eyes danced. "Even though they now let your kind in."

"Only to better serve and protect your kind." Parker snuggled up to Eric.

Their lips touched, first lightly, then in a crescendo of intensity.

Eric broke away, visibly reddened. "Don't mess with me now. I'm cooking," he said, returning to his pot on the stove.

"So am I." Parker slipped an arm around the younger man's muscular waist.

Their eyes met for a moment.

"When do I get to whisper sweet nothings in your ear?" Parker asked.

"Oh, please." Eric's nose wrinkled. "Not when I'm about to eat."

Parker pulled him away from the stove and playfully pushed him back against the cabinet. "Man does not live by bread alone," he said grabbing Eric's hips and pulling him close.

Eric drew his muscular arms about Parker's neck. "If a man lies with a male as with a woman, both of them have committed an abomination," he quoted from Leviticus, chuckling at the tickle of Parker's chin stubble against the tender flesh about his own Adam's apple.

"Don't worry," Parker said, inhaling the redhead's clean, spicy scent. "What I plan to do with you would be impossible with a woman."

Eric laughed throatily.

Parker felt the younger man's impressive hardness against his own body and pulled Eric in closer. "I detect a strong fundamentalist upbringing," he said.

"Always the detective." Eric breathed shallowly, rolling his head from side to side to allow Parker free rein with his neck. "I had perfect attendance in Sunday School," he managed to say, feeling Parker moving against him.

Parker took his attention away from Eric's neck and looked into his eyes. His hips continued their slow, subtle gyrations against Eric's groin. "Agnostic, myself," he said before pressing his open mouth against Eric's slightly parted lips.

Their tongues darted one to the other until they pulled apart gasping for air. Eric's hands dropped from around Parker's neck to the man's buttocks. He squeezed hard.

"Recovering Baptist," Eric breathed.

"Thought so." Parker bit his lower lip at the pleasure of Eric's grip. "I know a great twelve step program."

"Really." Eric pulled Parker tight against him.

"It's a religious experience." Parker groaned slightly.

"Hallelujah!" Eric laughed and threw his head back.

Parker deftly released the buckle of Eric's belt with one hand while undoing the waistband button with his other.

Eric looked down and raised an eyebrow. "I think you're hands are a little too practiced at that," he said.

"You'll thank God for these practiced hands shortly." Parker brushed his lips against Eric's lightly.

Eric threw his head back again, this time allowing Parker's lips to roam wildly about his neck.

The phone by the dining table clamored for attention.

"Ignore it." Parker breathed hotly against Eric's chin.

"The machine will get it," Eric gave Parker's ass a reassuring squeeze.

Their lovemaking foreplay continued despite the phone's insistence. The answering machine clicked on.

"Finally," Parker said quietly. He tugged at Eric's zipper and smiled as it burst open spontaneously against the mounting pressure behind it. He could hear Eric's voice droning the opening message on the answering machine. He stroked a hand up the outside of Eric's undershorts, admiring the throbbing hardness pushing out against the thin cotton. He became aware of the other voice on the answering machine.

"Parker! Eric!" The shrill female voice pierced through the sound of Eric's humming groans. "If you're there pick up the phone!"

The two men pulled apart slightly, looking at each other.

"I know you're there! Pick up the goddamn phone!" the woman screamed.

"Margaret?" They said simultaneously.

"Someone's trying to break in the house," Margaret whispered in a panic. "Please pick up the damn ..." There was a crackling click and the voice went silent.

CHAPTER 8

"**Goddamn it!**" **Margaret pumped the release** button on the phone, praying for a dial tone.

Frantically, her eyes scanned the open loft that served as her bedroom and study. She dropped the receiver onto her desk and ran to the door, making sure it was locked. Pressing her ear against the door, she strained for anymore unwelcome sounds over the pounding of her heart. Hearing a muffled, rustling sound, she caught her breath.

"Thank God," she mouthed silently. Whoever it was, was still messing around downstairs. The stairs would creak noisily no matter how delicately someone tried to walk on them. She would at least have some warning when they started up to her sanctuary. What would she do then?

She wrung her hands nervously. Where the hell were Parker and Eric? She fought back the tears and rising panic.

"Think!" she told herself. "Think."

Margaret tiptoed in bare feet across the smooth oak

floor back to her desk and grabbed up the phone again, hoping against hope. It was still dead. She stifled a sob and gingerly replaced the receiver.

"Cell phone!" Margaret clamped a hand over her mouth excitedly. Her eyes darted about the room for her purse. "Please, be here, please, please, please!" she whispered.

Enough light filtered through the floor to ceiling window behind her desk to see the obvious dumping places for a purse. Margaret bit her lip, remembering that she had tossed her bag on the kitchen table downstairs when she came home. She leaned against the window sill and peered through the mini-blinds, looking for any sign of friendly life below.

"Up shit creek without a paddle," Margaret muttered to the window. She returned to the bed and sat trembling in her nightgown, waiting. She shook her head and pounded on her knees with her fists. "Bullshit" she whispered to herself, fighting back tears.

If Parker and Eric weren't coming to her, then she was going to them. The thought suddenly returned to her that maybe she had dreamt the whole thing. What a wonderful relief if the whole thing had just been a silly nightmare. But, she couldn't stay in her house alone this night.

She got up and wiped her moistened cheeks with her hands. Taking a deep breath, she hurried over to her closet and pulled out a pair of jeans. She donned them quickly on the move to her bureau to grab a pull over sweater. Rather than take the time to lace up a pair of tennis shoes, she slipped on her power stilettos she had worn earlier that day, and tiptoed to her bedroom door. She stood for a moment, hoping against hope that she

was now fully awake and her little nightmare drama was
really over.

She grabbed the cold, brass doorknob tightly and
turned it ever so slowly, grimacing at the click of the latch
release which sounded like a sonic boom to her adrenalin-
enhanced hearing. She pulled the door open a crack and
tried to penetrate the dark hall beyond with eyes that were
now more adjusted to the dark. She could make out the
dark lines of the stair landing banister rail. No sign of
movement, no rustle of shadows in the dark were evident.
Margaret put a hand to her heaving breasts and willed
herself to breathe more deeply, more regularly. She still
felt like it was all a dream. She pulled the door the rest of
the way open and stepped out onto the landing. For a
moment, she breathed a little easier. It was all a dream.

With a little more confidence, Margaret moved to the
top of the landing. She stepped down onto the first riser,
almost laughing. Carefully she made her way down the
stairs, sliding her hand down the banister. She could see
dim, veiled light streaming in from the windows beyond
the end of the stairs on the main floor and she relaxed her
vigilance, feeling even more confident. The onset of
embarrassment made her thank God that the boys had
not picked up the phone.

She stepped down onto the carpeted floor of her
living room, remembering what Parker had told her about
his planned romantic evening. Parker and Eric— "Shit!"
she muttered to herself. She had to get to the kitchen
phone and hopefully it would be working. She had to call
them—tell them not to worry. She began to race herself
for the coming sarcasm she would have to endure from
Parker. But, anything was better than the seeming brush
with death she had previously imagined. Having gotten

her bearings in the light that managed to intrude from the street lights beyond the sheer curtains, she turned to make her way into the kitchen.

A sudden movement caught the corner of her eye. Margaret felt a sudden wrenching on her arm as she was jerked into the dining room. A pair of rough hands shoved her hard down into one of the chairs. Margaret was paralyzed. The unseen figure wrapped his thick arms about her, pinning her to the chair. Another hand clamped itself over her mouth.

"Shut up!" the raspy voice growled into her ear.

Margaret realized she was screaming. Fear had overwhelmed her and she fought to regain control over herself. She gasped air through her nostrils, demanding self-awareness, a clever head. She needed to think—to get a clear picture of what was happening. Her legal training cried out for her to find some way to negotiate for her life.

Margaret nodded her head, indicating she had understood the man. Here wide eyes panned side to side, trying to see who had her pinned down. It was clear to her now that there was more than one.

"All right, lady," the raspy voice of the other man whispered in her face. "You know why we're here." His features were hidden by a dark, woolen ski mask pulled down over his face.

Margaret blinked. Why *were* they here? Robbery? Money? She closed her eyes and nodded again.

Masked Man signaled to the man with thick arms who held her pinned down. Carefully, Thick Arms released the pressure against her mouth and slowly removed his hand.

Margaret gasped for air. "On the table in the kitchen," she managed to say despite the hyperventilation.

Masked Man left quickly, leaving her pinned in the chair by Thick Arms.

Margaret could feel his hot breath on her neck, laced with bourbon and cigarettes. That odor mixed with her fear churned her stomach and she fought the compulsion to wretch. She heard Masked Man dumping the contents onto the hard surface of her kitchen island. Mentally she tried to take inventory of her purse's contents for future reference—*future reference*—she shut her eyes tight but felt them tear up anyway. She agonized over whether or not there would be a future.

"Goddamn it!" Masked Man yelled out from the kitchen with obvious anger and frustration.

Margaret turned her head in that direction and saw the heavy, squat Masked Man bearing down on her. What had she forgotten?

Masked Man bent over her. Margaret forced herself to look at him—a pair of angry, bloodshot eyes glaring through the black ski mask.

"Where are they?" Masked Man asked in his familiar raspy voice. "You'd better tell me now if you know what's good for you!"

The heavy hand released her mouth momentarily.

"Where is what?" Margaret stammered. "Whatever it is you can have it!" Her voice rose to near hysteria. "Take whatever you want! Just take it and get out!"

Masked Man grabbed her face by the chin with one hand. "You know what we want," he insisted. "Now, where is it?"

Margaret's mind raced. "What?" she almost screamed. "Money? Jewelry? Credit cards? What?"

"Cut the crap, lady," Masked Man said. "You know what we're here for and you'd better tell me where it is or you're gonna regret it."

"If you tell me what it is, I'll tell you where it is," Margaret responded, letting anger represent her fear. "I'm not a damn mind reader!"

Masked Man straightened, then lunged at her as if he was going to hit her. Margaret screamed and struggled against her captor. Instead, Masked Man stepped back, laughing at her helplessness.

"Son of a bitch!" Margaret screamed at him.

The man signaled to her captor to shut her up and Thick Arms put a hand over her mouth once more.

"Take her upstairs," Masked Man ordered. "We'll search up there next. Tie her on the bed, then maybe we can convince her to cooperate. I'll finish up the search down here."

Obediently, Thick Arms all but lifted Margaret out of the chair. "Let's go upstairs, miss," Thick Arms said. He pulled her arms behind her back and clamped them together in a vice-like grip. Then he pushed Margaret toward the stairs.

Her ankle twisted slightly trying to keep up in the stiletto heels she was wearing. "For God's sake!" she pleaded. "Give me time to take steps. It's hard enough in these…" She paused with the sudden realization that maybe she wasn't so helpless. Maybe she had a weapon of her own.

Thick Arms pressed in close behind her as she started up the first stair riser. As he lifted her body up with the left foot solidly planted on the riser, she suddenly stamped downward with the left, dropping all her body weight onto the heel of her shoe as it hammered downward onto the main floor level and onto the instep of the man who held her hands pined behind her back.

The man screamed in pain and instantly released his hold on Margaret. She reacted instantly, leaping out of both shoes and racing up the stairs in her stocking feet.

"Fucking bitch!" she heard Thick Arms scream after her.

She did not look back, even as she heard Masked Man running across her hardwood floors from the kitchen. Once at the top of the stairs, she stumbled back into her bedroom, slamming the door shut and locking it behind her. She ran over to the window beside her bed, unlatched it and threw it open.

"Help!" she screamed at the top of her lungs, praying that someone would hear her, despite the fact that the window faced the street and the noisy tourist traffic beyond. "Help! Please!" she continued to scream.

The tears came again and she collapsed to her knees by the window. There was no way her bedroom door would hold against the two men outside. She sat waiting for the inevitable, fighting the paralyzing fear to think of some strategy for survival. But there was only silence.

After a moment, she forced herself to her feet and made her way over to the desk to try to get a dial tone on the phone. It was dead.

Parker and Eric raced down the mountain roads for town. Eric drove like a madman and all Parker could do was hold on for dear life.

"Anything?" Eric called out over the sound of the straining engine.

"Nothing," Parker shouted back. "All I get is a busy signal," he said, returning the Blackberry to the clip on his belt.

"Shit!" Eric said, hammering a fist on the steering wheel.

"What?" Parker asked.

"I forgot to get a gun or something," Eric replied angrily. "I should have…"

"Don't sweat it," Parker said. "I've got mine on me. Just drive!"

Eric spun the wheel, rocketing the Range Rover onto another gravel road. Parker wasn't sure if they were driving down the mountain so much as falling down the mountain.

"Did you call the sheriff?" Eric asked.

"I notified their dispatcher," Parker replied. "Sheriff's up at the glacier station handling some drunk students. We're closer so I told them we'd be first responders and get back to him if we needed any kind of backup."

"What do you think's going on?"

"Hell if I know," Parker said. "It's probably nothing serious." He could see Eric wasn't buying that explanation. "Or," he continued, "it could be Margaret's overactive imagination."

"But— " Eric began.

"How much further?" Parker asked, interrupting. He didn't like discussing what might be possible. In his experience, the worst case scenario was always the unthinkable.

Eric spun two wheels off the dirt road and onto city pavement. "Next turn," he said. His knuckles were white on the steering wheel.

Parker tried to think of something positive to say. "She'll be all right," he said for Eric's benefit. "She's feisty and resourceful." He sat forward trying to will the car to go even faster. "She'll be all right!"

Margaret sat down at her desk, listening intently for any sounds in the house. She sat quietly, not moving, for what seemed an eternity. The only audible sound was her own heartbeat pounding relentlessly in her ears. The quiet sent her imagination into overdrive and Margaret's mind raced through one horrible scenario after another, each growing more horrible.

Somewhere on the floor below a door slammed shut. Margaret stiffened. She got up from the desk hoping her attackers had gone, or maybe they had just wanted her to think they were gone. Warily, she tiptoed to the bedroom door and pressed her ear against it, listening. The tell-tale creak of the stairs echoed in the hall beyond her door.

"Oh, shit," Margaret whispered in panic. She dashed about the room frantically, looking for anything she could use as a weapon. "Shit, shit, shit!" was all she could repeat.

She turned sharply at the sound of the door knob turning. Her panic mutated to fear and anger. She grabbed up a heavy bronze paperweight from her desk and tossed it in her hand like a baseball.

The door knob jiggled again and Margaret heard the sound of metal scraping on metal. Whoever it was, was jimmying the door latch. She held the heavy paperweight at her shoulder, poised and ready to heave it at the intruder. She tried to swallow her pounding heartbeat back into her chest.

The bedroom door swung open violently. Margaret screamed and leveraged all her strength behind the throw of the paperweight. It sailed across the room, finding its mark with a heavy thud.

"Goddamn it!" A familiar voice hollered as the tall, shadowy figure in the door sank back into the hallway.

"Parker!" Margaret screamed. Through her tears she made out the red hair of another figure appearing at the doorway over the unlucky fallen one.

"Well," said the redhead, looking down at the still, prone body at his feet. "I told you we should have knocked."

CHAPTER 9

Parker pressed the ice pack to the side of his head squinting against the throbbing pain. He opened his eyes, trying to focus the blurs around him into intelligible shapes. A pair of strong hands was kneading the muscles about his neck and Parker emitted a trailing moan.

"How are you doing, old man?"

Parker recognized Eric's voice from behind him.

"Is it very bad?" Margaret was on her knees in front of him. She brought her face up to his. "I'm so sorry, sweetie."

He could hear the tears in her voice, but his head still hurt too much to make a sound. He moaned and struggled to his knees, an act he regretted immediately as the pounding in his head crescendoed dramatically. "Shit and goddamn it," he said weakly. He felt Eric's sinewy fingers slide under his armpits.

"Up we go," Eric said, easily pulling Parker to his feet.

"Wait, wait, wait, wait!" Parker moaned loudly. He gripped his head tighter, trying to keep it from blowing apart completely.

Eric helped him over to the king-sized bed and sat him on the edge.

"Can you ever forgive me, honey?" Margaret plopped down beside him.

"I'll forgive you just as soon as my head does." Parker cast her a sidelong glance, still holding his aching head. "What the hell did you bean me with?"

Margaret patted his cheek. "It was just the paperweight from my desk." She kissed one of the hands gripping his head. "The little brass one."

"You mean this little brass one?" Eric held up the heavy object from the doorway where he had gone to retrieve the offending weapon. "It only grazed you."

"Grazed?" Parker shifted his burry gaze from the paperweight to Margaret. "I'm amazed that you could pick the damn thing up, much less throw it across the room at me."

"Terror is a great motivator." She smiled innocently at him.

Parker released the grip on his skull, relieved that the pounding was easing and being replaced by a constant dull ache. He stretched the muscles in his neck. Eric sat on the bed behind him and resumed his neck massage. Parker sighed and leaned back against Eric's muscular chest.

Margaret watched, amused. "So," she said. "I guess this answers my question about what you two have been up to while I've been in mortal danger, waiting to have my throat cut, all alone, defenseless and helpless."

"Defenseless, my ass." Parker rubbed his head for effect. "I think if the truth be told, I'm the only one who's been in mortal danger around here."

Eric chuckled and rested his cheek against the top of Parker's head. "Now don't be mean," he said. "The phone lines *were* cut."

"That's right!" Margaret cut in excitedly. "Otherwise there would have been police all over the place before you arrived."

"Why didn't you call the police in the first place," Parker asked.

"I panicked, okay?" Margaret said. "When I heard someone messing around downstairs, my first instinct was to call you guys." She threw her hands up. "So sue me!"

"Where's your cell phone?" Parker asked, evenly.

"Well," Margaret stuttered. She looked around for a good explanation. "When the line went dead while I was talking to Eric's machine, I . . . why the hell didn't you pick up the phone and talk to me?" she asked, speaking faster. "Here I was, up to my tits in murderers, and you two are too busy fooling around to—"

"Where's your goddamn cell phone, Margaret?" Parker reiterated a little louder.

Margaret clenched her lips together and assumed her most put upon expression. "I don't want to talk about this anymore," she said.

"It wouldn't have been in your purse down on the kitchen table, would it?" Parker tossed the small phone into her lap.

"Just shut up, all right?" She threatened to throw the phone back at him. "How the hell was I supposed to know I would need my cell phone tonight, for Christ's sake?" She shuddered visibly. "Come on, G-Man, give me a break. I was so scared." Her chin quivered as she fought back a resurgence of tears.

Parker sighed and sat up. He took her hands in his. "Okay, okay," he said. "I had to give you a hard time because I've never been creamed by another lawyer before."

"I told you I'm a nasty bitch in a fight." Margaret grinned coyly at him through the tears.

"Yes you are, my sweet." He kissed her forehead.

"Oh look!" Eric chimed in from behind them. "The two sharks are making nice."

Parker made a grab for Eric's crotch, but the sudden movement threatened to rekindle the throbbing in his head.

"Can't get enough of him can you?" Margaret dried her eyes.

Parker rubbed his forehead. "For your information, my dear," he said. "I haven't managed to get *any* of him yet. You call at the most inopportune times."

"Well, excuse me," she said dramatically.

"If I didn't know better," Parker said through clenched teeth, "I'd swear you planned it this way."

Eric waved at the two of them to notice him. "Maybe it would help if Margaret checked about the house to see if anything was stolen," he said. "And then maybe someone would like to notify the police."

Margaret and Parker looked up at him.

"He's so down to business, isn't he?" Margaret said to Parker.

"He needs to get laid desperately," Parker answered.

"The two of you need to go get fucked," Eric said, walking over to the desk to deposit the paper weight.

Margaret stood up, stretching the tension from her neck. "Did the bastards, whoever they were, tear up the downstairs?" she asked.

"The contents of your purse were dumped out on the kitchen table." Parker stood and stretched as well.

"How did they get in?" Margaret turned sharply to face Parker. "For that matter, how did the two of you get in?"

"Do you always leave your back door open?" Eric asked.

"Open!" Margaret's mouth dropped open. "I keep this place locked up tighter than—"

"Careful," Parker interrupted, waving a finger at her.

"I was going to say Fort Knox," Margaret said, taking a swat at his hand. "I'm never out or in without all the doors locked. I lived in Chicago too long to change hard-learned habits of caution."

"Does anyone else have a key?" Parker asked.

"No one. Since I've lived here, I've never . . ." She paused.

"Well?" Parker looked at her inquisitively.

"Well, I mean, there is another key, of course, but it certainly doesn't have anything to do with this."

"I'll be the judge of that."

"No. I mean, there is another key," she said. "I keep one in my desk at the office for emergencies. But no one—"

Parker held up a hand. "Is there anyone at your office right now?" he asked.

Margaret thought. "Well," she said. "Bobby is probably there . . . the night guard. Why do—"

"Call." Parker pointed at the cell phone.

Obediently, Margaret picked up the phone and punched in the number.

Eric signaled for Parker's attention.

Parker raised his eyebrows and moved over to the

desk.

Eric nodded at the file folder on top of a stack of papers. "That's a personnel file from our office," Eric whispered.

While Margaret was occupied on the phone, Parker flipped the file open and perused the contents. He pointed to the name heading the file and raised an eyebrow at Eric. Eric moved the file aside to inspect the next one. The fourth and last file they encountered caught them both by surprise. Eric blinked his eyes at Parker.

Parker smiled and picked up the file. "Would it make you uncomfortable if I gave your file a once over?" he asked.

"If I said yes, you'd just enjoy it more," Eric replied with a resigned shrug.

Parker flipped the file open. "So true." He scanned its contents with overly enthusiastic interest.

Eric sighed and tried to look unconcerned. "I've seen that file, and it's rather a boring read," he said.

"Margaret must not think so."

"And how would you know what Margaret thinks?" Eric asked with a sneer.

"Now don't go getting upset," Parker said, flipping to another page in the file. "I'll let you know if there's anything here of concern."

Eric shot him the finger, but Parker refused to look up from the file.

"Well, I never would have thought," Margaret called out, hanging up the phone.

Both men turned to her.

"The key's missing?" Parker asked.

"Bobby said he looked all through my desk drawer," she said. "No key."

"Well, that tells us how," Parker said, dropping the file onto her desk.

Eric slid the file across the desk away from Parker. "Now all we need is the *who* and the *why*," he said.

"I need to call a locksmith." Margaret rose from the bed and paced in front of the bed.

Parker went over to her, took her hands in his, and pulled her back to the bed. "First things first," he said, sitting on the bed beside her. "From the looks of the downstairs, your intruder was looking for something."

"Robbery?" Margaret shook her head. "And how did they get by my security alarm?"

"Well, my dear," Parker began, patting her knee. "For one thing I noticed you had disabled the audible alarm."

"Disabled?"

"Turned it off," he explained patiently.

"Well," Margaret blustered, "I didn't see where that ridiculous beeping sound would scare anyone away." Margaret looked at him annoyed. "And these condos are so well insulated, that the neighbors wouldn't be able to hear it anyway." Her hands dotted the air for emphasis. "And besides, that's why I pay a monthly fee to a security company. My system is supposed to notify them of any break in and then they notify the police."

"Sweetheart," Parker said, shaking his head at her. "If the audible alarm had been on you might have known the moment someone broke in. And I assure you, it may well have scared them away."

Margaret batted her lashes at him.

"The rest of your system was disabled when the phone line was cut," Parker added.

"Shit!" Margaret put her head in her hands. "So much for a two thousand dollar security system."

Parker patted her knee again and tried not to laugh.

"I guess I'd better look around and see what was stolen," Margaret said, getting up again.

"Nothing was stolen." Parker pulled her back down.

"How would you know?" Margaret and Eric said simultaneously.

"Everything was dropped out of your purse, that's true," he said. "But your wallet was untouched. Money and credit cards left alone."

"Well, what the hell were they looking for?" Margaret asked.

"Ah. Now that's the question." Parker got up from the bed and walked toward the desk. "What, indeed?"

Margaret looked at Eric who could only shrug. "Rape?" she asked, wrapping her arms about herself.

"Well, dear," Parker stifled a snicker. "I'm sure if they had gotten upstairs and found you, the thought would have crossed their mind."

"Don't be insensitive." Eric punched Parker in the arm.

Parker ignored him. "Margaret, why are you looking through these personnel files?" he asked.

"I was just checking the backgrounds of our principal players," she responded with a shrug.

"Excellent," Parker said. "So you *do* consider him a suspect." He pointed accusingly at Eric.

"Wha . . .?" Eric began.

"A suspect?" Margaret looked at Parker questioningly.

"It's always the person you would least suspect." Parker gave her a knowing look.

"Well," she said, returning Parker's look. "I didn't want to say anything."

"What do you mean I'm a suspect?" Eric stood

askance. "You've got to be putting me on." He looked at Parker with growing irritation. "You can't be serious—"

"Well now, dear, let's be honest," Margaret interrupted. She assumed her most imposing demeanor. "What do we really know about you?"

"What?" Eric couldn't believe what he was hearing.

"And I mean, really." Margaret continued. "I think it's very interesting that right from the beginning of this case, you've ingratiated yourself to the main investigator. It's not the first time a criminal element has tried to influence an investigation by sexually compromising a federal agent."

"You've got to be kidding." Eric threw up his hands. "That's the most ass—"

"He has been asking a lot of questions," Parker volunteered. He folded his arms and eyed Eric suspiciously. "I should have checked to see if his bedroom was equipped for video surveillance."

"Video . . .?" Eric stared at him in shock. He caught a tell-tale quivering at the corners of Parker's mouth. "I knew it!" He pointed to Parker's face.

Parker's seriousness weakened perceptibly.

"Go ahead and laugh, you son-of-a-bitch!" Eric closed in on Parker still pointing. "You are so full of shit."

"Good save, Margaret," Parker managed, unable hold back his laughter.

Eric turned his glare toward Margaret who sat on the bed unruffled.

She pursed her lips. "Now wait a minute," she said. "I may be on to something here."

Parker put a hand over his mouth.

"I can't believe your encouraging him." Eric started

for her.

"Now Eric." She put up her hands defensively. "Everything you say can and will be used against—"

Eric grabbed her up from the bed. "I don't plan on saying anything." He began tickling her mercilessly. He grunted with satisfaction as she began writhing with laughter and screams.

"Help me you asshole!" she screamed at Parker.

"I'm not getting involved," Parker said, backing away.

Eric released Margaret and she fell panting onto the bed. He turned to Parker. "Now I am going to punish you severely."

"What did I do?" Parker tried to look innocent. "She's the one—"

"Now it's your turn," Eric said, diving at Parker.

Parker faked to the right and spun about out of harm's way. Laughing, he dashed for the bed and grabbed up Margaret for a human shield.

Eric stood across the room watching them. "I'll get even," he said with a smile.

Margaret stopped her struggling. "Now don't be a spoilsport," she said.

Parker released his hold on Margaret. "He's rather touchy right now," he whispered loudly into her ear. "But then, I can understand why. Your phone call interrupted our date at a time when things were getting somewhat," he winked at Eric, "intense."

"Do tell," Margaret said.

"I'd prefer to get back to discussing the robbery, please." Eric sighed.

Margaret and Parker exchanged disappointed glances.

"The question was," Eric continued, "what interest is my personnel file to you?"

Margaret started to speak.

"And this time," Eric interrupted, "something closer to the truth would be appreciated."

Margaret rolled her eyes and went to the desk. "There's no cause for alarm," she said, straightening the files. "While I was getting these others to check background on, I went ahead and picked yours up just to be sure no one had written anything derogatory since your recent and unfortunate visit with your boss."

Eric relaxed. "Thanks," he said meekly.

Margaret gave him a warm smile. "Don't mention it. Big Sister is looking out for you."

"Anything of interest in the other files?" Parker joined them at the desk.

"Well, not really." Margaret frowned. "Pretty standard stuff. Nothing that jumps out at you."

Parker picked up one of the folders. "Well, let's run each one of them down." He sat down at the desk and spread the file open.

"What are we looking for?" Eric moved behind Parker to look over his shoulder. "Like, drug arrests or something?"

"Already done that," Margaret said, leaning against Eric. "Of course, I didn't expect to find anything like that since I doubt the Forest Service would have taken a convicted felon."

"Ah," Parker said, smiling at them over his shoulder. "But the criminal mind is somewhat predictable. Most serious criminals have equally serious backgrounds that need to be covered up when moving from situation to situation." He scanned over the file's contents. "You look for things that don't match or add up." He tossed the file to the side and opened another. "Lies are difficult to maintain seamlessly." He scanned the file. "Someone with something to hide counts on the fact that an employer will take certain things for granted." He tapped a page in the file with his finger. "Like this."

Margaret and Eric leaned in for a better look.

"Educational background lists a B.A. in geology. That's a bit odd. It should be a bachelor of science." Parker flipped to the back of the file. "Let's compare it to the original application." He pulled the pages back and forth. "Ah, see here?" On the original app he's written B.S. So it was just a transcription error."

"That's a pretty small detail," Eric said.

"Investigation is in the details," responded Parker.

"Lying about educational background is a common ploy on employment applications," Margaret said. She patted Parker on the head. "Good bloodhound. Keep sniffing."

Parker snorted and reached for another file. He scanned it quickly under his companions' watchful eyes. He tossed it to the side and pulled another file out.

"Here!" He almost shouted tapping on the paper.

Margaret and Eric looked at the entry and then at each other.

"You two are hopeless," Parker said, flipping to the back of the file. "No. See there. He's entered the same Social Security number and place of birth on the original app. There's no transcription error this time."

Margaret squeezed his shoulder. "Are you going to share this little find with us, or what?" she asked. "Looks like a perfectly good Social Security number to me."

"Ditto," Eric offered.

"Oh, come on people. Look at it." Parker tapped a finger on the page again. "It's a 769 prefix." He looked from one to the other.

Margaret and Eric shrugged in unison.

"The file says he was born in Arkansas," Parker added hopefully.

"So far this is really fascinating." Eric said smugly.

Margaret giggled beside him.

"You two are useless." Parker reached behind Eric and slapped him on the ass.

"Ow!"

"You're not paying attention," Parker said. "Social Security prefixes indicate what state you were born in. 769 is the prefix for Florida."

"Are you telling me that you have memorized all the Social Security prefixes?" Margaret asked.

Parker nodded triumphantly.

"Get a life." Margaret turned to Eric. "Do you really want to get involved with someone who memorizes numerical demographics for a hobby?"

Eric patted Parker on the head. "Oh, it's not his mind I'm interested in," he said, bobbing his eyebrows.

"Fuck the both of you." Parker took another swipe at Eric's bottom, but the younger man parried the blow.

"Now, if you two can concentrate for a second." Parker returned his attention to the file. "This info is not something you would accidentally get wrong. Either the Social Security number is wrong or the birth state is wrong, or both. "Either way we have a falsified application for federal employment."

"Hmm." Margaret leaned in to give the file a closer look. "Arlee Bonner. Why am I not surprised?"

"My favorite homophobe," Parker said.

"Shall we drag his ass in for a little questioning?" Eric asked, clapping a fist into the other hand.

"Let's not be hasty," Parker said. "I've already requested the Bureau conduct a thorough background check on the son-of-a-bitch. I'll give them a call with this latest info and by tomorrow we ought to have the full rundown."

"So this good-ol'-boy's a suspect then?" Margaret's eyes narrowed.

"Believe me. Bonner's been a suspect since our little run-in yesterday," Parker responded. "But he's too stupid to be anything but a mule herder in a drug scheme as big as this one."

"We want the big boys," Margaret confirmed.

"As far up the line as we can go." Parker closed the file and stood. "Well, that's enough for one evening. It's getting late and I still haven't had my supper yet." He put an arm around Eric's broad shoulders.

"That won't take long," Eric said. "I just have to heat everything back up."

"Why don't we just stay here and I'll order out for pizza or something?" Margaret said hurriedly.

"Pizza?" Eric grimaced.

"We?" Parker questioned.

"Well, I mean . . ." Margaret's face drew up in a pout. "You're not going to go off and leave me here alone, are you?"

Parker moved between her and Eric and gave her the evil eye. "Margaret," he said in an emphatic whisper. "I'd like a little time with Eric tonight."

Margaret grabbed his hands. "I don't want to be alone," she pleaded. "I just need a blanket and a sofa. I won't get in the way. You won't even know I'm there. Honest."

Margaret!" Parker said trying to smile. "I think you'll

be just fine here now. Whoever broke in isn't—"

"Fine." Margaret threw up her hands dramatically. "Fine. No problem. You're right." She stomped over to the bed and plopped down. "Go on. I'll be just fine."

"Now, Margaret." Parker followed her to the bed with outstretched arms.

"No." She held up a hand. "Don't worry about me. I'm a big girl." Her eyes grew moist.

Parker turned back to Eric. "Shit!" he said, throwing his hands up.

"We're not leaving her here by herself after what's happened," Eric said, shaking his head.

Margaret gave Parker a triumphant snap of the fingers.

"Whose side are you on?" Parker looked at Eric, pleading.

Eric just smiled and shook his head.

"Oh, all right," Parker conceded. "Pack a bag." He stuck his tongue out at Margaret's smug expression. "And hurry!"

Margaret ignored him and took Eric's arm. "Come help me pick out a nightie," she said, pulling him over to her bureau. "Something appropriate for a cabin in the mountains."

"We'd better pack up these files to bring also," Parker said, sighing. "Where's your briefcase?"

Margaret snubbed him and turned back to rummaging through a drawer in her bureau. Parker looked about the sides of the desk and spotted a large catalogue case sitting on the floor behind the desk chair.

He hoisted the heavy case up onto the desk. "What the hell's in this damn thing?" he asked, grunting at the weight. Attached to the case was a small collapsible luggage cart. "So that's how you haul this thing around."

Margaret and Eric were too busy stuffing various items into her overnight bag to pay any attention to Parker's musings.

He shrugged and stacked up the file folders littering the desk. He stuck a hand into the case to make room for them. "What in God's name—" A clatter of shiny, spherical objects tumbled out of the files and scattered about the desk. Parker set the files down and picked up one of the small computer disks. "What are these?" he called out, holding up one of the disks.

Margaret paused in her packing to look up. "They're computer CD's, dear," she said, returning to her bag. "Anything else?"

"I mean," Parker said, annoyed. "What are they doing in the personnel files?"

"In the files?" Margaret looked puzzled. "What are you talking about?"

Parker collected the other CD off the desk. "Simply that these disks fell out of this stack of files," he said. "They weren't in any of the files we looked at."

"Maybe they were stuck between the files," Margaret ventured. "I can't imagine what they are. They probably got there by accident when the files were being collected for me at the Station."

Parker studied the CD's. "Margaret, can I borrow your laptop for a second?" he asked.

"All right," Margaret said with a shrug. "But don't go snooping around in my file directories."

"I wouldn't dream of it," Parker said, pulling the small grey laptop computer from the case and sitting it on the desk. He pulled a chair up and flipped the screen up, toggling the power on as he sat.

"Don't get into anything heavy," Eric cautioned. He carted Margaret's bag over to the desk. "We're ready to go."

"This'll just take a sec." Parker popped one of the disks into the CD-ROM drive. He manipulated the built in roller ball mouse and opened a directory of the disk. "Numerical file names," he said blankly.

"See if you can open one," Eric said from over Parker's shoulder.

Parker clicked the mouse and waited for the file to open. A page of unintelligible computer code scrolled up the screen.

"Gibberish," Eric intoned.

Parker stared at the screen. "We just need the right interpreter." He tried to memorize some of the number and symbol sequences.

"You can ponder all that later," Eric said, giving him a nudge. "It's getting late, and I'm tired."

"Right." Parker popped the CD out and closed up the laptop. "Straight to bed with you." He smiled up at Eric.

Eric grinned and shook his head. "Pig." He picked up Margaret's bag.

"I've got everything," Margaret said breathlessly, coming out of the bathroom carrying another bag.

"You get that one," Eric said, looking back at Parker from the door.

Parker reached a reluctant arm out.

"Such gentlemen," Margaret said. She handed the bag to Parker. "This'll be a lot of fun."

They started for the door as well.

"We'll make it a slumber party," Margaret continued behind the two men. "I'll make hot chocolate. We'll all get in bed and snuggle and watch old movies, and—"

"Margaret," Parker said.

She took his arm and squeezed. "Yes, dear."

"Don't make me hurt you," Parker said, not looking at her.

She smiled up at him, batting her lashes.

"You two snuggle," Eric called out, starting down the stairs. "I need a good night's sleep."

"Poor dear." Margaret squeezed Parker's arm again and sighed. "Maybe next time."

"Margaret?" Parker said, resisting the urge to throw her down the stairs.

"Yeah, hon?" she responded with a catty smile, slipping her arm into his.

"I hope," Parker said patting her hand, "you bleed to death on your next period."

"I love you too, sweetie." Margaret skipped down the stairs beside him.

They all loaded into the Range Rover and Parker almost shoved Margaret into the back seat.

Eric started the engine. "Don't you think the lady should sit in the front?" he asked, adjusting the mirror.

"The lady?" Parker asked with much irony. "The lady will be just fine—and alive, in the back seat."

Eric muffled a laugh and pulled the Range Rover away from the curb.

Margaret scooted forward and leaned on the backs of the front seats. "This is like being on vacation," she said. "A romantic cabin up in the mountains."

"It was romantic earlier," Parker said through clenched teeth. "Now it'll just be like a crowded summer camp."

"Parker, you're just being an ass about this whole thing," Margaret said with a pout.

"Don't pay any attention to him, Margaret." Eric pulled at the wheel to negotiate a winding stretch. "You're perfectly welcome at my house anytime."

She beamed and reached out to massage the back of Eric's neck. "So beautiful and so sweet," she whispered to him.

"He'll get over it," Eric said giving Parker a glance.

"I've known a few federal guys before." Margaret pulled up between the front seats. "It's the Washington environment. They're so used to getting what they want when they want it."

Eric laughed. "They need to cultivate a better sense of patience and forbearance," he said.

"They're so out of touch with the rest of us," she responded.

Eric nodded at Parker. "And they forget the subtle niceties of daily living," he said.

Margaret nodded. "Like romance," she said.

"How to get to know someone."

"How to woo a girl properly."

"How to take it slow," Eric added. "And release those pent up frustrations."

"You mean how to masturbate," Margaret said with a hand gesture.

The two of them howled with laughter.

"Are you ignoring us?" Margaret gave Parker's shoulder a slight punch.

"Huh, what?" Parker turned his attention from the side mirror outside his window.

"He is ignoring us," Margaret said. "How do you like that?"

"Of course I'm ignoring you," Parker said evenly. "I'm still mad at you."

Margaret sighed.

"Besides." Parker nodded at the mirror. "I believe we're being followed."

"What?" Margaret froze.

Eric turned his eyes to the rear view mirror and tried to make out the car behind the headlights following them at a distance.

Margaret's hand went into her purse. "This time I've got my cell phone," she said triumphantly holding it up. "Shall I call the sheriff?"

Parker shook his head. "No, no, not yet." He watched the bobbing headlights in the side mirror. "Let's make sure."

"Shall we take the road less traveled?" Eric asked.

"My thoughts exactly." Parker said, giving the younger man a peck on the cheek.

"Buckle up ladies." Eric down shifted. "It's going to be a bumpy ride." He turned sharply onto a single lane, gravel road spiraling upward away from the main road. The Range Rover lurched violently along the eroded road bed. Eric let out a whoop, grinning broadly at Parker.

"Eyes on the road, please," Parker cautioned. He grabbed for the hand strap over the door and held on for dear life. "And try not to enjoy this so much."

Margaret hugged the back of Parker's seat. "Are the headlights still with us?" She fell back against her seat with a loud squeal as the car slammed into a particularly deep rut in the road.

Parker gave up trying to make out anything in the bobbing side-view mirror and turned to look out the rear window. A tell-tale beam of light flickered around the hairpin curve they had just left behind.

"We still have company," Parker remarked. He

studied the shadow behind the lights. "Looks like some sort of small truck."

"Things are going to get steeper and rougher from here on in," Eric said. He tugged at the stick shift. "Here's where we find out whether or not they have four-wheel drive."

The Range Rover dug into the road bed, pushing and pulling itself up the mountain side.

"I hope this road goes some place." Margaret steadied herself in the back seat.

"Other than over a cliff," Parker added, tightening his own grip on the overhead strap.

"Trust me, my friends." Eric's muscle strained against his cotton shirt as he fought to keep control of the steering.

"If we were to let our man catch up to us for a moment, do you think we have enough horsepower advantage to outrun him again?" Parker asked.

"Catch up to us?" Eric frowned.

"Yes," Parker answered. He flipped open the glove compartment and pulled out a small camera. "I'd like to get a quick look at the occupant or occupants of that truck."

Margaret squealed with delight. "A picture's worth a thousand words," she said.

"There's a ninety degree cut-back up ahead," Eric said. "Once around the corner out of their line of vision, I'll stop the truck."

"Perfect." Parker checked out his camera.

"You be ready for that picture, though," Eric warned. "The moment they're over the surprise, I'm out of here."

"Roger, Ranger Red." Parker saluted.

"Shut up."

"Stop arguing, boys," Margaret called out from the back seat. "I hope that thing has a strong flash on it."

"Good point." Parker studied the small camera.

"Cut-back dead ahead!" Eric almost shouted.

"Damn!" Parker reached up to release the sun roof. A rush of cool mountain air engulfed the interior.

"Here goes!" Eric called out. He pulled the wheel hard and the Range Rover careened around the ninety degree turn.

Parker pulled up through the sun roof opening and stood up on the seat. "Allow some stopping room for the other vehicle," he yelled down at Eric over the roar of the straining engine.

Eric cleared the turn by a couple of hundred feet and then hit the brakes hard. He cut the wheel sharply causing the Range Rover to spin out a hundred and eighty degrees until it came to rest facing the opposite direction. He cut the head lights.

"Jesus H. Christ!" Margaret's muffled yell came from the floor boards of the back seat. Parker was barely hanging onto the sides of the roof opening, laughing.

Eric looked around at them sheepishly. "Did I mention fasten your seatbelts?" he asked.

Margaret scrambled back into position and fumbled for her seat belt. "If you weren't so pretty, I'd shove my patent leather heel up your nose." She snapped the seat belt buckle into its receptacle.

"Nice driving, hot shot," Parker said, regaining his stability. He checked the camera quickly to be sure all was in order.

"I can hit them with the headlights when they come around," Eric said, squinting at the growing haze of light filling the sharp turn directly in front of them. "Get ready!"

In a spray of dust, the pursuing truck's headlights rounded the curve. When its lights hit the Range Rover, Eric hit the high beams, blinding the truck occupants. The truck swerved sharply to the other side of the road and made a jolting stop as its driver's side, front wheel dropped into the shallow drainage ditch bordering the roadway. The flash from Parker's camera strobed over the truck. Its passenger door flew open.

"Guns!" Parker shouted.

In an instant, Eric threw the Range Rover into gear and sat down on the gas pedal. Margaret screamed some unintelligible profanity as the Rover skidded across the gravel road bed.

Parker was thrown backwards and the small camera flew out of his hand on the rocks below. He dropped down through the sunroof opening and pulled his own pistol from its shoulder holster. "Stay low!" he yelled up at Eric.

Eric sank down low into his seat while trying to negotiate the sharp cut-back in the opposite direction. The rear window shattered before the crack of rifle fire reached them.

Margaret interrupted her running litany of "Oh shits" with another piercing scream as the thousand shards of safety glass showered over her.

Once around the turn, Eric straightened in his seat and gunned the engine. He fought the wheel for control as the Range Rover rocked and skidded over the ruts and rocks.

Parker turned in the seat and pointed his pistol at the gaping hole that had been the rear windshield. He watched as the sharp cut-back receded from view.

Satisfied that they had a commanding lead, he glanced down at Margaret. "Speak to me, Margaret," he said. "You okay?"

Margaret continued trying to shake the small pieces of glass from her blonde tresses. "Don't worry about me," she stammered, giving him a death glare. Her bottom lip quivered. "Feel free to stop and take a few more snap shots."

"Now, Margaret."

"I don't like this!" She sat up sharply, snatching a quick glance behind her. "I want a gun!"

Parker reached a hand back to comfort her, but she jerked away. "How are we doing?" he asked Eric.

Eric cast him a quick smile. "We're doing great." He pulled at the wheel as the Range Rover almost leapt off the road. "I'll bet they're still stuck in the ditch back there."

"Give us another smile." Parker leaned in and gave him a peck on the cheek.

Eric tried in vain to stop his lips from curling upward. "Don't mess with me while I'm driving," he said.

Parker gave him another buss on the cheek. "I'll be back," he said, and scrambled between the front seats into the back with Margaret. She scooted away from him. Parker grabbed her and pulled her to him. "Excitement's over now," he said, holding her tightly to prevent her escape. "Let's go home."

"I want a gun," she reiterated less violently.

"We'll get you a gun," Parker assured her, brushing some residual glass from her hair.

"I hope you got a picture of those bastards!" Margaret let herself lean back into his chest. "I'm gonna kick some ass!"

Parker chuckled, deciding not to say anything about the camera.

"I'm the goddamn DA," she said through tears. "And I will not be shot at!"

"That's my girl," Parker said. He gave her a big squeeze.

"You track them down," she continued through clenched teeth. "But when you find them, their balls are mine!"

"Poor bastards," Eric said. He downshifted and pulled back out into the paved road.

"That's a promise, Blondie." Parker lifted Margaret's face to his and kissed her lightly on the lips. "When I catch those creeps, you can have first crack at their nuts."

"I want you to fuck those shits in the ass!" Margaret gave him a fierce look.

"You'll fuck their brains out!" Parker saw a slight smile break behind her tears. "You'll ram their sorry butts with that big fat, yard-long dildo you keep in your bedside table."

"Margaret!" Eric laughed.

She slapped Parker on the head. "I don't have any such thing," she said.

"Do too."

"Do not!" The tears disappeared and she smiled up at him. "It's certainly not a yard long anyway."

"Okay, eight inches."

"And it's not a dildo."

"Okay, your personal massager," Parker said with a nod.

"And it so happens, I only use it to ease my carpal tunnel symptoms."

"Of course." Parker nodded again in complete

agreement.

Eric groaned in the front seat. "Pigs," he said.

"I'm not going to sleep a wink tonight," Margaret said. "I'm sure it's no secret to these bastards where Eric lives."

"Don't worry," Eric said. He glanced back at her with a smile. "I have an excellent security system."

"So did I," Margaret said. "Or at least I thought I did."

"We'll be quite safe, I assure you." Eric pulled off the main road again. "There's also my shot gun collection."

"I like that much better," Parker said.

Margaret seemed to relax. "A shotgun I can shoot," she said.

"Grizzly Curry, mountain woman." Parker laughed.

"I'm serious," she said. "My dad taught me. He had visions of family hunting trips."

"You go hunting?" Parker looked incredulous.

"Don't be ridiculous." Margaret frowned at a chip in the polish of one of her nails. "I could never harm a defenseless animal."

"Then you won't be much use with a gun against these guys," Eric said.

"I'll blow their fucking brains out." Margaret pointed an imaginary gun at Eric.

"Ah the sanctity of human life," Parker said.

"Humans are savage scum." Margaret laid her head back on Parker's shoulder. "I know. I have them locked up in cages every day."

The Range Rover came to a bumpy stop.

"We're here." Eric turned off the engine. "All human scum follow me."

They climbed out of the Range Rover and grabbed up

Margaret's bags.

"Oh," Margaret said. She looked up at the small cabin framed in the moonlight. "Eric, it's charming."

Parker started up the path ahead of them. "I'll get the gate," he said.

Eric raised a hand to stop him, but changed his mind. "This ought to be interesting," he said to Margaret.

"What's that?" she asked.

"An excellent test of my security system."

"Oh dear." She covered her ears. "I hate loud noises."

"It's . . ." Eric cocked his head to one side. "It's sort of a silent alarm."

They watched Parker as he sat her bag down and fumbled with the gate latch. Eric began to chuckle.

"What?" Margaret smiled up at him.

He shook his head. "Just watch."

The gate swung open and Parker grabbed up the bag again.

"Hurry up, you two," he called out. He looked back at Margaret and Eric. "What are you grinning at?" He shook his head. "Fine. Stand out here if you like." He started through the gate.

A low rumbling growl froze him in his tracks. He looked around to find himself surrounded by several pairs of snarling fangs gleaming up at him from the darkness. They began to inch closer to him.

"Eric!" Parker heard the laughter behind him. "Eric, goddamn you!"

"Stand!" Eric commanded.

The fangs disappeared and Parker was surrounded by four massive Rottweilers with wagging tails.

"You can relax now," Eric said.

Parker remained still and let the dogs sniff him for a

moment.

Margaret skipped through the gate. "Puppies!" She went to her knees and the big dogs swarmed over her, licking and panting.

"Our people are supposed to prefer cats." Parker stepped carefully through the squirming dogs. He looked back at Eric. "I shall kill you later."

"Don't say that too loud," Eric warned. He reached down to pet one of the dogs. "They might hear you."

Parker started up the path toward the cabin with a wary eye behind him.

"They're beautiful dogs," Margaret said.

"Only to my friends." Eric bobbed his eyebrows at her.

Margaret managed to get to her feet despite the dogs. "I hope those bastards try to come here tonight." She scratched one of the more insistent animals behind the ears.

They stumbled through the dogs and caught up to Parker on the porch.

"All I want to know," Parker said, "is where your little pets were earlier when we were here?"

Eric slipped a key in the lock. "They were in their pens," he said, pushing the door open. "The gate has a solar powered, automatic release on it to let them out after dark when I'm not here. Otherwise, I have a switch by the kitchen door to keep them in or let them out as I choose."

"Now that's an automatic security system." Margaret stepped into the room. "Oh, I love it!" she exclaimed. "It just screams testosterone."

"Keep an eye on her," Parker said. "Or she'll be in your underwear drawer."

"My under—" Eric began.

"Don't ask." Parker hauled the heavy bag inside. "Where should we put her?"

"Now, I don't want to be any trouble," Margaret said, rushing up into the kitchen.

Parker gagged.

"I can sleep on the sofa." Margaret inspected the contents of the still warm, covered pots on the stove. "I can sleep anywhere."

"And have," Parker said under his breath.

Margaret ignored him. "This looks wonderful," she said, sniffing one of the pots. "Who's cooking?"

"Hungry, Margaret?" Eric smiled and joined her in front of the stove.

"You don't think it's too late?"

"It's never too late for vegetarian," Eric said. He turned on the burners under the pots.

"I'll set the table." Margaret began searching the cabinets.

"Good, she's occupied." Parker slipped up behind and wrapped his arms about Eric's waist. "Now's our chance."

Eric stirred the contents of the large stew pot. "Now's our chance for what?" He chuckled and leaned back against Parker.

"Flights of ecstasy," Parker murmured in his ear.

Eric adjusted the flame under the large pot. "And here I thought," he said, turning to give Parker a devastating smile, "you didn't like vegetarian."

CHAPTER 10

"**Fucking idiot!**" **The fat man's voice boomed,** echoing off the metal walls of the post and beam outbuilding. "I told you to follow them?" He stalked the perimeter of the large shed.

A squat, muscled man raised a pleading hand. "Boss, we—"

"Shut it!" Fat Man lingered in the shadows, breathing heavily. "You goddamn fuckups!"

A thin, black man who had been standing guard by the door cleared his throat. "They got a picture of my truck!" he said.

"No shit!" Fat Man spun at him. "What about follow and stay out of sight did you not understand?"

Thin Man scratched his head. "But, boss, they caught us by surprise," he protested.

"They caught you by surprise?" Fat Man kicked dirt at him. "You fucking asshole! And what about the goddamn woman?"

A large black man with thick, muscular arms stepped nervously out of the shadows. "She..." Thick Arms thought quickly. "We couldn't find it."

"We searched through everything," said another, squat man from the opposite corner. "She didn't have it."

"You searched through everything?" Fat Man asked, spitting on the floor. "Bullshit! You should've made her tell you where it is. She has it. We know that. If you hadn't..."

"What's done is done!" Squat Man said. He walked up to the fuming, fat man. "She got away from us because this idiot couldn't hold onto a woman." He gestured to Thick Arms who dropped his head ashamed. Squat Man faced the fat man. "It doesn't matter now. Even if they have it, it doesn't mean they know what they have or how to use it. We're wasting time. We need to act now! They'll be up at Borenson's cabin."

Fat Man waved a beefy hand in the air. "Don't you go off half-cocked and be stupid, too, Bonner." He paced the floor, stirring up dust. "You're right about one thing. We don't know how much they know yet—what kind of reports that fag, White, has filed."

"The last shipment will be dropped soon." Bonner checked his watch. "Once we move it through and collect, we'll all be out of here!"

Fat Man spat on the ground by Bonner's feet. "You'll be out of here," he said pointedly. "I have no intention of giving up my reputation and going on the run at my age!" He jabbed a pudgy finger in the air at Bonner. "We're gonna do things right and we're gonna do them my way!"

"Whatever." Bonner turned away, throwing his hands up in the air. "But we'd better do something fast before we have an army of federal agents descending on the Park."

Fat Man made a guttural, growling sound. "Fuck!" he said and spat on the dirt floor again. He paced around the others. "We don't know what they have and, at this point, we have to assume they have everything that was on your goddamn computer!"

Bonner remained silent.

Fat Man stopped in front of him. "Everything!" He turned to the other men. "We have to contain this now. It's already out of control and the best shot we have at this point is to delay in further outside interference as long as possible."

"Meaning?" Bonner joined the other men.

"Meaning," Fat Man said, "we have to get our hands on them and everything they've compiled about our operation to date."

Thin Man scratched his head again. "But what about the other night's shipment?" he asked. "How're we gonna make that up? The spicks ain't gonna like that."

Fat Man glared at him. "You let me worry about our Venezuelan friends," he said. "And we haven't lost anything. That so-called lost shipment is already in transit."

"How, boss?"

"Because, you dumbass, that fag G-Man locked it up in the safe back at the ranger station until the Denver guys could retrieve it." Fat Man glared at each of the other men individually. "I'm tired of all the screw-ups. You dumb shits have yet to get it through your thick skulls that this is not some playground game. We've had it easy up to now, but I told you it wouldn't last. Someone was bound to get suspicious." He turned on Thin Man. "But I had no idea we'd get sent to ground because one of our own was too lazy to keep up his part of the bargain."

"I've done my part," Thin Man said desperately. "It

wasn't my fault that—"

"Fucking yeah it was your fault!" Fat Man said, jabbing his finger in the black man's face. "It was your job to keep that goddamn faggot Borenson distracted when we had drops. You were supposed to keep him out of the high range drop points. You!" Fat Man gave the much taller black man a shove. "No one else! You!"

"It's not my fault he's so damn suspicious," Thin Man protested. "I did my part.

"Oh, yes," Fat Man said icily. "You did your part all right. It was your stupidity that blew this apart completely. You had to get trigger happy!"

Thin man backed away. "They caught me by surprise," he said. "They saw the shipment drop. What else was I supposed to do?"

"Use your head, idiot!" Bonner shouted from the side. He held a heavy black semi-automatic pistol in his hand pointed at Thin Man's temple. "There were a million other things you could have done."

Fat Man nodded ominously. "You've become more trouble than you're worth," he said, turning his back on Thin Man. He looked at the other players. "Anyone got any objection to cutting this asshole loose and taking his share?"

The other men shook their heads. They know Fat Man had made up his mind and there was no use arguing differently.

Fat Man looked back at Bonner. "Get it over with," he said without emotion.

Thin Man dropped to his knees, pleading. "Wait!" he cried. "I can make this better. You'll—"

He was interrupted by a loud, cracking sound in his right ear. The bullet exited the other side of his head before he began to fall backwards onto the dirt floor which hungrily began to soak up the flood of blood and brain matter.

The other men stood still in the ensuing quiet. Bonner holstered his weapon and kicked the body at his feet.

Fat Man clapped his hands together. "All right. Now we start taking care of business. Keep your radios handy. Look for opportunity to round them up, one at a time or all together, doesn't matter to me. Just get on the horn and let me know. Don't try and plan it yourselves, goddamn it, you've already fucked up enough!"

Fat Man put his hands to his hips. He thought a moment and then went over to a metal locker beside the door. He pulled out a set of keys and took off the pad lock. "No more fucking around!" he said, swinging the locker door open. "Lock and load!"

The men surrounded the gun safe. Bonner reached in for a box of 9mm ammunition.

"Take the rifle too," Fat Man said, pulling out a long, sleek gun case. "We may need some sharp shooting and you're supposed to be very good at that."

The corner of Bonner's mouth curled up. "I'm damn good at it," he said, caressing the gun case.

Fat Man motioned for the others. "And not just pistols," he said. "Grab one of the automatics and several full rounds." He stood back while the men rummaged in the safe. "If we have to do any shooting, I want to be damn sure we take everyone and everything out!"

The men stuffed their pockets with ammo clips.

"Now." Fat Man nodded at them. "Stubs, you stay in the truck and monitor radio traffic for that next shipment." He pointed at the thin black man. "And for fuck's sake, Stubs, keep the damn truck out of sight now that it's had its picture taken!"

Stubs lowered his head and headed out the door.

Fat Man pointed at the much larger, black body builder. "You let Brentlinger know and then you get your ass up to Borenson's place," he said. "I want to know where they go and when." He leaned into the man's face. "And stay the fuck out of sight!"

Thick Arms nodded and backed up for the door. "Will do, boss!" He disappeared out the door.

"What about me?" Bonner raised the rifle case.

"You!" Fat Man spat on the ground again. "You get back to the station."

"Why, boss, I—"

"You were supposed to erase all those computer files."

"I did!"

"Bullshit! I checked.   Your files had not been erased—they were moved elsewhere and copied."

"There's no way—"

"Don't argue!" Fat Man boomed. He cocked his head at Bonner. "How the hell did they get your computer files?"

Bonner shrugged. "I can't—"

"You can't, shit!" Fat Man shook a finger in Bonner's face. "There's only one person with access to your private files."

Bonner's eyes widened.

"What?" Fat Man asked sarcastically. "A goddamn light bulb turn on in your empty, fucking head?"

It was Bonner's turn to spit on the floor. "That goddamn bitch!" he said.

"That goddamn bitch," Fat Man waved his hands in

the air, "has fucked you up one side and down the other. You find out what she gave them and how much they know."

Bonner kicked the dirt. "And then what?" he asked.

Fat Man looked at Bonner like he was stupid. "I don't give a fuck!" he said. "Just make it look like an accident. Drag her up to the rocks and throw her off, for fuck's sake!"

"What about Borenson and that G-Man?" Bonner asked.

Fat Man shrugged. "Stay in contact with Stubs. An opportunity will come up and I want to be ready to take advantage of it." He smiled at Bonner. "Remember, there's a major drug smuggling operation going on up here. When the feds find the bullet riddled bodies of our problems piled up in the mountains, I don't think there will be any question who's responsible. You know what a mean bunch of fuckers those Venezuelans are." He laughed causing the thick folds of flesh around his midriff to jiggle.

Bonner listened but did not laugh. All he could think about was the woman who had betrayed him. He left Fat Man laughing over Thin Man's body, kicked the door open and headed out to his own truck. He stored the rifle behind the seat and shoved the heavy, black pistol into his belt. He climbed up into the cab and started the engine. Muttering under his breath, he peeled out of the gravel parking area onto the service road.

"Bitch!" he yelled at the top of his lungs and gunned the small truck around a sharp corner. "Fucking bitch!" He gritted his teeth and glared at the road ahead.

Fat Man stood in the center of the shed, eyes fixed on the door. After a moment, his gaze shifted to the gun locker. He shuffled over to it and shut the heavy, metal door, pulled out his keys and started to set the padlock. He stopped, changing his mind and pulled the door back open. He deposited his own small pistol on a shelf and extracted another one similar to the pistol Bonner had taken. He pulled out an ammo clip and slid it into the bottom of the handgrip until he heard the tell-tale click. Satisfied, he shoved the pistol into the pocket of his khaki parka and locked up the gun safe.

Fat Man started for the door, pausing over the crumpled body still oozing into the dirt. His eyes now narrow dark slits.

"Stupid shit!" He spat on the body just as he had seen Bonner do.

He thought for a moment and smiled to himself.

"Pay day," he said lightly, and headed out the door.

CHAPTER 11

What do you think?" Parker scrolled through the computer screen.

"You've got me," Eric answered. He leaned over Parker to study the screen, almost cheek to cheek. "Some sort of graphic generating code."

"I agree." Parker turned to look at Eric up close. He breathed deeply. "You smell good."

Eric grinned and pretended to ignore the comment. "Those number lists seem to be a data set of some sort," he said.

"You always smell good." Parker brushed Eric's cheek with his nose. "Even when you're all hot and sweaty."

"How would you know?" Eric straightened, laughing. "When have you seen me hot and sweaty?"

"After you showered last night." Parker wrote down some of the numbers from the screen in a list. "When you got into bed all warm and toasty. You smelled good then too."

"I wasn't hot and sweaty when I got into bed." Eric

studied the list Parker was making. "Besides, Margaret was in between us." He pointed to the numbers. "Those are colons, not decimal places."

Parker squinted at the screen. "Damn, so they are." He scribbled the changes to his list. "Where is that meddling, interloping, nosey, annoying little wench anyway?"

"Hey, now." Eric pulled at the back of Parker's hair. "You're talking about my girlfriend. And she's still in the shower."

Parker groaned. "Well your girlfriend is starting to piss your boyfriend off."

"Who says you're my boyfriend?" Eric dropped his arm over Parker's shoulder. "We haven't even held hands yet."

Parker tapped his pen on the paper, still studying the numbers. "I was planning to hold more than your hand last night," he said. "Before little Miss Margaret came into the bedroom whining." He set the pen down. "Could these represent hours and minutes?"

"I don't blame Margaret for being scared down on that sofa by herself," Eric said. "Especially after what she had been through." He leaned over again. "No, those numbers are too big, even for sidereal or Greenwich Mean Time."

"She's enjoying frustrating me," Parker said. He reached up and took Eric's hand. "We're holding hands—"

"Longitude and latitude!" Eric almost yelled.

"What?"

Eric shook Parker. "Degrees longitude and latitude," he said, excitedly. "Those numbers are expressed just like degrees of longitude and latitude."

Parker looked at the numbers and broke into a smile. "Bingo. Good work, Dr. Watson. I think you may be right."

"How can we be sure?" Eric knelt on the floor beside Parker to better see the screen.

"I've got an idea." Parker exited the CD directory and clicked on the Internet icon. "There's a weather satellite data compiler we can pull down." He typed in the address and they waited the few seconds it took the browser to find it. A few more keystrokes and the compiler was being downloaded.

"The suspense is killing me," Eric said.

"Patience, my love." Parker's hands flew over the keyboard as he ran the compiler and referenced it to the data file in the CD drive. "Damn! Incompatible file format." Parker read the message on the screen. "So much for that."

"It doesn't have to be weather data," Eric said.

"No shit, Sherlock," Parker said. He reached up for Eric's hand again. "What's your next idea?"

"Well." Eric eyed the list of numbers once more. "They could simply be positional data. You know, pointing out the location of something."

"That could be." Parker thought a moment. "But it doesn't seem logical. There are so many numbers. That's an awful lot of positions."

"Are you boys still playing with your toys?" Margaret was standing at the bathroom door, wrapped in a towel. She dried her hair with another. "I've got to get to the office soon."

"Keep your towel on, counselor," Parker said. "We're solving crimes over here."

"You always investigate crime while holding your

partner's hand?" She wrapped her hair up in the towel.

"Only when he can get away with it," Eric said.

"Careful, Eric," she warned. "You know these Washington types. He's probably picked up a cute little number at all his ports of call."

"What?" Parker sat up sharply.

"Only kidding, dear," Margaret said. "Have you had too much coffee or something?"

"No . . . It's what you said." Parker looked down at the number list. "Ports of call."

Margaret looked at him. "Maybe you haven't had *enough* coffee," she said.

Parker ignored her. "Look," he said to Eric. "It makes sense. This could be a travel route. These could be various stopping points—"

"Or pick up points," Eric interjected.

"Exactly!" Parker turned to Margaret. "Pretty good for a blonde, my dear."

"I haven't the slightest idea what you're babbling about." Margaret put her hands on her hips. "Just because you slept your way to the top, doesn't mean I did."

Parker held a hand out to Eric. "Five bucks says she's not a real blonde," he said.

"You're on." Eric slapped his palm.

They dove for the stairs.

"Get the towel!" Parker shouted.

Margaret screamed and dashed up the stairs out of reach. "Men!" she shouted down at them from the loft. "Go play with yourselves. I've got to get dressed." She headed for the bedroom.

Eric and Parker returned to the computer.

"So," Parker said, "what we need is a navigational compiler."

"Something a pilot would use to plot a course," Eric said.

"Exactly." Parker typed search parameters into the Net browser.

"Not just pilots," Eric said. "Also look for navigation in general."

"That's even better." Parker added the parameters. After a moment, search options began to list down the screen.

"What do you think?" Eric asked.

"Six of one, half a dozen of the other," Parker replied. "You pick."

"Page through them," Eric said. He watched the screen as Parker moved through page after page of listings. He pointed to the screen. "Wait."

"Okay." Parker paused the screen. "Which one?"

"Go back a page."

Parker backed up one page.

"There." Eric touched a finger to the screen. "Look here."

Parker read the option. "Why military applications?" he asked.

"It just occurred to me," Eric said. "When a hiker is injured far off the beaten path, we search them down and then use a GPS device to pinpoint the exact position. The air rescue service can then plot an exact course to our location to ferry out the injured."

"A what?"

"A GPS, global positioning system," Eric explained. "One of the paramedics was a Gulf War veteran. He said it was the same way they effected rescues in the war." He rapped his knuckles on Parker's temple. "Jeeze," he said. "You sure you're FBI?"

"Okay. Military applications it is." Parker said, ignoring him. He highlighted the option and double-clicked the entry with the mouse. Within seconds a directory of download options scrolled down the screen.

"That one," Eric said excitedly. He pointed to the directory listing.

"GPS-based course plotting for pilots," Parker read. "Let's pull it down and see." Parker manipulated the mouse and downloaded the software. "Well, let's see what the program thinks of our data."

He ran the program and referenced it to the data disk. Eric crossed his fingers under Parker's chin.

"How about a kiss for good luck?" Parker looked up at him.

Eric laughed. "You don't let any opportunity go by, do you?" He bent over Parker. "I hope you shaved close this morning."

Before Eric could say anymore, Parker took the man's head in his hands and drew Eric's mouth to his own. Their lips parted and tongues battled for supremacy. Parker forgot the computer completely. All his senses were caught up in the kiss. He reveled in Eric's freshly showered scent, the warmth and strength of his lips, and the hungry urgency of his probing tongue.

Eric pulled away slightly, leaving a small gap between their open mouths. Both were breathing hard. Parker opened his eyes at the interruption, and looked up into Eric's gold-flecked, hazel ones. The heat of their bodies mingled in the minute space between them. Parker pressed his lips toward Eric's, but Eric again pulled away, preventing the connection.

"Give a guy a breather," Eric said with a smile. He allowed his nose to brush lightly against Parker's.

"Oh, my God!" Margaret called out from the loft at the top of the stairs. "Man-on-man action. That makes me so hot!"

"Margaret," Parker said under his breath.

"Margaret," Eric said with a chuckle. He straightened.

"Margaret!" Parker called out, turning in the small desk chair. "I swear, I'm going to hurt you."

"That's the thanks I get for saving you from committing a mortal sin." Margaret sashayed down the stairs, adjusting an earring.

"Look!" Eric said. He pointed to the computer screen.

Parker turned quickly. "Well, well," he said, looking at the screen. "We have a match."

"What's that?" Margaret joined them at the computer. She studied the geographic map and the red line moving across it from point to point.

"It's one of the CD's you had," Eric replied.

"It was navigational data," Parker added. "See, it's plotting a course from point to point."

"What kind of course?" Margaret frowned.

They all stared at the screen.

"Why are you messing around with these disks anyway?" Margaret asked. "I picked them up by accident. It's not like they have any relevance to the case."

"I'm one of those who believe nothing happens by accident," Parker replied.

"Click on one of the course points," Eric said.

Parker complied. Instantly a small information window opened giving the geographical coordinates of the point as well as a description of its location.

"That's a small airport outside of Denver," Parker said. "Look at the date and time out. It's only about thirty minutes' difference from the time in."

"Something was picked up or dropped off, I'll bet." Eric bent closer. "That was three days ago."

Parker hummed softly. "But there's something more important about that date."

"I'll be damned," Margaret said. "That's the day of the murders."

"Bingo." Parker moved the cursor to the next point north of the airport. "Let's see where this baby is." He clicked on the point and its small information window popped up.

"That's in the Park," Eric said with a puzzled look.

"Two miles northwest of Bear Lake," Parker read aloud.

"That's Climber's Ridge, I'd bet a dollar to a donut," Eric said.

"The site of the murders." Margaret picked up one of the CD's. "Here." She handed it to Parker. "Try another one."

Parker replaced the old CD with the new and tapped the drive drawer back in.

"What's the matter, Margaret?" He manipulated the mouse to access the new data file. "Still think they're not case related?"

"Oh, shut up!" Margaret punched Parker's shoulder lightly. "How the hell did these things get in with the personnel files from the Park Service?"

"This is a bit too convenient to be an accident," Eric said.

A new map plot appeared on the computer screen.

"If you ask me," Parker said, studying the map with the others. "I'd say we have a friend somewhere close to the action."

"That looks like the same map as before," Margaret said. "See. There's the small airport outside of Denver. There's the point up in the park—"

"No, wait." Eric put his hand on Parker's and moved the mouse cursor to that point. "This point isn't the same. Click here."

"Whatever you say, my love." Parker smiled up at Eric and clicked the mouse.

"There! What did I tell you?" Eric pointed to the small information window that appeared. "That's a different longitude and latitude. I'd say that it's a pretty good guess that's up in the high range at Granite Point."

"Where you wrestled me to the ground?" Parker asked.

It was Eric's turn to ignore. "That's another one of the areas I suspected illegal trespassers had been messing around." He pinched Parker's arm. "That's where we ran into Bonner."

"Ah, Bonner." Parker rubbed his much abused arm. "My second favorite park ranger."

"Shall we check the other disks?" Margaret asked.

"We can later," Parker said. He removed the CD from the computer. "I think we can safely assume the other disks will plot routes to the other points in the Park that Eric is concerned about."

"What now?" Eric straightened.

"Now we have two leads to follow up on," Parker answered.

"The airport?" Eric asked.

"And our friend at the ranger station," Margaret said. "Got any blank CD's in that desk?"

Eric opened a drawer and pulled out a handful of the faux-metallic disks.

Margaret took several. "You boys do the airport," she said, slipping the blank CD's into her briefcase. "I'll handle the ranger station."

"Now, Margaret," Parker said. "Don't you think you've had enough excitement for a while?"

"It's daylight now," she said. "And there will be plenty of people around. I think I'll be all right."

"If you say so." Parker shut off the computer.

"But I'll take my gun now," Margaret continued.

Parker looked up. "Beg your pardon?"

"You said you'd give me a gun." Margaret tapped a black, patent leather pump on the hardwood floor. "I'll take it now." She smiled. "Just to be on the safe side."

Parker looked at Eric.

"Well," Eric said with a shrug. "You did promise."

"I know how to shoot, if that's what you're worried about," Margaret said. "I've been to the firing range many times."

Parker shook his head. "A pistol is quite different from a shotgun," he said.

"You point it, you pull the trigger," she said. "What's so different?"

"Good grief, Margaret." Parker rolled his eyes.

"I've got a small twenty-two in the gun cabinet, Margaret," Eric offered. "You can take it."

"You sweet man." She hugged him. "I'll take it."

"Just don't go shooting up the ranger station," Eric said.

"As long as no one pisses me off!" Margaret straightened her jacket. "It's time for the DA to clean up this town."

Eric chuckled and went to retrieve the pistol from the gun cabinet at the back of the room.

"If she takes your gun," Parker called after him, "what are you going to use for protection?"

"I've got you, babe." Eric said, unlocking the cabinet. "And my little friends in here."

"Mary, Mother of God!" Parker stood to get a better look at the cabinet's contents. "What are you, a one man militia?" He joined Eric by the cabinet, admiring the contents. "Does the ATF know about this?"

"Eric." Margaret walked slowly to the cabinet. "Is there something you're not telling us?" She stood, hands on hips, looking over the large collection of pistols, rifles, and shotguns. "This is *some* phallic obsession you've got going here."

"You want the gun or not?" Eric held out the small, chrome pistol.

She took it and balanced it in her hand. "This'll do nicely." She deposited it carefully in the inside pocket of her jacket. "I feel better now."

"I wish I did." Parker shook his head at her. "Let's face it, you're dangerous enough as it is." He poked a finger at Margaret's jacket. "Don't shoot yourself in the tit."

Margaret sniffed. "Nothing worse than a queen with tit-envy!" She started for the stairs. "Let me get my bag and I'll be ready to go."

Parker watched her climb the stairs. "Let this be on your conscience," he said to Eric.

"She'll be all right." Eric pulled a menacingly heavy shotgun from the cabinet along with a box of shells.

"What are you going to do with that?" Parker's eyes widened.

"I just want to take it along with us."

"Elephants again?"

"Here," Eric said with a smirk, handing the box of shells to Parker. "You carry this." He shut and locked the cabinet.

Parker watched him, amused. "You're a real hoot," he said. "One surprise after another."

"Now I won't know if you really like me," Eric said, "or you just covet my gun collection."

"Can I hold your pistol?" Parker put his hands on Eric's hips and pulled him close.

Eric rolled his eyes, but allowed himself to be pulled in closer. "Little boys should never play with loaded guns," he said.

"You let Margaret have one." Parker pouted.

"Yes." Eric wrapped his free arm about Parker's neck. "But her's isn't loaded."

"Thank God," Parker said, sighing.

"We just better hope she doesn't find out," Eric added.

"Find out what?" Margaret was halfway down the stairs carrying her overnight bag.

Eric and Parker looked at each other.

"Nothing," Parker said. He smiled at Eric. "Red's just got a crush on you is all."

Eric batted his long red lashes at her.

"I knew it." Margaret dropped the heavy bag at Parker's feet. "I know what makes him tick now." She stroked Eric's cheek. "I've got his pistol in my pocket."

Parker picked up the bag. "Well, there you have it. You already had the balls, Margaret. Now you've got the penis too."

"Oh, honey." She turned and headed for the door. "I've had plenty of those."

CHAPTER 12

A cool mist had enveloped the higher elevations that surrounded the valley at the base of Rocky Mountain National Park. The small village of Estes Park, along with several surrounding miles was bathed in a chilly drizzle condensing from the blanket of gray nimbus clouds that seemed to menacingly delay the morning's full sunrise.

Parker pulled his light jacket about him and looked for a way to bridge the gap between his seat and the driver's in order to get closer to Eric. "How about a little heat?" Parker leaned closer and stretched his arm over the back of the driver's seat. "Don't you think it's a little chilly this morning?"

"No." Eric smiled at him. "It's a balmy summer's day for these parts."

"And me without my sunscreen." Parker ran his fingers through the silky blush of straight hair at the nape of Eric's neck. "I love your hair."

Eric stretched his neck, accepting the full benefit of Parker's massaging fingers. "And here I always wanted hair like yours," Eric said.

"God, why?" Parker asked. "It's so ordinary."

"Exactly!" Eric turned the Range Rover out onto the main highway to Denver. "Imagine being thirteen and having stand-out-in-a-crowd reddish hair and spots."

"They're freckles." Parker stroked a pale, translucent patch of freckles streaming down Eric's neck from his ear.

"Freckles, spots . . . whatever. It's all flashing neon on someone who's just trying to fit in."

"Yeah, but now you're a man."

"Thanks for noticing." Eric cocked his head at Parker.

"The most goddamn beautiful man I've ever laid eyes on."

Eric laughed. "Obviously you don't get out much."

"I'm not joking," Parker said softly. "If I were a painter, I could make looking at you a life's work."

"You have some set of lines." Eric shifted in his seat. "We're only about twenty minutes away from that airport."

Parker shook his head and smiled. "You don't take compliments well, do you?"

"What are you talking about?" Eric blinked.

"I mean . . ." Parker leaned in closer "every time I try to say something nice about you or tell you how I feel about you, you get antsier than a nun in a biker bar."

"Such a talent for metaphor," Eric said, rolling his eyes.

"If it really makes you uncomfortable, I'll stop . . . for a while," Parker said.

Eric guided the Range Rover down the highway in silence for a few moments. "Just because I'm not used to it, doesn't mean you have to stop." He kept his eyes on the road.

"Good." Parker resumed toying with the hair on the back of Eric's head. "I have to talk to someone about you, and I'm mad at Margaret right now."

"I like Margaret a lot," Eric said.

"I like her too," Parker said, "but of late she's been a pain in the ass."

"Your ass."

"All right—a pain in my ass."

Eric winked at him.

"I'm frustrated and horny as hell," Parker said. "And she's not helping things."

"Oh, I'm sure she'd be happy to take care of your little problem for you," Eric said.

Parker pinched the nape of Eric's neck. "Now don't you be a smartass."

Eric's laughter was infectious.

"I want to be serious for a minute," Parker said.

"That can be dangerous."

"I'll risk it." Parker pulled his hand back and turned in his seat to face Eric. "I've been pursuing you rather doggedly."

"Like a dog in heat." Eric nodded.

"Now you're the queen of metaphors."

"Sorry." Eric's hazel eyes twinkled. "Go on with what you were saying."

"I was saying that it's pretty clear I want you . . . badly."

"Yeah, that's pretty clear," Eric agreed.

Parker toyed with the zipper on his jacket. "How shall I put this?" he said.

"Succinctly."

Parker resisted the urge to cold cock the younger

man. "All right." He took a deep breath. "Do you want me?"

Eric pulled out to pass an eighteen-wheeler. He waited until after he had cleared the lumbering truck to answer. "I'm not very good," he began, "or should I say not very experienced . . . or more correctly, a little out of practice—"

"Succinctly, please."

Eric rolled his eyes and chuckled nervously. "Touché." He stared at his hands grasping the steering wheel. "I'm not quite sure of all my feelings," he said.

Parker pulled one of Eric's hands from the steering wheel and held it gently in his. "Who's ever sure of all their feelings?" He caressed the palm of Eric's hand. "How do you feel about me right now?"

Eric shifted in his seat again.

"Ants in your pants?" Parker asked.

"Shut up!" Eric said with a nervous laugh. He took a deep breath and thought for a moment. "I've been alone up here for quite some time. I had almost convinced myself I liked it that way." He looked at his hand in Parker's. "Until that night up at Climber's Ridge." His eyes met Parker's for a moment before he turned his attention back to the road.

Parker's heart sped up. "The night on Climber's Ridge," he said. "You mean, when I kissed you?"

"Yeah." Eric blushed.

"I thought you hated that kiss."

"Don't be ridiculous." Eric felt the heat about his ears as blood gorged the capillaries. "It was a great kiss. I've hated the thought of being alone ever since."

"Keep talking." Parker put Eric's hand to his lips.

Eric caught his breath as he felt Parker's warm lips

press against his hand. "I've been trying very hard not to fall..." Eric took a deep breath. "Not to fall for you."

"And how's it going?" Parker asked.

"Not very well."

"Good." Parker smiled at him.

"I can't help but think—" Eric paused.

"Go on."

"Well, you know," Eric began. "When this little vacation of yours is over, you'll head back to Washington, and I'll have to go back to being alone again."

"So," Parker said. "I'm a hit and run artist."

"Wham, bam, thank you, ma'am." Eric tried to smile.

They rode in silence, listening to the steady swishing of the windshield wipers and the drone of the engine.

"You know." Parker squeezed Eric's hand. "Maybe I'm not so crazy about being alone either."

Eric considered this. "Yeah. But it's different."

"Oh?"

"You've been out for quite a while," Eric continued. "You know a lot of gay people."

"Oh, really?" Parker laughed.

"You've made speeches to gay organizations. You've been interviewed in gay publications. Hell, you've been featured in *The Advocate*."

"My, you've been a busy boy."

"It's amazing the info you can Google," he said with a knowing smile.

"So I've made a few speeches."

"So you're out there," Eric said, "and you don't exactly strike me as the celibate type."

Parker smirked. "Well, I have to admit, between the Bureau, sex, criminal investigation, sex, court testimony, sex—"

"Here we go."

"—I'm just a busy little bee," Parker finished.

"That's not entirely what I mean." Eric sighed. "I'm just saying that your *lonely* argument is hard to swallow."

Parker studied the younger man. "Do you want to know the last time I had sex?" he asked.

"Not really."

"Well, I'm going to tell you anyway," Parker said. "It was before the speeches, before the interviews, and certainly before *The Advocate*."

Eric looked incredulous.

"It's true," Parker said. "When I first went into the Bureau, I was involved with this young attorney . . . a Congressional aide . . . I thought I had a pretty good thing, until all the publicity started." Parker looked out the window. "He couldn't take the light of public scrutiny—like I'd betrayed him or something."

"Tough break." Eric kept his eyes on the road.

"Maybe." Parker shrugged. "But I'd made the decision not to hide anymore. No more closets."

"I can't believe that someone as good looking as you—"

"Why thank you kindly," Parker said.

"— and as openly gay as you," Eric continued, "has not been . . . doggedly pursued."

"Well." Parker laughed. "I admit I haven't been without offers."

"Aha!"

"Now wait a minute," Parker said. "I've had opportunity. I've just been lacking in motive."

"Oh sure," Eric said.

"I haven't met anyone that particularly interested me," Parker said, "and, quite frankly, I've been pretty much putting all my energy into the career."

"But now I've changed all that." Eric shook his head.

"You don't think you could?"

"No."

Parker leaned forward and kissed Eric's cheek. "I think you could," he whispered into Eric's ear.

Eric's face went crimson again and he grinned at the steering wheel. "I'm not sure how good I'd be at all this," he said.

"You're good at it without even trying," Parker assured him.

Eric slowed the Range Rover and pulled off the highway onto the exit ramp. "There's the airport." He pointed to a turn-off.

"What?"

"It's a small municipal airport," Eric said pointing. "See those hangers?"

Parker looked in the direction of Eric's finger to a row of small metal buildings. "Not much of an airport," he said.

Eric followed the series of signs staked in the ground along the roadside to the small terminal building. He pulled into a parking space and tried to pull his hand free from Parker's grasp to put the car in park.

Parker held on tightly. "Before we get out," he said, "I want to know something."

"Shoot." Eric sat back in his seat.

Parker turned Eric's face to his. Eric's twinkling, gold-green eyes made him blink. "We have a lot of potential," Parker said. "Our children would be knockouts."

Eric smiled broadly.

"Anyway, let's both be open to the possibilities," Parker urged. "If there's a possibility that you can want me as much as I want you . . . don't let fear stand in the way."

Eric took a deep breath and swallowed. "You're a persuasive guy," he said.

"We could be so good together."

Eric hesitated.

"All right," Parker said, "don't answer now. Think about it for a while."

"Thanks."

"But not too long." Parker released Eric's hand. "I'd like some feedback—positive or negative—by the end of the day."

"Deal." Eric nodded.

They got out of the Range Rover and started for the sidewalk.

"Hey, G-Man." Eric stopped at the door of the airport terminal.

"Yeah, Yogi." Parker drew his hand back from the door knob.

"Thanks for not giving up on me yet." Eric smiled down at his shoes.

Parker put an arm about Eric's shoulder and reached to open the door. "I don't give up easy," he said. "Besides, where you're concerned, I can't help myself."

The terminal was about the size of a large living room. A long counter spanned the width, serving as passenger and luggage receipt on one end, and a small snack bar on the other. A thin, young man with dyed, jet-black hair sat on a stool behind the counter, yawning over a magazine.

Parker sized him up instantly. "Let me handle this," he whispered to Eric and strode up to the counter.

The young man looked up surprised. "Can I help

you?" His face brightened as he got a good look at Parker.

"Hi." Parker smiled down at him, noting the tell-tale skin blotches and the barely complete mustache and goatee. "I hope you can." He gave the boy's magazine a light nudge with his finger. "You have to sit in here all day, by yourself?"

"Beats digging ditches," the young man said.

"I'll bet."

"It's okay for a summer job." The boy stood. "My dad runs the shuttles to Aspen and Vale. Are you interested in a flight?"

"Summer job?" Parker cocked his head to one side. "You're at the University?" He leaned over the counter, resting on his elbow. He looked into the boy's eyes with a steady gaze.

"Like I said." The boy didn't blink. "Beats working." He bit his lip and smiled up at Parker.

Parker laughed. "And I'll bet you're a real hard worker," he said suggestively.

"If it's something I enjoy." The boy took a deep breath and rested his head on his hands, inches from Parker.

Eric coughed in the background and the boy straightened, suddenly aware of another's presence.

"My friend and I," Parker nodded to Eric, "would like to charter a helicopter ride, if that's possible."

The boy eyed Eric with interest. "Sure it's possible." He smiled back at Parker. "Where you want to go?"

"Just for a ride," Parker said. "You know, look at the scenery and what-not."

"What-not is nice." The boy pulled a clipboard from under the counter. "Let's see. There's Stan Brentlinger.

He mostly ferries big shots to and from Denver, but he does a pretty good tour about Rocky Mountain National Park."

"What are our chances of hitching a ride with him today?" Parker asked.

"I think something can be arranged for you," the boy said. "Stan was talking with another client earlier, but I don't think it was about any trips today."

Parker reached a finger out to tap the clipboard in the boy's hand. "Where can we find old Stan?" he asked.

"He's out in hanger five." The boy giggled. "You want me to call him up here for you?"

"No, don't bother." Parker picked a piece of lint off the boy's sleeve. "We'll pop out and see him." Parker turned to leave, but stopped short. "I'm sorry." He turned back to the boy. "What was your name?"

The boy's face lit up. "Todd . . . Todd Arrington," he said quickly.

"Thanks, Todd." Parker reached out a hand.

"No problem." Todd shook his hand. "You two have a nice flight."

Parker withdrew his hand along with the small slip of paper the boy had passed to him. "Thanks again, Todd. Be safe," he said with a wink.

"Always." The boy leaned against the counter and gave Parker the once over.

Eric rolled his eyes at Parker's self-satisfied smile and opened the door. "Having fun?" Eric asked a little too sweetly.

"Oodles," Parker replied, exiting the small terminal.

"He gave you his phone number, didn't he?" Eric followed him out.

Parker paused, and opened the small slip of paper in

his hand. "Well, I'll be," he said, feigning surprise. "He certainly did."

"What would you do with that little boy?" Eric asked.

"Well," Parker said, stuffing the paper in his back pocket. "To quote your girlfriend, Miss Margaret . . . what couldn't I do with him?"

"Pigs!" Eric grabbed at Parker's back pocket and snatched the paper from it.

Laughing, Parker tried in vain to turn away. "Hey, that's mine!"

"You'd better be careful," Eric warned. He wadded the small paper up and tossed it into a nearby barrel. "I haven't thrown a bitch fit in a long time. I'm overdue."

"I like a forceful man." Parker snuggled up against him.

Eric tried not to smile. "Get your butt down that sidewalk," he said in his most gruff, drill sergeant voice. "We've got work to do." He gave Parker a good slap on the behind.

"I kind of like that too." Parker started down the walk toward the hangers, rubbing his butt. "Would you do it some more later?"

Eric threw up his hands. "It scares me to think that you stand at the forefront of American justice," he said.

"That scares a lot of people," Parker said. He took Eric's arm. "Now, come along dear. We have a honeymoon trip to plan."

Eric rolled his eyes and allowed himself to be lead through the random collection of hanger buildings. Without warning, Parker dove between two of the metal buildings, dragging Eric with him.

"What the—" Eric began.

"Shhh!" Parker put a finger to his mouth.

Eric stood silent, watching the walkway from the shadows with Parker. After a moment, he heard the sound of faint footsteps coming closer down the walkway. Eric gave Parker a questioning look. Parker smiled slightly, pointing to the walkway. A familiar figure walked past them without taking notice of their presence.

"Bonner," Eric whispered through clenched teeth. His eyes narrowed and his face clouded as the figure moved quickly away from them.

Parker peeked out around the hanger. Satisfied that Bonner was out of earshot, he turned back to Eric. "You think Bonner's planning a honeymoon trip, too?"

"I'd say that cinches it." Eric shook his head. "We're definitely on the right track."

They stepped back onto the walkway and continued toward hanger five.

"Can you act real nelly?" Parker asked as they reached the hanger door.

"What?"

"You know. Can you act all girlie . . . access your feminine side?"

"Are you kidding?"

"Never mind. I'll be the woman and you be the man." Parker rubbed his butt again. "You're so good at it anyway."

Eric frowned. "What the hell are you talking about?"

"We have to have an undercover persona for this little meeting," Parker said. "It rarely works to march in saying, I'm the FBI, tell me what you know."

"Fine." Eric shrugged. "But do we have to do the stereotypes?"

"You uncomfortable with that?"

"Well . . . yes, if you want to know the truth."

"Don't be so self-righteous." Parker unbuttoned his shirt a little more. "Some of my best friends are queens of the first order. Besides, it's what most ignorant straight men expect. We'd be a little too threatening to their manhood if they thought they couldn't tell any difference between them and us."

"As long as I don't have to talk with a lisp or anything," Eric replied.

Parker laughed and patted Eric's cheek. "God, you'd be so cute if you did," he said.

"Sorry."

"Oh well." Parker feigned disappointment. "Put your arm around my shoulder."

"Why?"

"Because you're queer and you love me." Parker drew Eric's arm up around his neck. "All right, let's do it. Camp is my middle name."

They stepped around to the hanger opening. A man in coveralls was cleaning the windshield on a small, single-engine plane. He climbed down from the step stool when he spotted Parker and Eric at the hanger door.

"What can I do for you?" he asked as he cleaned his hands with the same wiping rag he had used on the plane.

"Are you Stan, the helicopter pilot?" Parker asked. He reached up to grab Eric's hand to keep it around his shoulder. "The one who does tours of the National Park?"

The man's expression changed visibly when he got a better look at the two men standing in the hanger door. "Yeah, I've got a helicopter."

Parker looked at Eric adoringly. "We're in the right place, honey," he said. He walked up to the man, hoping to divert attention away from Eric's crimson face. "We'd like the deluxe tour." He palmed two hundred dollar bills into view. "All the most beautiful and romantic spots." He held out his hand. "Hi, I'm Parker."

The man hesitated before shaking Parker's hand. "How long do you want to be out?" He eyed the money in Parker's hand.

"Oh, I don't know," Parker said. He turned back to Eric. "What do you think, dear, an hour or two?"

Eric had regained his composure somewhat. "Whatever you want," he attempted a smile, "dear." He tried not to stare at Parker's change in mannerism. The FBI agent was somehow looser, less restrained in his stance and gestures. "We can go out as long as you want."

"I'm already feeling spoiled." Parker giggled and threw his arm about Eric's waist to draw him up closer. "Let's go for about an hour. I want to go to lunch at that big mall before it closes . . . you know . . . the one we passed on the way in." He turned to the pilot who was eyeing them both with misgivings. "Unless you serve a picnic lunch on the tour?" Parker pulled at Eric's arm and continued before the pilot could answer. "Oh, that would be super, Eric. A picnic in the sky. That would be stunning!"

"I'm sorry," said the pilot. "I don't serve any food."

Parker pouted. "Well, okay. We'll need to be back by lunch, then." He snuggled against Eric's arm. "When do we leave?"

The pilot blinked his eyes before pocketing the cash. "Chopper's out back on the pad." He gestured behind him.

"Chopper!" Parker giggled. "You actually call them that."

"It . . . it's out back." The pilot gestured again.

"I'm so glad you suggested this," Parker said to Eric. He pulled Eric toward the door. "I've never been in a heli . . . I mean a chopper." He giggled again for the benefit of the pilot.

The two men left the hanger and headed around back to find the helicopter.

"I'm not sure what to make of your feminine side." Eric shook his head at Parker.

Parker snapped his fingers side to side. "Get over it, girl."

"I hope you don't do drag." Eric laughed.

"Don't you think I'm beautiful?" Parker assumed a hurt expression. "I think you're beautiful."

"As a man, your beauty is peerless."

"You romantic dog you." Parker batted his eye lashes.

"But you'd make a really ugly woman." Eric chuckled.

"Ugly?"

"Fug-ugly!"

Parker looked at him puzzled.

"That's mountain-talk for fucking-ugly," Eric said.

Parker frowned and gave Eric's shoulder a good punch.

"You brought the subject up." Eric squeezed Parker's arm.

"That's okay," Parker said. "You like regional expressions. Fine. Later, we'll see if you can squeal like a pig."

Eric gave a karate yell and dove for Parker's midsection. Before Parker could react, Eric hoisted him up over his shoulder and continued down the walkway.

Parker tried to laugh but, doubled over Eric's shoulder, he couldn't get enough breath.

"What will the pilot think?" he managed to stutter.

Eric kept his hold around Parker's thighs. "He'll think exactly what he's been thinking," he replied, and gave Parker's butt a hard slap.

"Ooo, baby!" Parker reached down to give Eric's buttocks a squeeze. "I kind of like this position."

Eric sat Parker down on the helicopter pad. "Well now we know who'll carry who over the threshold," he said.

Parker stood facing Eric, an arm draped over the younger man's muscular shoulder. "Ever done it in a helicopter at two thousand feet?"

"No," Eric said, eyeing the small helicopter, "and I don't intend on becoming a member of the Mile High Club now."

"Be creative!"

"Be serious." Eric nodded toward the hanger. "Here comes old Stan."

The pilot walked hurriedly from the hanger, carrying a small case, his eyes glued to the ground.

"I think we've embarrassed him," Parker whispered in Eric's ear.

"Look what he's carrying," Eric whispered back.

Parker immediately recognized the laptop computer case in the pilot's hand. "Are we ready to be off?" He called out.

"Yeah," the pilot said, breathing heavily from the short walk. "We're all clear." He slipped a key into the helicopter's door latch and swung it open. "Just climb up here in the back and strap yourselves in."

"This is too exciting." Parker reached up to grab the door sides for leverage. "Give me a push, dear," he said to Eric.

With a smirk, Eric grabbed Parker's buttocks and

shoved him up into the cockpit.

Parker looked back at him with a smile. "Thanks."

Eric merely cocked his head to one side and climbed up into the seat beside Parker and latched the door.

After completing his exterior checks, the pilot climbed into the front. "There are some headsets on the back of the front seats," he said. "If you put them on, we can communicate above the noise of the rotors." He flipped various switches and the large blades overhead began to spin.

Parker slipped on the headset in front of him. "Roger, over and out," he said into the attached microphone. "Cool." He nudged Eric. "Say something, Eric."

"Something."

"I can hear you," Parker said excitedly, almost bouncing in his seat.

The pilot ignored their banter and proceeded to set up his laptop in the seat beside him.

"Is that a computer?" Parker asked. He tapped Stan on the shoulder.

"Huh?" The pilot started. "Oh, yeah."

"Do you fly the plane with it?"

"Helicopter," Eric interjected.

"Do you fly the helicopter with it?" Parker said ingenuously.

Stan shook his head. "It's just for navigation," he said. "It's connected to this GPS that can tell us where we are at any given moment. The computer compares that with our destination and lets me know what heading corrections to make."

"I see." Parker stared at him blankly.

"It just makes sure we don't get lost," the pilot explained. He pulled back on the joy stick and the small helicopter rose in a gust of wind.

Parker let out a whoop.

"Not so loud, Parker." Eric pointed to the earphones.

Parker giggled and snuggled against Eric's shoulder. The pilot circled the small airport, before taking off in a northward heading.

"Oh, Eric, I just remembered." Parker pulled a CD from his jacket. "Eric's just a whiz with computers," he told the pilot. "Last night he got on the national web, or whatever you call it—"

"The World Wide Web," Eric offered.

"Yeah, that's it," Parker said. "He got on the Web and pulled down some navigation program and plotted a course to some of the best spots in the Park." He waved the CD at the pilot. "Here. It's all on this little disk thing."

"I don't know," the pilot said. "This software is pretty specialized. I doubt it can interpret what's on your disk."

"You might give it a try, though," Eric said. "The data on this disk was also generated by a GPS-based software."

The pilot eyed the small disk without enthusiasm. "Well, it's your time and money." He slipped it into the laptop's disk drive. "I'm telling you though, this program is highly specialized." He manipulated the trackball mouse.

"No harm if it doesn't work," Eric said.

They watched while the small computer clicked and whirred.

"See," Stan began. "I told you. . ." He stopped mid-sentence, eyes wide with surprise.

Even though he couldn't see the small computer screen from the back, Parker knew the course plot schematic had come up.

"From the look on your face, I'd say we have a match," Parker said with a sparkling smile.

"Good," Eric said, leaning over the seat for a look. "This'll save some time getting to the spots we'd like."

Stan's face went from surprise to dark concern as he studied the small schematic. "Where did you say you got this?" he asked hesitantly.

"You can get anything on the Web these days," Eric answered. "It's a hobby of mine."

"That's all you do," Parker said pouting. "You used to spend time with me when you came home. Now all you do is sit in front of that blasted computer." He nodded to the pilot. "Thank God, he can't have sex with the damn thing."

"Who says you can't?" Eric asked with a laugh.

"This map looks familiar." The pilot's suspicions were not completely allayed.

"I hope so," Eric agreed. "I'd hate to think we had a pilot who wasn't familiar with the area." He laughed. "No seriously, I just plotted the main tourist spots we'd heard about or seen in the brochures." He pointed to the screen. "That first point is Climbers Ridge—which is another hobby of mine."

"Can you imagine anyone enjoying climbing a rock?" Parker shook his head. "If I wanted to take risks, I could think of a few more interesting ones than that."

Stan was not put off. "This plot comes from off the screen to the airport here." He looked hard at Eric. "The first plotted point is the airport."

"Yeah, damn program?" Eric said, nodding. "I did it on my PC back home. When it asked the point of origin I entered Houston, Texas. I had no idea it was going to make that the first plot point."

"I don't see Houston on this plot," Stan countered.

"This is Greek to me," Parker said with a yawn. He hoped his comment gave Eric enough seconds to think.

Eric just smiled and put his arm about Parker. "Yeah," he said. "The program wasn't too sophisticated. Instead of saving my plot as one continuous file, it broke it up into pieces that would only take up one screen view. Damn thing saved my plot as almost twenty different data files. I had to go through each one of them before I figured out which file had the Park coordinates on it."

Parker relaxed into Eric's arm. "That took a good two hours of my snuggling time," he said.

"Sorry, dear," Eric offered.

Parker sniffed diffidently.

Without further word, the pilot banked the small helicopter into the heading indicated by the course plot.

Parker pulled Eric's arm tight about him and settled back comfortably into the curves of Eric's muscular torso. He covered the microphone on his headset. "I like undercover work," he whispered into Eric's ear.

Eric chuckled and held Parker tightly.

"It's rather roomy back here," Parker added into the microphone.

"It's not that roomy," Eric answered, giving him a look. "So I'd suggest you just enjoy the ride."

The pilot shifted uncomfortably in the front seat.

It wasn't long before the topography below them began to change dramatically. The roar of the chopper blades pulled them ever higher into more mountainous terrain, skimming several hundred feet above the ground below.

Parker continued his new bride charade and Eric his

patient new groom. Parker would occasionally *ooo* and *ahh* at the scenery below, or nuzzle Eric's neck affectionately. He kept a covert check on Stan, the pilot's shaky equilibrium and growing agitation.

Parker covered his microphone again. "I think he's reaching critical mass," he whispered in Eric's ear.

Eric was frowning. He nodded at the pilot who was hunched over in his seat, talking excitedly into his headset. He had apparently turned off the passenger headsets and was relying on the helicopter's roaring engines and rotors to cover his conversation.

Parker sat forward and leaned over the front seat. "Is everything all right up there?" he called out.

The pilot started. "What?" He switched off the radio and hit another switch to engage the passenger headsets.

"I said, is everything all right? Our headsets were off and I noticed you talking on the radio."

"Had to check in with the tower," Stan said with a shrug. He made a slight course adjustment. "Didn't want to let it disturb you."

Parker smiled reassuringly. "You won't disturb us. I'd love to hear some official radio talk." He settled back into Eric's arms. "All part of the total ambience."

"Climbers Ridge." Eric tapped on the window.

Parker leaned across him for a better view. "Doesn't look so high from up here." He felt the bottom drop out of his stomach as the helicopter began a sharp descent.

"We can see fine from up here," Eric said to the pilot. He frowned his concern to Parker.

"On to the next point!" Parker said to Stan good-naturedly.

The pilot ignored them and continued the descent.

"Damn it!" Eric said to Parker. He covered his

microphone. "If we get any lower the turbulence from the blades is going to wreck havoc with the ecosystem below."

Parker leaned into the front seat again. "Hey, Stan! We've seen enough here, let's move on to the next place."

The pilot concentrated on his controls and didn't answer.

"Stan!" Parker called out again. He tapped the pilot's shoulder. "What gives?"

Eric threw off his headset. "What the hell! He's trying to land this goddamn thing."

"Stan!" Parker shook the pilot's shoulder. "What the hell are you doing?"

"You wanted a picnic," Stan answered finally. "This is a good place for one."

"What did he say?" Eric asked, angrily replacing his headset.

"He said this is a good spot for a picnic."

"That does it!" Eric pulled Parker back into the seat and leaned into the front himself. "You take this goddamn thing back up!" he said to the pilot. "You land this chopper and I'll see to it your license is pulled. This is a violation of federal law."

The helicopter sat down on the ridge mesa with a jarring thud.

Eric fell back into his seat. "Son-of-a-bitch!" he yelled.

Before Eric could react further, Parker grabbed him by the arm and held him back. "Steady, Red," he said.

Eric stared at the barrel of the pistol pointing at him from the front seat. "What the—"

Stan waved the pistol at him. "Now you two love birds step out of the chopper carefully," he said with a sneer. "And don't try anything. I'd hate to have to clean your blood off my upholstery."

Eric pulled slowly at the latch and swung the door open.

Parker smiled and batted his lashes at the pilot. "Stan," he said. "I hope you don't think you're getting much of a tip for this!"

CHAPTER 13

Margaret gave her breast pocket a pat. She had taken a detour by the sporting goods store and bought a small box of bullets for the petite gun nestled snugly next to her left breast.

"Men are such children" she said to herself and adjusted the motley silk scarf tied about her neck before entering the ranger station. Satisfied with her power-dressed appearance, she breezed into the station's visitor area, and made her way around the racks of information brochures to the service counter.

"Hello," she called out, setting her heavy briefcase down on the counter. "Anybody working the front desk?"

A door opened and the short, brunette ranger stepped out.

"Oh! Hi, Ms. Curry," the woman in uniform said, recognizing the DA instantly.

"Hi . . . Alice, isn't it?"

"Yes, ma'am." She straightened some stray papers on the counter. "What can I do for you today?"

"Well, Alice, it's like this." Margaret opened her briefcase. "When I was here the other day to pick up these personnel files," she pulled the files from her case and plopped them onto the counter, "these disks were in among them." She pulled the two diskettes out and splayed them over the top of the files.

Alice looked at the CD's and attempted a halting smile. "Yes, ma'am?"

"Well, it's very curious, Alice."

"Yes, ma'am?" Alice's voice had weakened.

"Do you know who pulled these files for me?" Margaret tapped the CDs with a blood red nail.

"Yes, ma'am, I ..." Alice cleared her throat. "The Superintendent asked me to pull the list you faxed over." She shifted nervously. "I pulled all that you requested, didn't I? I—"

Margaret raised a hand. "The files were fine, Alice," she said. "It's these computer disks I'm interested in."

"Yes, ma'am."

"Alice?"

"Yes, ma'am."

"One more *yes ma'am* and I'm going to have to charge you with felony annoyance."

"Yes, ma' ... I mean ... Ms. Curry," the ranger stuttered.

"Call me Margaret, please." Margaret smiled disarmingly.

Alice let her breath out. "Thanks ... Margaret." She laughed and relaxed visibly. "Sorry, but Superintendent Bledsoe is very strict about how the public is treated."

"Think of me as just one of the girls around here," Margaret said. "I'm just another government employee like yourself." She brushed a particle of lint from her sleeve. "So what if I can order the police to have you shot."

Alice's mouth fell open.

"Lighten up, Alice." Margaret laughed to emphasize she was joking. "It's just us girls."

"Well," Alice said, visibly relaxing, "that's a phrase you don't hear around here very often."

"I know the feeling, dear," Margaret said. "Men just can't stand it when we don't stay home, barefoot and pregnant." She picked up one of the disks. "Now, seriously, about these CD's?"

"Did they have something important on them?" Alice drew her shoulders up.

"Very important," Margaret said. "As a matter-of-fact, the information on these CD's is directly related to an ongoing murder investigation."

"Murder investigation?" Alice's eyes almost bulged.

"Murder investigation," Margaret stated flatly.

"Oh, my God!"

Margaret leaned into her. "Are you telling me you didn't know these CD's were material evidence in a murder investigation when you slipped them in among these files?"

"No, honestly," Alice protested. "They were just a bunch of numbers. I . . ." She stopped.

"So it was you," Margaret said triumphantly.

Alice almost moaned. "Dammit!" A hand went to her forehead.

"Alice," Margaret said, reaching out a hand to pat Alice's arm. "If you didn't know what the significance of the data on these disks was, why did you slip them to me in these files?"

Alice banged her forehead several times with a

clenched hand.

"Talk to me, Alice." Margaret pulled the girl's hand down. "This is very serious. Do you know something about the murder at Climber's Ridge?"

"No! No." Alice shook her head violently. "I didn't have any idea." Her eyes moistened. "Oh, God!"

"Calm down, Alice." Margaret took both of Alice's hands in hers. "Between you and me, now. What's the deal with the CD's?"

"I thought they might help Eric." Her face softened noticeably.

"Help Eric?"

"You know," Alice said. "With his trouble with the Superintendent."

"I'm not following you, Alice."

Alice took a deep breath. "I knew one of the men was causing trouble for Eric. Bledsoe had me in the office taking notes when the complaints were being made."

"He had you taking notes?"

"Well," Alice said bitterly. "Secretarial work is about the only reason Bledsoe would have a woman ranger on the staff. So that's what I do."

"Men!" Margaret nodded her understanding. "I've been there, dear."

"So," Alice continued. "When Arlee finished making his filthy complaints—"

"Arlee?" Margaret queried.

"Arlee Bonner."

"Of course." Margaret rolled her eyes.

"When he finished his complaints, I kept an eye on him," Alice said. "He went to his desk, and I saw him copy some files off the computer onto some CD's."

"These are Bonner's disks?"

"Well, copies of them," Alice said. "I manage the network here at the office, so I called up his workstation on my screen and watched him copy the files from his hard disk directory onto the CD's. Then he deleted them from the hard drive."

"I see," Margaret said, nodding.

"I thought the files might have something to do with his complaints against Eric—some proof that he was making it all up."

"How did you make the copies if the files were deleted?"

Alice shrugged. "Nothing is ever really deleted from the hard drive until you write over the data."

"So you restored the deleted files?" Margaret asked.

"Yes, ma'am."

Margaret raised an eyebrow.

"I mean, Margaret," Alice said quickly.

Margaret nodded again and smiled. "You looked at the files?" she asked.

"Yes," Alice said. "But they were just a mess of programming code and numbers."

"So why slip them to me?"

"Well," Alice said, looking down at her hands. "I thought, just because I didn't understand, it was no reason to think you couldn't. You have to be pretty smart to be a lawyer. I thought, after you found the CD's, you'd be curious enough to figure out what they contained."

"I appreciate your faith in me." Margaret laughed.

"Well, apparently I was right," Alice said, smiling down at the counter.

"Which computer is Bonner's?"

"It's in the other room," Alice said, pointing. "Why?"

"I want to see what else is on it," Margaret

responded.

"That's easy." Alice raised the counter gate and motioned Margaret inside. "I restored his files from the network. There's nothing in his private drive anymore. I've stored it all elsewhere."

Margaret gave the ranger an appreciative look. "And I bet they think you're just the pretty receptionist who can't do anything but file," she said.

"Oh, I can type, too," Alice said with a light laugh. She sat at her terminal and typed in her passwords. "What do you want to look at?"

"Surprise me." Margaret stood behind Alice, looking over her shoulder.

Alice opened a directory file and ran her finger down the screen over them.   "These are all gibberish, like the ones I slipped to you," she said.

"Are there any others?" Margaret asked.

Alice scrolled down through the directory.   "That's pretty much all there was."

"Damn." Margaret straightened. "I'd kill to know what else he's been up to."

"Well." Alice pursed her lips, hesitating.

"What?" Margaret put a hand on Alice's shoulder. "Out with it, girl!"

"I'm the network administrator," Alice stammered. "If I want, I can see every website Bonner's visited over the past . . . couple of months or so, depending on disk space." She looked up at Margaret. Margaret's smile made her shudder.

"Everything?" Margaret pointed at the screen. "Show me websites."

Alice alternated mouse clicks with a few typed words. Another directory scrolled onto the screen.

"These are the web sites he's visited in order of date," she said, manipulating the mouse.

Margaret crouched beside Alice for a better view. She glanced over the list. "More," she said.

Alice scrolled down further.

"Wait!" Margaret covered Alice's hand over the mouse. "That one!" She pointed.

Alice clicked on it. "It's the Continental Airlines website," she said.

"Can you tell what he was checking there?"

"Not particulars, no." She clicked several more times. "Wait a minute!" She typed vigorously. "Looks like he bought a ticket. This is his e-mail and there's a confirmation message." She brought the e-mail up.

"Belize!" Margaret hummed to herself. "Old Bonner's going to Belize."

"He hasn't put in for any vacation time that I know of." Alice shrugged.

"I think, Alice, that this is not for a vacation," Margaret said. "More like a relocation."

Alice's eyes widened.

"Can you cancel the reservation?" Margaret asked.

"I can try," Alice said, liking the idea. She called up the airline's website and entered the confirmation number. She maneuvered the mouse deftly, clicking and then typing. "Done!" she said, dropping her hands in her lap.

"Well, that was easy," Margaret said, nodding with satisfaction. "At least we know that, whatever Bonner's planning, there's gonna be a slight hitch in his get-away plans."

"He pays his bills online, too," Alice said. "I can probably cancel his credit cards, turn off all his utilities, and take out his cell phone for good measure."

Margaret could not help but laugh. "Damn, girl! I'm gonna have to keep you on my good side."

"Just a thought," Alice said with a shrug. "I'm not gonna lose any sleep being nasty to a scumbag like Bonner."

"Well," Margaret replied. "Save it for when I've left." She bobbed her eyebrows. "What I don't know, I can't charge you with."

"Oh, well." Alice pushed back from the keyboard. "What now?"

"Okay, here's the plan." Margaret stood. "I'll have some of the forensic guys here this afternoon. They're gonna want to download your entire network contents."

Alice's brow furrowed. "Is that legal?" Her voice shook.

"They'll have a warrant, don't you worry," Margaret said. She put a hand on her shoulder. "Are you okay with that?"

"If it'll help Eric."

"You like Eric?" Margaret patted her hand.

"Sure. You've seen him." Alice grinned.

"Really nice ass." Margaret's eyes twinkled.

"Really nice everything," Alice said shyly.

Margaret suppressed a giggle. "Would the idea of him being gay bother you that much?" she asked. "I mean, would it really be such a big deal?"

"Hell yes!" Alice said emphatically. "I think that would be grounds to shoot myself."

"Sometimes a girl's just gotta face facts, honey," Margaret said. "It's true what they say—all the really good men are gay." She shook her head in mock despair.

"It's not fair." Alice sighed again.

"You could say the same thing about that gorgeous FBI man," Margaret said.

"It's true then?" Alice asked after a moment's silence. "That Eric's gay?"

Alice nodded.

"I'm afraid so, honey," Margaret said.

Alice shook her head sadly. "There goes a year's worth of fantasies," she said with a long sigh.

"Girl." Margaret tossed her hair. "You don't have to have sex with a gay to enjoy him."

"What?" Alice looked at her puzzled.

"Heavens no, dear!" Margaret pulled out her lipstick to re-apply. "They love to cuddle and snuggle and dish and all the really fun things."

"I should live so long." Alice giggled.

"The best girlfriend is a beautiful gay man."

They laughed in unison.

Alice took in a deep breath. "I just can't believe these CD's have anything to do with the murders at Climber's Ridge," she said. "What the hell kind of information was Arlee Bonner compiling in that form. Some sort of code?"

"That's a good question." Margaret dropped the disks back into her briefcase. "But we've already narrowed the answer down."

"What is it?" Alice asked. "Swiss bank accounts? Coded messages to South American drug lords?"

"Nothing so dramatic," Margaret said. "Parker and Eric are on it, and I'll leave it at that."

"I understand." Alice thought a moment. "Are you going to have Bonner arrested?"

"In due time," Margaret said. "In due time. For now, we'll just wait and see."

"I'll keep an eye on him around here," Alice volunteered. "Give me your cell phone number and I'll keep you informed."

Margaret dropped the lipstick back into her purse. "Where is sweet, little Arlee now?" she asked.

Alice shrugged again. "His shift doesn't begin until the afternoon." She nodded at the phone on the wall behind her. "I could give him a call at home and see if he's there."

"No, no." Margaret held up a hand. "That won't be necessary." She gave Alice a hard look. "You're sure Bonner doesn't know you copied these files?"

"Absolutely. He'd have had a cow and a half if he knew I was in his private drive."

"Good." Margaret grabbed up her briefcase. "Let's keep it that way. Not a word."

Alice's eyes widened.

"I'm serious, Alice," Margaret said. "Not a word to anyone about the files or this conversation."

"Whatever you say."

"And no more messing around in Bonner's private drive, okay?" Margaret patted her hand again.

"Okay."

"Okay, I'm outta here." Margaret headed back toward the reception area. "But do keep your eyes and ears open." She slipped her business card into Alice's hand. "My cell phone's on the back. Call me about anything out of the ordinary, anytime day or night."

Alice eyed the card. "No problem. If Bonner's involved in these murders, I want to help put him away, anyway I can," she said emphatically.

"Good girl." Margaret slipped out from behind the reception counter. "Now don't worry." She leaned in conspiratorially and patted Alice's hand again. "We're gonna nail these bastards!" Margaret turned to leave.

"Hello, Ms. Curry, said the squat, heavy set man blocking her way. His toothy smile sent a chill down Margaret's spine. "Or should I say, Margaret?"

Margaret heard Alice gasp behind her.

"Arlee Bonner, I presume," Margaret said, facing him squarely. "And it's Ms. Curry to you."

Bonner pushed the barrel of a thirty-eight into Margaret's ribs. "Get behind the counter with your spy," he said menacingly.

"Bonner." Margaret fought the tremor in her voice. "You're in deep enough shit as it is. If I were you—"

"If you were me, you wouldn't have anything to lose either . . . nothing to prevent you from snuffing out a nosey lawyer and a busybody clerk." He nudged her with the gun. "Now do what I told you."

Margaret moved slowly around the counter to join Alice who was literally frozen with fear. She could feel the weight of the small gun in her jacket pocket as she put her own quivering arm about the terrified girl.

"Take it easy, Alice. We'll be all right," Margaret said, trying to look unfazed.

Bonner moved around them to study the computer screen. "What have you been doing here?" He turned on Alice. "You little bitch! What did you do?"

Anger overtook Alice, emboldening her. "Go to hell!" she said, glaring at him.

"I ought to…" Bonner drew his hand back as if he would slap her. "It doesn't matter anyway," he said. "The two of you aren't gonna be any more of a problem after today."

"Bonner, "Margaret said, swallowing. "Surely you

can't be so stupid as to think you're going to get away with this?"

"Get away with what?" He waved the gun at the two women, laughing. "I haven't done anything to you yet."

"What's that supposed to mean?" Margaret said. "What are you planning?"

"None of your business, bitch!"

"You are not gonna outsmart the FBI," Margaret said defiantly. "It's all over with. You just haven't figured it out yet."

"Margaret," Alice said, putting a hand on Margaret's arm.

Margaret took a deep breath, realizing that perhaps she shouldn't upset Bonner any further.

"To the back door, ladies." Bonner said. He started around the counter, keeping his pistol leveled at Margaret. "My truck's just outside. We're going for a little ride in the mountains."

Margaret pulled Alice with her. "My office knows I was coming here to see you, Bonner." She hoped she looked confident. "If I don't check in within the hour, your ass is as good as cooked."

"That's funny," Bonner said with a malevolent leer. "I just called your office, before I came in. They had no idea where you were. As a matter of fact, your secretary said that, if I happen to run into you, to remind you she would be out the rest of the afternoon for a dentist appointment."

Margaret cleared her throat and tried to look unconcerned.

"Consider yourself reminded," Bonner said. "Now move it."

CHAPTER 14

Parker stepped down from the helicopter onto the rocky top of Climber's Ridge. Eric dropped down beside him.

"Well," Parker said. "I suppose making a run for it is out of the question."

Eric kicked a pebble over the nearby rim. "Nowhere to go but down," he said. "And without climbing gear, there's not much hope of that."

Parker turned back to the chopper. "So," he said to the pilot. "What now?"

"Now you wait," the pilot said. "Shut the door and back away from the chopper." He waved the pistol for emphasis.

Eric latched the door and moved across the ridge with Parker until they were clear of the helicopter.

"Well, Mr. Big-Shot-G-Man," Eric said. "I suppose you have a plan of action?"

Parker shrugged and made himself comfortable on a large boulder. "Improvise," he said. "Make the most of the situation."

"What the hell does that mean?" Eric sat down beside him.

"We could make out."

"That's your answer for everything," Eric said, rolling his eyes.

"Love conquers all." Parker put a hand on Eric's knee. "We'll know more when the others arrive."

"The others?" Eric rested his head on Parker's shoulder.

"If he was going to kill us he would have done it by now." Parker smiled. Eric's manner had grown more relaxed and intimate with him as the day progressed. "We're waiting for something and my guess would be the other major players in this little game." He relished the cool scent of Eric's hair.

Eric straightened and looked around. "You're probably right." He squeezed the hand Parker had rested on his knee. "So kiss me."

"What?" Parker's brows went up.

"I thought you wanted to make out."

"Now?" Parker couldn't believe his ears.

"Okay, you want to just sit and stare at the rocks?"

"Like hell!" Parker turned and slipped an arm over Eric's shoulder. "Let's give old Stan an eyeful."

"Just so you know." Eric tried to sound smug despite the rising heat in his face and the grin he was fighting to suppress. "I'm not one to make a habit of public displays of affection."

"Well, let's not let that beautiful pink blush go to waste."

Parker bent his face around to Eric's. Their lips met, tentatively at first. Then Parker pulled Eric to him, tightly. Their tongues spiraled, exploring each other. Parker felt

Eric's arms tighten about him. The redhead's skin was hot and inviting against the cold breeze cutting across the escarpment. As their lips parted, Parker felt the soft caress of Eric's long lashes against his cheek. He held Eric's face up in his hands, marveling at his reflection in the younger man's moist, hazel eyes.

"That was a great kiss." Eric grinned, a little embarrassed.

"That was an awesome kiss." Parker nibbled on Eric's upper lip. "You smell good. You taste good. You feel good. You kiss good." He stroked Eric's cheek. "I keep wondering what else you do good?"

"I hope we get out of this so you can find out." Eric chuckled.

"Why wait?" Parker kissed Eric's brow.

"I'm not very good in crowds." Eric nodded toward the chopper.

"That's okay." Parker kissed Eric's cheek. "I could kiss you all day."

"We might not have that long."

"*Carpe diem.*" Parker pressed his lips against Eric's again.

They held each other tighter, more urgently. For a moment, Parker forgot where he was. He pulled away breathing heavily, taken aback at the magnitude of his need to lose himself in Eric's embrace.

"Sorry," Eric said, looking at the ground.

"Sorry?" Parker lifted Eric's eyes to his own. "Why?"

"I thought . . ." Eric looked confused. "Maybe I was a little too . . . needy."

"No." Parker almost laughed. "The more you want it, the more I want to give it to you."

Eric's smile beamed. "I guess I'm not very experienced at figuring out what someone else is thinking or feeling," he said.

"Don't worry about that." Parker said. "Go with your own feelings." His conscience prickled at his own failure to say what *he* really felt. Something pulled his gaze to the chopper. "Heads up!"

The pilot was carrying on an animated conversation with the shortwave radio in the chopper.

"Looks like a call's coming in," Parker said.

"Don't suppose you read lips?" Eric asked.

"No." Parker attempted a light-hearted chuckle. "But I'd say it's bad news for us at any rate."

"Do we rush the chopper?"

"Only if we're suicidal," Parker said. "Let's just maintain a wait-and-see attitude and keep our eyes open for any opportunity."

"All right." Eric slipped his hand into Parker's. "I'll do that on both counts, the chopper pilot . . . and you."

Before Parker could respond, the pilot clipped the shortwave mike back on the instrument panel and restarted the powerful engines.

"Now what?" Parker jumped up. "Hey!" he yelled at the pilot and waved his hands in the air.

The helicopter door opened and the pilot tossed out a heavy rope. Without a word he lifted the chopper off the escarpment. Eric and Parker hugged the ground, struggling to keep from being blown over the edge by the powerful vortex generated from the chopper blades. The helicopter ascended quickly and with a sharp turn, headed back in the direction they had come from.

Parker sat up, brushing dust out of his hair. "Well, my dear, this is a fine mess we've gotten into," he said.

Eric scrambled over to the coiled rope. "At least he

left us a way down." He uncoiled some of the rope and tested its strength. "Perfect," he said, carrying it over to the edge of the escarpment.

"I'm not sure I like where this is going," Parker said. He followed Eric as close to the edge as he could before his lungs clenched with a familiar panic response.

"We can do this." Eric sensed Parker's hesitation and anxiety. "I know you must have climbed plenty of ropes and such at the Langley training grounds."

Parker grimaced. "None of them were over a sheer rock face, two hundred feet up, with a boulder field for a landing site," he said.

"Why do you think they left us a way down anyway?" Eric asked, scratching in the dirt along the edge of their high perch.

"What do you mean?"

"Well, why not just leave us up here exposed to the elements?"

Parker shrugged. "Maybe they just didn't want to add murder of a federal agent to their list of sins," he said. "Especially since you're intent on killing us yourself!"

"We're in luck," Eric said, paying no attention to Parker's whining. He brushed dirt away from an old piton that had been left behind from some previous climber's attempt. "We can tie off on this." He hastily knotted the rope through the small steel loop and tossed it over the edge.

"No way, José!" Parker shook his head.

"The length is right," Eric said. "But there isn't enough rope to knot it at intervals. At least we'll be going down which is a lot easier than climbing up."

"For you . . . easier for you," Parker said. "I'm staying right here. You go for help."

"Bullshit!" Eric reached a hand out to Parker. "Come here."

Parker shook his head.

"I'm serious," Eric said.

"So am I." Parker backed farther away from the ledge.

"I can't believe you're this afraid of heights."

"I can't believe it either," Parker said. "But there we have it."

"How can they still let you out in the field?"

"They don't know about this," Parker said with a shrug.

Eric raised an eyebrow.

"This is a recent development," Parker explained.

"Recent?"

"Ever since some dipshit terrorist wanna-be hung me by the heels out a window on the twenty-sixth floor of a high rise in Dallas."

"No shit!" Eric stood. "The twenty-sixth floor? How'd you escape?"

"I promised to tell them ever frigging civil defense secret I knew."

Eric's eyes widened.

"I'm kidding." Parker tried to smile. "I reminded them of the cadre of well-armed agents waiting for them on various floors, and pointed out I'd be much more useful as a human shield."

"Good thinking," Eric said with a smirk.

"Out of the fire and into the frying pan."

"This is no different." Eric took Parker's hand.

"Like hell!" Parker said. "I'm already in the frying pan. I'm sure as hell not jumping into the fire!"

"Calm down." Eric put his arm around Parker.

"I am calm," Parker managed between clenched teeth.

"I'm an expert climber," Eric offered. "I can get us down without a hitch. Trust me, I don't intend on letting anything happen to you." He bussed Parker's cheek. "I have very definite future plans for you."

Parker smiled weakly. "That's why I don't want to go over that edge," he said.

"You know you have to." Eric gave Parker a little tug. "You've got to get over this. You can't afford to let an unreasonable fear rule you like this."

"Unreasonable?" Parker pulled Eric back. "I think I stand firmly in the company of all sane and reasonable men by refusing to dangle two hundred feet above a boulder field by that little rope."

Eric pulled Parker around to face him. "Other men don't have me there helping them down," he said.

Parker looked into Eric's warm, hazel eyes. "Damn you!"

"That's better." Eric guided him slowly to the edge. "Just keep your breathing steady. You should know how to deal with fear better than I do. Now do it!"

Parker nodded and forced himself to take slow, deep breaths. He threw his head back to let the crisp, cool wind hit him square in the face. Eric stood next to him, a supporting arm wrapped tightly about Parker's waist.

"All right." Parker relaxed his hold on Eric's arm. "Let's do this thing."

"Good man." Eric squeezed Parker's waist. "Just keep your mind and your eyes on what your hands and feet are doing."

Parker peered out over the edge of the high escarpment. "Shit!"

"Don't look down, dummy!" Eric began pulling the

rope up. "We're going to have a safe and easy descent."

"Do tell."

"Let's have a look at your belt." Eric held the end of the rope in his hand.

Parker inspected his belt.

"Looks like a good piece of leather," Eric said, checking the end stitching.

"It had better be, considering what it cost." Parker shrugged. "What's my belt got to do with this?"

"It'll be one of your main safety nets," Eric said. "Now watch."

Eric wrapped the rope once around his waist, slipped the end through his belt and then brought it down between his legs to the rear.

"This is a make-shift rappelling setup," Eric said. He pulled the rope through his legs, demonstrating the friction control created by the rope circling his body. "This distributes your body weight directly to the rope without it having to transfer through your arms and hands. This way your upper body strength is used mainly to control your rate of descent."

"That makes sense." Parker took the rope from Eric and recreated the process on himself. "Why through the belt?"

"Let go of the rope," Eric said.

Parker did so.

"You see?" Eric said pointing. "Even if you were to lose your hold on the rope, you're still tied to it by your belt. You can't fall away from the rope. Unless you're knocked unconscious or something, you'll be able to reestablish your grip."

"Unless I'm knocked—"

"Ignore that," Eric interrupted. "That's not going to

happen."

"Says you." Parker retested the setup. "What now?"

"Don't wrap the rope around your waist," he said. "The man on the bottom ... that's me ... does the rappelling. You just slide down the rope." Eric pulled the rope through Parker's legs until the G-Man was fully threaded.

"Ouch!" Parker rubbed his crotch. "That got a little hot."

"Oh yeah." Eric chuckled. "That's another little safety tip."

"Do tell."

"Keep your vital parts to one side or the other of the ropes path."

"Thanks for bothering to tell me that."

"Oh, you'd have probably figured it out for yourself before any lasting damage occurred," Eric said.

"I'm a lefty myself." Parker adjusted himself delicately. "Now what?"

"I go first." Eric began threading the rope around himself. "That way I can keep an eye on your progress. If you lose your grip, I'll be there to block your fall until you can get your hold again."

"I like that part," Parker said. "How much of a head start should I give you?"

Eric turned his back to the edge and positioned himself in front of the piton. "Give me about ten to twelve feet," he said. "Then I'll stop and talk you through getting started."

"Okay."

"Remember," Eric cautioned. "Keep your hands on the rope and your feet on the rock face. Walk your way down until you get the hang of things. Then we'll try a few short hops to speed our descent."

"Couldn't I just lash myself to your back and ride down."

"You lazy, old fairy!" Eric laughed. "I'm not lugging your fat butt anywhere."

"Fat! Who you calling fat?" Parker gave his ass a pat. "There's nothing but prime beef back there."

"Well you can drag your own prime butt down this rock, old man."

Parker feigned shock. "Now you're calling me old," he said and shot Eric the bird.

Eric was too busy checking his setup. "Now," he said. "Get down on your knees on the ledge with your belt as close to the ground as possible."

"That sounds kinky," Parker said.

"Just do it."

Parker did as he was told and lay on his stomach facing away from then ledge.

"This will keep you from being jerked to the ground when my weight takes hold of the rope," Eric explained, making sure the rope was tightly secured to the piton.

"Doesn't look like much." Parker eyed the small metal cleat jutting from the rock.

"Don't worry. It'll hold us both easily." Eric straddled Parker. "I know what you're thinking so don't say it," he said, looking down at Parker's leering expression.

"I'm not saying a word."

"Brace yourself," Eric cautioned. "I'm going to let myself over the edge using you for a hand hold until I clear you.

"Hey, mountain boy!" Parker watched Eric's progress admiringly.

"Are you paying attention?" Eric said.

"Yes, mother," Parker replied. "I have to go to the bathroom."

"What?"

"I hope I don't have to take a piss when I start down." Parker eyed Eric from between his legs. "You might get a little wet."

"You're a sick motherfucker," Eric said, and lowered himself down Parker's back and legs until he was clear.

"It's the call of nature," Parker said.

"I'm not into that sort of thing," Eric replied, leaning back into space until he was standing out from the rock face.

"I've yet to find out what exactly the hell you are into, my beauty," Parker mumbled to himself.

"What?" Eric's voice echoed in the canyon below as he slowly walked down the rock face backwards.

"Nothing!" Parker said.

"Okay," Eric called up to him. "Now it's your turn. Let's get this show on the road."

For a moment, Parker considered changing his mind. He cursed himself silently, angry at his own hesitation and hoping that the anger would overcome the fear. He concentrated on the rope running through his belt and how he might slide back over the edge without looking like a total fool.

"Parker," Eric's voice called up to him. "Are you still there?"

"It's kind of hard to move with this rope pulling me against the ground," Parker called out.

"Just slide backwards on your stomach," Eric said. "Keep an eye on your belt though, and make sure it doesn't come loose. Once the belt clears the edge, it'll be smooth sailing."

Parker forced himself to push backwards on his belly toward the edge. He backed closer until his feet dangled out into space. His chest felt like it might explode. He cupped his hands over his nose and mouth and struggled to slow and deepen his breathing by inhaling his own carbon dioxide. The technique worked better than he expected and he was able to grab hold of the rope again.

"Thanks, Eric," Parker said.

"What for?" Eric said, puzzled.

"For not rushing me."

"Don't look down." Eric smiled up at him.

Parker caught his breath for a moment and jerked his head up to look straight ahead at the rock face.

"You're doing fine," Eric reassured him. "Just slide down the rope like a fireman's pole. It'll support you. Don't worry."

"Don't worry, he says," Parker mumbled. He complied anyway, wrapping his legs about the rope as he slowly slid over the edge and down the taut rope. When he had cleared the rim, he paused a moment, assessing his situation, and convincing himself that the rope was secure.

"How are you doing up there," Eric called up, his voice closer and more reassuring.

"Doing good." Parker swallowed.

"Okay," Eric said. "I'm going to let myself down a little farther. The more distance there is between us, the less you'll feel the rope jerk about when I move." As Eric began to move, the rope fibers tightened among themselves causing an ominous elastic creaking sound to echo about the two men.

"What's that?" Parker felt the panic starting to return.

"Everything's fine," Eric called up. "It's just friction

in the rope."

Parker nodded to himself. He knew that was true in his head even before he asked. He didn't like the way his fear made him mistrust his own intellect.

"All right." Eric's voice broke through Parker's self-deprecation. "Let's start down together. You keep your eyes forward on the rock face. I'll keep track of the distance between us and the distance to the bottom. Your job is to keep your hold on the rope—"

"No problem there," Parker interrupted.

"—and maintain a slow steady descent," Eric finished. "Let's go."

Parker felt the rope jerking between his legs as a signal that Eric was on the move. He slowly began to slide down the rope. By forcing his mind to analyze every detail of his descent, he fought the powerful urge to look down. His upper body strength was excellent and he mentally patted himself on the back at how effortlessly he held his weight. Parker lowered himself with a deliberate pace, keeping mental note of every movement and sensation. He knew the best way to keep the fear and panic at bay was to convince himself that he was in total control of the situation.

"We're halfway there, old man," Eric called up. "I didn't think you had it in you."

Parker hugged the rope and smiled. He caught himself thinking how much he loved this guy. "You watch your mouth, boy," he yelled into the stone wall. "Or I'll slide down this rope and knock you off." The sound of Eric's laughter strengthened him.

"Now, I am having a little trouble keeping ahead of you," Eric said. "Take it easy. Were in no rush."

"Speak for yourself," Parker quipped. Nevertheless,

he slowed his descent. The fear was all but gone. Now he fought to suppress an overwhelming feeling of power and elation which he knew could be more dangerous under the circumstances than fear.

A sudden spray of dust struck Parker's face. His body tensed as he heard the loud, unmistakable echo of a rifle report. He looked up and saw several more small explosions of dust in the rock face about the rope, followed by the time-lagged cracking report of a rifle. "Eric!" he yelled, feeling the panic return.

"I hear it," Eric yelled back. "Keep moving—as fast as you can!"

Parker felt the rope go suddenly slack. He slammed against the rock face and felt himself begin to tumble backwards, still gripping the loose rope. "Shit!" was all he could manage as the horizon revolved in front of him, until all he could see was the fast approaching boulder field some hundred feet below.

CHAPTER 15

Margaret fought the stiff manual transmission on the small truck, almost stripping the gears as she downshifted. Besides the fact that she hadn't driven a standard in over five years, the gun pointing at her across Alice's stomach, made the driving even more difficult. That and the fact that three adults simply didn't fit comfortably on the front, bench seat.

"Sorry." Alice's voice quivered as she tried to give Margaret more room to maneuver.

"You're fine, Alice," Margaret said through gritted teeth. "It's this damn transmission!" A final tug pulled the stick into gear and the screeching of the gears settled into a loud hum.

"Take it easy with my truck," Bonner almost yelled.

"Eat shit," Margaret mumbled under her breath.

"Turn left up here," Bonner said, unconcerned.

"But that's a service road—" Alice began.

"Shut up!" Bonner raised his pistol at her for emphasis, and then shook it at Margaret. "You just drive where you're told, lady," he said to her.

"It's hard to concentrate with you waving that gun around," Margaret said, struggling once more to downshift into the turn.

"That's what happens when you stick your nose in where it doesn't belong." Bonner flashed her an acid smile.

The truck bounced mercilessly from pothole to pothole along the narrow gravel road. Margaret kept the truck on the road as best she could and hoped that Bonner's gun didn't have a hair trigger. "The road's blocked up ahead." Margaret nodded at the chain link gate spanning the width of the road. She slowed the truck and came to a stop in front of it.

"Get out," Bonner commanded. "Just you, Miss DA." He leered at Alice and said, "you stay here and keep me company."

"I'm not getting out until you tell me why," Margaret said. She hoped her expression was one of bold defiance as she put a comforting hand on Alice's thigh.

"I want you to open the gate," Bonner said ingenuously. "Think you can handle that?"

Margaret gave him the evil eye and fumbled the door open.

"Take the keys with you," Bonner said. "The small key with the red jacket opens the padlock...and don't try anything. You bolt and your girlfriend takes a bullet."

Margaret gave him another look and grabbed the keys from the ignition. She stumbled over the uneven roadbed to the gate, cursing her spiked heels. The road was surrounded by dense forest and underbrush on both sides. Behind the gate was a graveled clearing with a series of metal storage buildings and aluminum carports covering various tractors and small bulldozers.

She played with the padlock for a minute. Keeping her back to the truck, she looked about for any signs of life. In the distance, she could hear the noise of tourists arriving. Judging by the distance they had come and the terrain, Margaret guessed that Bear Lake Park must be nearby. Still, she knew that the service area would be far enough away from the lake that park guests would not even know it existed.

She unlocked the gate and pushed it open enough to be able to drive the truck through. She caught a glimpse of Bonner out of the corner of her eye. He was watching her every move and keeping the gun pointed at Alice's head.

Margaret headed back to the truck and did her best to avoid eye contact with her captor. "Now what?" she asked, climbing back up into the truck cab.

"Just drive through," Bonner said. "As long as you follow instructions we won't have any problems."

Margaret ignored him and started the engine. With a grinding of gears she put the truck in first and pulled slowly through the gate into the open enclosure.

"Pull over to that building." Bonner waved the nose of his pistol at a gray steel storage building to the rear of the enclosure.

Margaret did as she was told, stopping the truck in front of its large, sliding metal doors.

"Now what?" she asked.

"Now kill the engine and get out." He nuzzled Alice's ear with his nose. "This time we all get out."

Alice shook with revulsion and scooted across the seat to Margaret. Margaret quickly opened the door and pulled Alice out of the cab with her.

Bonner kept his pistol trained on them and slid across

to the driver's side. "Now ladies." He stepped down out of the truck. "We're going for a little hike up into the Park."

Bonner clipped a hand-held shortwave radio to his belt and reached into the truck behind the seat. He pulled out a long leather carrying case. Both Margaret and Alice stared wide-eyed at the unmistakable shape of the case.

"What are you planning to do with that?" Margaret almost stammered.

Bonner caressed the length of the rifle case. "You never know," he said smiling down at the weapon case. "We might run into a grizzly or something."

"You're crazy if you think I'm going to go trudging around in the woods." Margaret backed away further, pulling Alice with her. "I'm wearing heals and a dress."

"Suit yourself." Bonner turned the pistol on Margaret. "I guess I'll just have to kill you here."

The two women held each other.

"There's no need for that, Arlee," Alice said, finding her voice at last. "She'll be just fine." She looked desperately at Margaret. "I'll help you Margaret."

Margaret eyed the muzzle of the pistol. "Considering the alternative," she said, "I suppose I have no choice."

"I'm so glad you'll be joining us, Miss Curry," Bonner said, sneering. "It's a beautiful day for a little walk in the woods."

"Yeah, yeah," Margaret said, glaring. "Where are we headed?"

Bonner waved them forward with his pistol. "To Climbers Ridge." He pushed the nose of the pistol into Alice's back. "Up the back trail. You know the way."

Alice took Margaret's arm and guided her to another, smaller gate at the rear of the enclosure. Alice unlatched it and helped Margaret down into what seemed like a path of round, fist-sized stones that meandered upward into the surrounding Aspen groves.

"It's a dry creek bed," Alice explained. "Well, actually more of a natural runoff. When the snow melts higher up, this bed can fill with a torrent of rushing water in a matter of seconds."

"In the meantime," Margaret said, trying to balance on the bed of rocks, "don't tell me, it's the back trail to Climbers Ridge."

Alice smiled at her. "It's pretty convenient," she said with a shrug. "If you've got the right shoes on."

"Great!" Margaret sighed.

"Enough talk." Bonner jumped down onto the rocks behind them. "Get moving. I don't have all day."

With Alice's help, Margaret headed upward. She fought to keep her balance, stepping carefully among the fist-sized rocks on her tiptoes. As they progressed, the slope of the climb became steeper and steeper. Margaret's ankles and calves quickly fatigued from her tip-toe gait.

Alice helped Margaret step over a sizeable dead pine that had fallen across the narrowing gully. Blindly, Margaret stepped down onto an unstable conglomerate of large gravel and her ankle turned.

"Oh!" she cried out, falling forward. She managed to twist her body in the fall and landed on her side in the loose gravel.

"Margaret!" Alice went to her knees beside her. "Are you all right?"

Margaret pushed up on her hands. "Goddamn it!" She rolled over to a sitting position and smoothed her dress down to cover her thighs. "I've broken a heel off!" she said, pulling her empty shoe up out of the sand and gravel.

"Let's have a look." Alice took the shoe from her. "You didn't hurt yourself badly, I hope!"

"Get up!" Bonner commanded. "You're not hurt."

Margaret ignored him. "I'm fine, Alice," she said. "I just twisted my ankle a little is all. Nothing serious." She struggled to her feet. "Can we fix the shoe?"

Alice shook her head. "The heel's completely off and the tip is broken." She held it up for Margaret to see.

"Great," Margaret said. "Now what?"

"Go barefoot for all I care," Bonner said with growing agitation. "Now get moving!"

"She can't walk barefoot up this stream bed," Alice said. She motioned for Margaret's other shoe. "Let me have it."

Margaret slipped the good shoe off and handed it to Alice. "What are you going to do?" she asked.

Alice knelt by the fallen tree and set the shoe on end against the tree's trunk. Picking up a stone, she brought it down hard against the three-inch heel.

"Hey!" Margaret almost screamed. "My Guccies!"

Alice let fly with the stone once more, successfully breaking the other heel off. She handed the flat shoe to Margaret. "Now they match," Alice said with a weak smile.

Margaret frowned at the two ruined shoes. "Oh well," she said and slipped the shoes back on her feet. "At least it'll make climbing around on these rocks a little easier."

"Move!" Bonner yelled.

The two women started once more up the steep creek bed. Bonner followed them closely, mumbling angrily. With her heels missing, Margaret found her progress through the stones and crevices much easier. Now that

Alice was no longer having to assist her with every step, their pace almost doubled, despite the ever steepening terrain.

"How much farther?" Margaret asked, panting.

"Not much," Alice said, casting a glance back at Bonner.

They climbed up the creek bed another few hundred feet. Margaret did her best to keep up with Alice. She almost slid in a patch of loose gravel and grabbed for Alice's arm for support.

"Slow down, Alice," she said, regaining her balance. "Let's not be in too big a hurry."

"What's going to happen to us?" Alice asked in a whisper.

"I'm sure nothing good," Margaret responded.

"He's going to kill us up at the ridge, isn't he?" Alice fought back tears.

"Now, we don't know that." Margaret pulled Alice along to maintain a comfortable distance from Bonner. "If they kill us, it'll put more heat on their operation than they could stand."

"Do they know that?" Alice stopped. She climbed up the edge of the creek bed where years of foot traffic had worn a path up to a glade of blue spruce.

"Well." Margaret took Alice's hand for a little help climbing out of the creek bed. "If they don't have enough sense to figure that out, you can rest assured, I'll remind them at the appropriate time."

Alice did not appear overly relieved. "I hope you're right." She pointed up the path. "Climbers Ridge is just through there."

Margaret stole a glance back at Bonner. He was standing none too patiently behind her, adjusting the weight of the rifle strap over his shoulder and speaking into the small radio. "Come on, Alice," Margaret said, starting for the line of spruce.

The air had grown considerably cooler and she hugged her arms about herself to stifle the chill. She felt the hard metal nestled in the breast pocket of her jacket. Margaret smiled reassuringly at Alice.

"Don't worry, Alice," she said, trying to reassure. "We'll be all right."

"I hope you're right," Alice responded, less confidently.

They threaded their way through the stand of young fir with Bonner close behind. The trees stopped at a steep hill that climbed up about twenty feet. A smooth path was worn up the side with only an occasional rock jutting outward for a step.

Alice started up the path first with Margaret at her heels. The incline was steep enough that Margaret found it necessary to use both feet and hands to make the climb. As they approached the hilltop, Margaret could see the summit of Climbers Ridge rising up against the horizon. They scrambled up onto the flat grassy mesa that stretched several hundred yards before them to the foot of the climbing cliffs.

"All right ladies," said the gruff male voice.

Margaret caught her breath and turned to find Bonner right there with them. She was surprised at how fast the short, stocky man could move when he wanted.

"Have a seat over there," Bonner ordered, pointing to a patch of gravel and grass off to the side of the path. "And get comfortable."

Margaret and Alice obeyed. They knelt in the gravel together. Margaret tried to rest her weight on her hip with her legs out to the side.

"Damn it!" Margaret cursed softly. She adjusted her skirt. "That finishes my last pair of panty hose."

Alice gasped suddenly and grabbed Margaret's arm. Margaret followed her eyes to Bonner who was lying on his stomach at the top of the path. He had unzipped the rifle case and was pulling the gleaming weapon free.

"What the hell are you planning, Bonner?" Margaret's hand went instinctively to the metal object in her jacket.

Bonner mounted a scope on the rifle. "You just stay quiet and stay still, and you won't get hurt," he said, loading several missiles into the weapon.

He snapped a small, two-pronged stand onto the tip of the rifle. Flattening out on the ground, he stretched the rifle out before him. He sighted through the scope and made several adjustments to the focus.

Margaret watched him taking aim. For a moment, she felt frozen in time—relieved that the rifle wasn't pointed at her, and at the same time, afraid for the moment to take any action. Instinctively she followed his line of sight out across the expansive plateau and up to the rocky cliff called Climbers Ridge. A hint of movement just below its summit caught her eye. She stared hard against the bright sunlight, unsure of her own senses.

"What are you planning on shooting?" Margaret asked, not taking her eyes off the cliff. Her eye caught another sliver of motion on the cliff side. "Who's up there?" she said, louder.

Bonner continued to ignore her. He pulled the bolt on the rifle, pulling one of the powerful bullets into the firing chamber.

Margaret felt the panic rise in her chest. Against all reason, her thoughts fixated on Parker and Eric. Her insides imploded.

"No!" She screamed into the breeze.

The rifle exploded once, then again. Bonner jerked at the bolt, sighted, and fired three more times.

Margaret watched in horror as the two indistinct figures plummeted down the side of the cliff. The rifle report continued to echo for several seconds as she stood paralyzed, forcing herself to grab hold of reality once more. She found herself facing the cliffs with Alice sitting at her feet. The trembling girl's arms were locked about Margaret's waist.

As if she had rehearsed it a thousand times, Margaret's hand slid into her jacket to the hard, metal object nestled there. She gripped the butt of the small pistol and wrenched it out to arms length, pointing directly at Bonner.

Bonner was too busy securing his weapon with his type's usual macho, self-absorbed vanity to take notice of the blonde's hysterical gesturing. He heard the several loud cracks and for a moment wondered how his rifle's report could still be sounding.

Margaret fired at random, trying to hold the pistol steady with both hands. All she could do was hope one of her bullets would find their mark as long as she kept pointing in Bonner's general vicinity.

In an automatic reaction, Bonner rolled away from her, leaving the rifle on the ground. He felt a sudden burning in his right leg and chest. "Goddamn it!" he cursed, and rolled over the side of the hill.

Margaret heard the dull clicks and knew she had emptied the small pistol. She watched Bonner roll over the edge of the hill. He tumbled down the steep, rocky hillside, grunting or crying out in pain as he bounced from one sharp rock to another. He rolled into the stand of spruce, crashing against one of the small tree trunks in a shower of pine needles.

Margaret inched over to the side of the hill, still pointing the empty pistol. Alice recovered quickly enough, grabbed up the rifle from the ground, and joined Margaret. They watched Bonner pull himself to his knees. He looked up the hillside to where the two women stood pointing their weapons down at him. Wincing in pain, he dragged himself into the trees.

Margaret and Alice stood frozen for a moment.

"You son-of-a-bitch!" Margaret screamed down at the trees.

Alice left her side to study the ground where Bonner had been shooting from. "I think you might have hit him," she said.

"What?" Margaret blinked down at the trees.

"I think you got him. Look." Alice pointed down at the sand and gravel.

Margaret pulled herself away from the hillside and studied the area of ground Alice was pointing at. There were several patches of dark, wet stain.

"We have to help Eric and Parker," Margaret said suddenly. She started to run across the expanse toward Climbers Ridge.

"What do you mean we have to help Eric and Parker?" Alice called after her. She started off in pursuit.

"I just know that's who Bonner was shooting at," Margaret answered as Alice caught up to her. "I just know it!"

"Oh, my God!" Alice almost stumbled.

They continued sprinting across the grassy flatland.

"What about Bonner?" Alice asked with a backward

glance.

"I hope he bleeds to death." Margaret stopped short of the boulder field to catch her breath. She studied the rock face looming in front of her. "I saw them fall from somewhere up there," she said, pointing. She climbed into the mass of huge stones.

"Watch out for copperheads," Alice warned, following her.

"Copper . . . goddamn it!" Margaret forced herself to continue toward the base of the cliff. "God, don't let them be dead," she muttered over and over. She kept her eyes glued to the spaces between the rocks at her feet and struggled closer to the rock face.

Alice was better dressed for the task and climbed through the boulder field with relative ease. She reached the foot of the cliff ahead of Margaret and searched about the base frantically. "I don't see anything, Margaret," she called out. "Are you sure it was in this area?"

"I'm positive," Margaret yelled back. Despite her answer, she looked up to the summit, searching for some reassuring landmark. "Look! There!" She shouted and pointed up to the rock face. "There . . . at the top. You can still see some rope dangling."

Alice shielded her eyes from the sun and tried to spot what Margaret was pointing at. "I can't see it." She shook her head. Her vision was obscured by the sun's brightness as well as by several small trees jutting out from the side of the rock face about three-quarters of the way down.

"They should have fallen right near where you're standing." Margaret scrambled over the boulders as best she could. "We've got to find them!"

Alice climbed over the rocks searching.

"Parker!" Margaret yelled at the top of her lungs.

"Eric!" She held little hope of being answered. "Can anybody hear me?"

A sprinkle of dust and gravel rained down from the rock face above her.

"Margaret?" A voice called out weakly.

"Eric?" Margaret looked about her desperately for the source of the sound. "Do you see him, Alice?"

"Not over here." Alice threw up her hands, but kept scrambling around among the boulders.

"Margaret? Is that you?" The voice called down from above them.

"Eric!" Margaret shouted. "Goddamn it, where are you?" She strained against the bright sunlight.

"Up here!" Eric tried to wipe the blood from his eyes. He was glad he had tied the end of the rope about him under his arms. "I can't see you for a ledge below." He became aware of the heavy weight draped over his back, pushing his head down against his chest.

"Eric, are you all right?" Margaret backed away from the rock face for a better sight line. "Is Parker with you?"

Eric gasped. "Parker!" He suddenly recognized the source of the weight above him. "Parker!" He reached up to shake the still figure draped over his back. "Parker!" His relief was audible as he felt the weight stirring. "Parker, are you all right?"

A low moan answered him.

"Parker!" Eric took a moment to survey his own injures.

"Eric, answer me!" Margaret almost screamed.

"I'm okay," Eric called out.

"Thank God!"

"Just some cuts, bruises, and some bad rope burns." Eric looked at his raw, bleeding hands.

"What about Parker?" Margaret was still unable to see him. "Is he with you?"

"Yes!" Eric found one of Parker's arms and checked it for a pulse. "He's alive, but I think he's unconscious."

"Eric," said a trembling voice from overhead.

"Parker!" Eric grinned through the blood and dirt. "Are you okay?"

"Am I hearing things or is that Margaret's voice?" Parker managed. He was afraid to move.

"Yeah," Eric replied.

"Then I'm not okay," Parker said with a moan. "I'm obviously dead and in hell."

Eric managed a laugh. "She's here to rescue us," he said.

"Just don't say anything and maybe she'll go away," Parker said.

"I heard that!" Margaret had backed up enough to finally see beyond the ledge into the cluster of dwarf pines.

She saw the two men dangling at the end of a rope, the other end of which was tangled in the gnarly branches of one of the trees jutting out from the rock face. "I see them," she shouted to Alice.

Alice rushed to her side and the two embraced, laughing through tears.

"How badly are you hurt?" Eric asked. He gave Parker's hand a squeeze and felt Parker shift his weight slightly.

"I feel like I've sprained every tendon in my body," Parker said. "But I think I'm in one piece. My head feels like it's been hit with a hammer, and I've got one hell of a rope burn on my stomach—thanks to your making me thread the damn rope through my belt."

Eric chuckled. "That damn rope through your belt saved your miserable life," he said.

"Yeah, yeah, whatever." Parker looked up to where the rope was caught in the tree branches. "Are we going to hang around here forever or just until the rope comes loose."

"Where is it caught?"

Parker studied the tree more closely. "It's wrapped up in this little pine that's sticking out of the rocks about ten feet above us," he said.

"That was a lucky break," Eric said.

"See for yourself."

"I can't. Your butt's on my neck," Eric said, trying to turn his head.

"What are you two doing?" Margaret called up with impatient concern. "Are you going to stay in that cozy position all day or are you coming down anytime soon?"

"Margaret!" Parker yelled.

"Yes, Parker," she called back.

"Shut up!"

"I love you too, sweetie," she answered.

Parker chanted a litany of obscenities under his breath. "Do you think it's safe to move much?" he asked Eric.

"Only what's necessary," Eric replied. "Let's not take any chances."

"What do you suggest?"

"Can you get your belt unbuckled?" Eric asked.

"Yeah, I think so." Parker fumbled with his buckle. "Then what?"

Eric looked down. "The ledge isn't but about seven or eight feet down. If you can crawl down my back and legs, you'll almost be standing on the ledge."

"Does it look solid?"

"Well." Eric studied the narrow outcropping. "It's probably been there for several million years."

"That's how I get down, but what about you?" Parker got his belt loose and began to roll over to face the back of Eric's head.

"Once your fat butt is off my back, I'll be just fine," Eric said, grunting as Parker's weight shifted about.

Parker wrapped his arms about Eric's neck and leaned into his ear. "You sure like to talk about my butt, don't you?" he said.

Eric tried not to laugh. "You give new definition to the words *horny bastard*," he said and jerked his ear away from Parker's nibbling.

Parker slid down the length of Eric's body. Hanging from Eric's ankles, his own feet dangled about two feet above the narrow ledge below. It was another good ten to twelve feet down to the boulder field where Margaret and Alice stood watching.

"Well, let's see if I can land without losing my balance and falling off the ledge," Parker said.

"Anytime, now," Eric said with a sarcastic edge. "But there's no rush. I can't feel the rope cutting into my bruised armpits anymore."

"Bitch, bitch, bitch!" Parker released his hold and dropped lightly to the sandy ledge below. His left leg almost collapsed under him and he pushed his weight back against the cliff before the momentum of his fall took him over the edge. "Speaking of bruises," he said looking up at Eric. "I've got a few doozies of my own." He massaged his left hip and thigh gingerly.

Eric struggled to get free of the rope tied about his chest. Like Houdini out of a straight jacket, he slid out of the loop of rope. Closing his injured hands into as much of a fist as he could, he hooked his wrists into the loop to maintain some semblance of a hold. "Guide me down to the ledge," he said to Parker. He straightened his arms and extended as far down as possible until he could feel Parker's hands on his feet. "Ready or not, here I come." He allowed the rope to slide free of his wrists.

Parker kept his arms up and allowed Eric's body to drop through. When Eric's feet hit the ledge he threw his arms about the younger man and pulled him back against the rock wall of the cliff. The two men pressed in against the cliff, holding each other tightly and breathing heavily with relief after the exertion.

Margaret and Alice also let out a sigh of relief.

"What did I tell you, Alice," Margaret said. Realizing she was still holding the empty pistol, she returned it to her jacket pocket. "They can't keep their hands off each other."

"Very depressing, I have to admit." Alice released the built-up tension with her laughter. "But kind of cute in a way."

"Come on, you two," Margaret yelled up at the two men. "We need to get out of here. Bonner may be back with some help if we're not careful."

"Bonner!" Parker's voice bit the breeze as he broke the embrace with Eric. "He's responsible for this?"

"Completely," Margaret said. "He kidnapped Alice and me, dragged us up here!" She pointed to her shoes. "By foot mind you, ruining my new Guccies—"

"Margaret," Parker interrupted. "Tell us your little story later." He turned to Eric. "Give the old man a hand down, kid."

"Sure, pops," Eric said with a smile. He took Parker's

hands and lowered him over the edge of the ledge.

Parker released his grip and dropped the remaining six feet or so to a gravely patch between two large boulders at the bottom of the rock face. Eric then swung himself over the ledge, supporting his body on his elbows. He dropped the remaining distance to join Parker.

Margaret and Alice scrambled over to them. Margaret hugged both men and kissed them effusively. Alice stood to the side, smiling and wringing her hands.

"All right, Margaret." Parker laughed. "You can stop now. We're glad to see you, too."

"Hi, Alice," Eric said, acknowledging his fellow ranger. "Nice to see you out of the office for a change."

"Nice to be out in the wild again." Alice beamed.

"You say Bonner's gone for help?" Parker asked, suddenly all business.

"Well, we're really not sure," Margaret replied.

"She shot him," Alice said matter-of-fact.

"Shot who?" Parker's eyebrows went up.

"Bonner," Margaret said with a snarl. "I shot the bastard."

Parker looked to Alice who nodded her agreement. "What did you shoot him with?" Parker asked.

"With the gun Eric gave me, of course." Margaret straightened her shoulders.

"With the . . ." Parker looked at Eric.

"I bought some bullets for it," Margaret said. "Thank you very much."

"If he's gone for help," Parker said, sighing. "How do you know you hit him?"

"There was blood," Alice quickly offered.

"And," Margaret added, "he wasn't in the best of

shape after rolling off the hill back there and smashing into the trees at the bottom." She pulled out the small pistol again, brandishing it with much bravado. "If you had bothered to give me something a little bigger and more powerful, I would have punched the little weasel's time clock permanently."

Parker quickly relieved her of the pistol. "Thank you, Calamity Jane." He turned to Eric. "Where's the nearest phone?"

"At the information booth down at Bear Lake," Eric said, studying the horizon for any sign that they weren't alone.

"Bear Lake," Parker said. "I'm not swinging on vines or tight rope walking over any more streams. Is there another way down there?"

"We came up the stream bed," Alice said to Eric. "From the service compound."

"That takes a little more time," Eric said. "But it is a pretty easy hike."

"Bullshit," Margaret muttered.

"All right," Parker said. "Let's move out. We've got some offensive strategy to plan."

They followed Parker out through the boulder field.

"You know what else?" Margaret said, dangerously close to a whine.

"What, Margaret, dear?" Parker asked without turning around.

"It's also way past lunch time."

Parker stopped dead in his tracks. He jerked his head about to face her. "Are you saying you want to stop off for lunch?" he asked, incredulous.

"My blood sugar's low." She looked like a hurt spaniel.

"There are soft drink and snack machines at the information booth," Alice said. "I'd kill for a diet soda."

"I could hold out for a little while on a bag of chips," Eric said hopefully.

Parker turned from them and continued through the boulders, shaking his head.

"What's wrong with him?" Margaret asked.

"Probably smells a Twinkie in the distance," Eric said.

Parker threw his hands up at the titter of laughter behind him. "Amateurs!" he mumbled, heading out into the open meadow.

CHAPTER 16

Parker signaled for everyone to stay down and stay quiet. He gave Margaret a particularly hard look since she had complained non-stop all the way down to the service compound. They crouched in the creek bed, peering out over the embankment and through the chain-link fence into the compound of metal buildings.

Parker checked the small pistol he had taken from Margaret. "It would be nice to have a bullet or two left," he said in a low voice. Margaret started to speak, but Parker shushed her. He turned to Eric. "What do you think?" he asked.

"Looks pretty quiet," Eric said.

"Look," Alice whispered to Margaret. "The truck's still there."

Margaret nodded. "Right where we left it," she whispered.

"Interesting." Parker handed the small pistol back to Margaret. "Here, maybe you can throw it at someone."

"Don't tempt me," she said, putting the pistol inside her jacket.

"So." Parker turned back to reconnoiter the compound once more. "There's a good chance my man, Arlee, is inside one of the buildings."

"Unless he was picked up by someone else," Eric cautioned.

"That's true," Parker said. "In which case they probably left a welcoming committee behind."

Margaret and Alice exchanged worried glances.

"I don't see any phone lines, though." Parker looked about. "No utility poles."

Alice spoke up quickly. "He had a radio," she said.

"What?" Parker started.

"He had a shortwave radio," she explained. "He was talking to someone on it when he was bringing us up here."

"Well." Parker shook his head. "Thanks for telling us."

Margaret gave his arm a punch. "Don't talk mean to her!" She got right in his face. "We had a hell of a lot more to worry about, what with being almost murdered and everything."

Parker grabbed her up in a bear hug and bussed her cheek. "Yes, my little blonde rose." He turned to Alice. "No offense, Alice."

"None taken." Alice shrugged and smiled.

"But just for the record," Parker continued. "Is there any other important little fact either of you would like to tell us about?"

"Yeah, your zipper's open." Margaret gave him a poisonous look.

Parker's eyes shot down to his trousers, which were securely fastened. He looked back quickly to her, then smiled. "Bitch," he said flatly.

They all laughed softly.

"All right ladies," Parker said, releasing Margaret. "Let's get this show on the road." He reached down, lifted his pants leg up, and pulled a small semi-automatic pistol from a holster strapped to his calf.

"Now I know what made that funny bruise on my side," Eric quipped.

"Why didn't you tell us you had a gun?" Margaret punched Parker on the arm again.

"You didn't ask." He rubbed his arm. "And if you hit me again, I'm going to start hitting back."

He scrambled up the embankment, narrowly escaping a well-aimed kick from Margaret. Keeping his eyes glued to the buildings beyond, he carefully released the latch and eased the gate open. "You all stay put until I've checked things out," he said to the others. "Any sign of trouble, get down to Bear Lake and call for help."

"You heard him," Eric said to the women.

"That goes for you, too, missy," Parker reiterated to Eric.

"Bite me," Eric said. "I'm checking out the fence perimeter for any surprises. I can stalk through the underbrush as well and as quietly as a cougar."

"You don't have a gun," Margaret cautioned.

Eric held up a deadly looking Bowie knife. "I'll be just fine," he said, eyeing his weapon.

"Where the hell did that thing come from?" Parker asked.

Eric only smiled and disappeared into the surrounding vegetation.

Parker bent down to the two women. "Stay low," he said. "And get the hell out of here if for any reason you think something's not kosher."

Margaret reached up from the creek bed and grabbed Parker's head. She planted a solid kiss on his lips. "That's for good luck, G-Man."

Parker broke free and wiped a hand across his mouth. "Margaret," he said, trying not to grin. "You know your lip color doesn't go with my complexion."

"Maybe you should check out a mirror," Alice said from behind Margaret. "I think it brings out the blue of your eyes."

"Don't encourage her, Alice," Parker said and made his escape through the gate.

Parker crouched low and darted in a zigzag across the open, gravel compound to the first building. Taking cover between two utility trailers, he peered over them for any sign of movement or noise about the compound.

He looked back to the gate and was satisfied to see both women barely visible, watching him from the creek bed. He considered his next move. The space to and around all of the buildings was completely exposed. He looked about for any potential shield, wishing he had his protective vest. His only hope was that Eric was in a position to watch his back from the perimeter. He studied the surrounding forest for any sign of the redhead, but all was quiet.

He glanced back at the women's position one more time and then darted across the open space to the first building. The door had a heavy padlock on it. Parker tried the door anyway, just to be sure, and it was secure. He had been constantly checking about him for any sign of trouble. Still, everything remained remarkably or, he thought, unnervingly quiet. He made himself relax a little. If anyone was going to attack from the perimeter, they would have done so while he stood out in the open.

He straightened and walked confidently to the next building, but not before once more checking the position of the women. Margaret gave him a small wave, but he gestured for them to stay put for the moment.

By the time he got to the door of the next building, he was out of the women's line of sight. The metal door was not padlocked and slid upward easily. A shovel had apparently slipped from the side wall to rest up against the door and its heavy handle fell through when Parker raised the door. It struck him squarely on the side of the head.

"Goddamn it!" he yelled angrily without thinking. The shovel fell to the ground with a heavy thud. Parker rubbed his sore temple and stepped into the dark interior of the metal shed.

He saw the body immediately, lying on the plywood floor at the foot of several large crates in the back of the ten-by-twenty structure. Parker jumped over the shovel and knelt down beside the body. The invading sunlight from the doorway was suddenly blocked by shadow.

"Parker," the high pitched voice stuttered.

Parker instantly swung his pistol to the doorway and found himself aiming at Margaret's face. "Margaret!" He cried out. "What the hell?" He got up from his knees.

She stood at the door holding up a large rock. Next to her, Alice was holding a tree branch like a baseball bat.

"I told you two to stay in the creek bed," Parker said.

"But," Margaret stammered, looking down at Parker's pistol, "we heard you yell. I thought—"

"Margaret!" Parker lowered the pistol and relaxed his muscles. "I didn't ask you to think. I told you to stay put or get away at any sign of trouble. Coming to my rescue was not an option."

"Oh, shut up!" Margaret lowered her rock. "We have no intention of running away from trouble."

"Are you all right?" Alice stepped into the shed. "What's that you're . . ." She stopped, seeing the body at Parker's feet.

Margaret saw the body as well. "Who is it?" she said, taking a step backwards.

"Bonner." Parker knelt beside the body once more.

"No shit!" Margaret said.

Alice also backed away slightly. "Is he dead?" she asked.

"As a door nail," Parker said, checking the body. "Looks like he's been shot in the leg and the right side several times."

Margaret gasped. "I killed him?"

"Not you." Parker shook his head. "Someone else popped him between the eyes." He pointed to the gaping, bloody hole in the body's forehead. The facial features were horribly swollen and nearly unrecognizable. "Looks like someone was cleaning up loose ends."

Parker jumped up suddenly, holding his arms out to both women. "Get in here quickly!" He leapt for the entrance, pulling both women in behind him and grabbed for the overhead door. Before he could pull it down he heard an ominous click.

"Stop right there, Agent White."

Parker turned his head slowly to find the twin barrels of a Mossberg shotgun aimed at his head. "Hello, Superintendent Bledsoe," he said evenly. "Fancy meeting you here."

Margaret and Alice stared in disbelief.

"Superintendent!" Alice stammered.

Her boss' large frame filled one side of the doorway.

Three other men in Park Service uniforms encircled the door, holding small Uzi machine guns at the ready.

"Take his gun," Bledsoe commanded. The set of his jaw made Parker think he was just itching to pull the trigger.

One of the men grabbed the pistol from Parker's hand.

"I see you've found Bonner," the Superintendent continued. "He's an idiot . . . and a careless one."

"Well, Dan," Margaret spoke up from the rear of the shed. "Some stupid career move you're making."

"Shut up, Curry." Bledsoe almost growled at her. "The only stupid career move here is your meddling." He turned the shotgun on her. "Now you're just one more . . ." He looked at Parker. "How did you put it? One more loose end to clean up."

Margaret's heart jumped into her throat. "You pull that trigger, Dan, and you'll destroy all hope you ever had," she said.

"She's right, Bledsoe," Parker interjected. "A battalion of federal agents will descend on this place. Every man, woman and child in the district will be investigated more thoroughly than an IRS audit. You've left a money trail somewhere, and they'll find it."

"That's the best you can do? I expected more," Bledsoe said. The gun barrel dropped slightly. "There's nothing tying me in any way, shape or form to this business that any of you thick-headed, paper cops could uncover. When the three of you are out of the way, I'll be home free." His face clouded suddenly. "Where's Borenson?" He yelled at the other men. "We're missing one, you idiots!"

Parker fought the urge to scream for joy. They didn't

have Eric. "Eric's dead, you son-of-a-bitch!" he lied, letting his heightened emotions work for him.

Bledsoe brought the shotgun up under Parker's chin. "What do you mean he's dead . . . how?" he asked.

Parker turned away and gave Margaret and Alice a look. "Back at Climbers Ridge," he said. "He didn't survive the fall when your bastard hit man there shot out our rope." He looked back to the body and kicked dirt at it. "If you hadn't killed this son-of-a-bitch, I would have."

"One less for me to worry about." Bledsoe shrugged and pursed his lips. "Well, we'll just have to restage your accidental death and include two more." He turned to his men. "Take them back up to the Ridge and make sure that fag, Borenson, is dead . . . then finish them off." He looked down. "Then get rid of this body." He gestured at the corpse on the floor of the shed. "I don't want the smell attracting any attention this close to all the tourist traffic."

Parker exchanged a glance with the two women. Margaret started to smile her understanding, but Parker shook his head slightly. His expression made it clear that she should look sad and hopeless and nothing more.

Bledsoe started to leave, but thought better of it. "All of you stay at the Ridge," he ordered his men. "That last big drop should be coming in a couple of hours. Spot where the drop is and I'll be along in the chopper with Stan to pick it up just before sunset."

"You're not going to get away with this, Bledsoe," Parker said, putting his arms about the women.

"I already have, faggot." Bledsoe sneered. He headed for Bonner's truck.

"All right, you heard him," one of the men said. He was shorter than Parker, but clearly a muscle builder, judging by the biceps swelling out of the short-sleeved work shirt. "Give them a trash bag Stubs," he said to the tall, thin, goateed black man. "Let's put out the trash first."

The black man nicknamed Stubs pulled two large green trash bags from a cardboard box dispenser sitting on a nearby shelf. He handed it to Parker with a toothy grin.

"What am I supposed to do with this?" Parker asked, already knowing the answer.

The muscle builder gestured with his Uzi. "Bag the body," he ordered. "Might as well make yourselves useful while you still can." He tried to match Bledsoe's parting sneer. "And the other one, too."

"Other one?" Parker looked in the direction of the man's nod. A large green trash bag lay against the back wall stuffed with what was the unmistakable shape of a large man's body. Parker shrugged, unwilling to argue about anything that could stall for more time. He stole a glance past the men and through the doorway hoping for some sign of Eric. "Where do you want them?" he asked without emotion.

"The dumpster out front," Bledsoe said with a chuckle. "What else do you do with garbage? They'll get a proper burial in the landfill."

Parker ignored him and went to work. He grabbed the bagged body by the feet and grunting, dragged it across the dirt floor. It was heavy, but Parker managed to jerk it along over the rocky ground out to the dumpster under the watchful aim of Bledsoe's men.

He left his load at the bottom of the large metal container and returned to the shed. "Anyone have a problem handling a dead body?" he asked of the two women.

"Handling . . ." Margaret stopped short. "You want us to help?"

"Well," Parker said. "Bonner's close to two hundred fifty pounds of dead weight. That's not easy for one person to handle."

"I'll help," Alice offered. She took one of the trash bags. "Just tell me what to do." She followed Parker's lead and started peeling the plastic trash bag open.

"You all bag him and then I'll help move him," Margaret said with a pleading look. "If that's okay?"

Parker gave her hand a reassuring squeeze before kneeling once again beside the body. He tried to lift one of the legs, but the whole body seemed to move with it. "Rigor mortis," he said with professional detachment. "Well, at least it's easier to carry a stiff body than a limp one."

Margaret stood over the body wringing her hands. "I don't even want to know about your last date," she said in a weak attempt at levity.

Parker busied himself slipping the first bag over the body. "My last date ?" He tried the bag over the corpse's head. "That would have been you, wouldn't it?"

Margaret rubbed the end of her nose with a one-fingered salute.

Alice struggled to get her bag over the body's head. "This is not in my job description," she said, struggling to get the bag down over the body's shoulders.

Parker rolled the body from side to side as they worked the bag down over it. He tied the bag at the feet. "You girls take the feet," Parker said.

Margaret helped Alice grab the plastic bag at the feet and lifted with all their strength. Parker balanced his end

of the bag and backed toward the door. The men parted
for the body to get through, but kept their Uzis pointed at
its bearers. As the captives carried the body across the
compound to the large dumpster at the main gate, Parker
again took the opportunity to look for any sign of Eric
hiding in the surrounding bush. There was none.

"Let's set it down here for a moment," Parker said to
the women.

The two women complied gratefully. Margaret's eyes
quickly scanned the fence around the compound. Parker
knew what she was looking for.

"Do you see—" Margaret began to whisper.

"Keep your mind on what we're doing," Parker
interrupted firmly. He looked at the men with the Uzis.

Margaret bit her lip. She hadn't realized the men had
circled in about them so close. "Is there room in the
dumpster?" she asked quickly.

Parker hoisted the heavy metal lid of the dumpster
open. "We'll manage," he said. He gave the women a
quick but meaningful smile.

The three grabbed up the bag with Bonner once more
and pushed it up over the rim of the dumpster. The body
dropped into the half empty container with an echoing
thud. Working together they made short order of
Bonner's corpse.

"Now what?" Parker said to the muscle builder who
had followed them out to the dumpster.

"Now we'll take a little hike," the man said. The lack
of overt fear in his hostages seemed to be irritating him.
"All right," the muscle builder snapped. "Let's get going.
You people know the way." He waved them toward the
rear gate.

Margaret took Alice's arm. "Not again," she moaned.

"You'll make it," Alice assured her.

Parker pushed between them and wrapped his arms over their shoulders. He pulled them along quickly ahead of the armed men. "Stay in front of me," he said softly. "If you hear me yell *run*, you damn well had better run."

"No talking!" the muscle builder ordered. "Now break it up."

The two women moved quickly ahead of Parker. The rear gate was still standing open and they climbed back down into the dry stream bed. Parker followed them, purposely maintaining a good five feet or so distance from the women, which in turn kept the armed men following behind him an even greater distance from his two companions.

As they made their way up the gully, Alice stole a glance back to Parker. He gave her an urgent look and motioned her to move faster, keeping his gestures in front where the men trailing could not see.

Alice turned and looked straight ahead. "Can you go faster?" she whispered to Margaret.

Margaret was breathing heavily. "Faster?"

"Parker wants us to move faster," Alice answered. She gave Margaret a side-long glance.

"All right," Margaret said. "If he wants faster he's got faster."

The two women picked up speed. Even though the terrain steepened to an excruciating angle, they struggled to keep their pace through the litter of sharp rocks and fallen debris. Parker let the distance between them widen even more. The pace forced the men behind him to relax the grip on their weapons and concentrate more on negotiating the hazards of the creek bed.

Parker heard a whistle of air behind him followed by

a sharp crack. He turned his head quickly to see the black man, Stubs, fall forward on his face. The back of his head was gushing blood.

"Stop!" shouted the muscle builder. He crouched down in the stream bed and brought his Uzi up.

Parker again signaled to the two women to get down low. The man in the rear let go a volley of shots into the forest around them.

"Hold your fire," the muscle builder shouted. His eyes darted back and forth to both sides of the stream bed. "Check and see if Stubs is okay," he ordered the man at the rear.

The man knelt down beside the still, bleeding form. "I don't get no pulse," he said, frantically feeling about on the body's neck.

Parker crouched down. Except for the panicked breathing of the two remaining armed men, everything was quiet around them. He nodded to Margaret and Alice who, in the confusion of the moment had managed to move even farther ahead. They also sank to their knees at Parker's signal and kept inconspicuously low to the ground.

The muscle builder noticed Parker's low-to-the-ground posture. "We're sitting ducks here," he said to his partner. "Stay low and keep moving." He pointed his weapon dead center at Parker. "Get moving." He looked out above the stream bed. "Anything else happens and I'm going to kill you first thing," he said loudly for anyone who might be listening.

Parker turned and motioned for the two women to move on as well. He watched the forest along the sides of the creek bed out of the corners of his eyes and tried to minimize the distance between himself and the muscle builder.

Parker heard another whoosh of air and turned in time to see a fist-sized stone strike the muscle builder hard on the side of his neck. Its sharp edges cut deep into the flesh. The man's hands went to his neck, his attention momentarily diverted from the others. Parker dove for the gun, simultaneously kicking the man's feet out from under him. Margaret and Alice scrambled up out of the creek bed and made for the cover of the trees.

"Hey!" shouted the man guarding the rear. He brought his Uzi up. "Stop!" He fired a burst at the two women as they ran into the trees. Another whoosh of air seared the air and another sharp stone struck the man clean in the face. He went to his knees clutching at his bleeding face.

The needles of a low Spruce whipped open and in a blur of red, Eric jumped into the creek bed onto the back of the unfortunate man. He clubbed the man on the back of the head with a two-inch thick, stripped tree branch he was carrying and the man fell over unconscious. Eric grabbed up the man's weapon before turning to Parker's struggle with the muscle builder. Parker grabbed up one of the large stones from the creek bed and bashed the muscle builder over the head with it. The quiet returned.

"Hi baby," Eric said as he extracted a couple of ammunition clips from the jacket of the unconscious man at his feet. "Miss me?"

Parker pulled the other Uzi from the muscle builder's limp grasp. "You know it, lover boy," he said, giving Eric a wink. "I haven't been able to think of anything but you."

Eric stepped over the body. "You all right?" His concern was very evident to Parker.

"You're my hero," Parker said, stepping over the muscle builder to meet Eric. He put a hand about the redhead's narrow hips and pulled their bodies together. He looked deep into Eric's hazel eyes. "I'm so glad to see you." His lips parted and found Eric's. They kissed without urgency, a long and languid kiss.

"My turn." Margaret's voice cut through the men's embrace.

Parker interrupted the kiss. "Kiss Alice then," he said, and gave his lips back to Eric.

The two women watched them kissing for a moment.

"I say let's each go find a club, pop them on the head, and take them cave woman style," Margaret said, finally.

"That's a problem," Alice responded. "We both want the same one."

"That's right." Margaret shrugged. "Poor Parker. Nobody wants him."

It was Eric's turn to break the kiss. "I do," he said, blushing.

Parker stuck his tongue out at Margaret.

"You're pretty good with that rock tosser." Alice pointed to the stick in Eric's hand.

"Yeah," Parker said. "What is that thing?"

Eric held up the stick. "It's a stone-age weapon." He reached down and selected a good size stone from the stream bed. "I was pretty good with it as a kid."

He wedged a flat stone into a six-inch slit cut into the business end of the stick which made it resemble a stone-age axe. He extended the stick behind him and whipped it forward like a casting rod. The stone flew from the end of the stick and struck a nearby tree trunk with enough force to shave away the bark.

"As good as any slingshot," Eric said with a satisfied

smile. "And easier to construct."

The muscle builder began to stir and groan.

"Better we tie them up," Parker said. He knelt beside the muscle builder. "Pull the laces out of his boots," he said to Eric. Parker took the man's cap and put it on his own head. "Do you like my disguise?" he asked Margaret.

"Very effective," Margaret said with a sarcastic look. "Especially the blood."

"Here, I'll finish this, Eric," he said. "Get the other guy's cap and see if he's still alive. We might need to tie him up too."

"What then?" Margaret took a few steps back.

"Then we get our butts back up to Climbers Ridge as fast as we can."

Margaret moaned. "I was afraid you were going to say that."

CHAPTER 17

A rumbling in the distance seemed to vibrate the crystalline air as it blew in gusts above the tree line of the high range. Climbers Ridge jutted high above the mossy tundra and rock below. Behind it an ominous curtain of black spilled relentlessly over the distant mountain peaks, ever closer.

Margaret stood under a sheltering blue spruce at the edge of the tree line, looking up at the Ridge and the boiling thunderheads in the distance. "I am not a happy camper." She sighed heavily.

"We are definitely going to need to find shelter pretty soon," Alice said. She stood on the other side of the tree. "That storm's real close."

"Great." Margaret waved to Parker and Eric who were trotting across the open mesa toward them. "Now I not only have blisters on my feet, a ruined pair of shoes, and shredded panty hose, but I'm going to get soaked to the skin and die of exposure."

Alice chuckled. "Actually, I'd be a little more worried about the lightening," she said. "It can be pretty bad up this high, especially standing under these trees."

"We found a good spot in the boulders up there to hide in and watch for the drop," Parker said as he and Eric ran into the spruce stand.

"There's a storm coming," Margaret said, pointing to the darkness slowly closing in on them.

"And it's going to be a doozy," Eric said. "What would you say, an hour to an hour and a half away?" he asked Alice.

"No more than that," she said. "There's always the possibility it'll stall for a while before moving on this way, but I doubt it."

"Not the way our luck is going, anyway," Margaret said.

"We should have the drop pretty soon," Parker said. "There's just enough sunlight left for a small plane to buzz the area and then get out safely."

"I assume someone has a plan." Margaret looked at Parker questioningly.

"Grab the drugs, then the murdering crooks," Parker said. "Then return home for a hero's welcome. A perfect plan if I do say so myself."

Margaret rolled her eyes. "Such attention to detail," she said. "How ever did you think of it?"

"Come on, Margaret." Parker threw an arm around her shoulders. "Get with the program. We're going to improvise. Seize the moment. If no one shoots you, you'll have a good time."

"Gee thanks." Margaret resisted the urge to knee him in the groin.

"Listen." Eric shushed them.

They tried to listen through the distant, rumbling thunder.

"It's a plane," Parker said, cocking an ear to the south.

"I don't hear anything," Margaret said. Her eyes squinted in concentration. "All I hear is thunder."

"I hear it now," Alice said. She looked at Eric excitedly. "Coming from the south, right?"

Eric nodded.

"Places everyone," Parker shouted. He started for the boulder field. "The show is about to begin."

Eric followed close behind him, an Uzi draped loosely over his shoulder.

"And stay put this time," Parker called back to the women.

"Male chauvinist queer," Margaret yelled after him.

"I haven't heard that one before," Alice said, laughing.

The two women watched Eric as he trotted across the tundra, his movements strong and graceful.

"I could look at him for hours," Margaret said, exchanging a look with Alice.

"That's not what I would like to do with him for hours," Alice said a little sheepishly.

"Alice, you tramp," Margaret said in mock moral outrage.

The two women laughed and slapped hands in a high five salute.

Parker and Eric scrambled into the boulder field at the base of the cliff. They quickly found the hiding spot they had scoped out previously and crouched down between three refrigerator-size boulders, sitting shoulder to shoulder.

"Here we are again," Parker said, giving Eric's knee a squeeze.

"What is it about this place that keeps pulling you back?" Eric asked. He snuggled in beside Parker. "And keeps making you drag the rest of us along with you."

"That's easy." Parker listened for the sound of the plane. It was much closer now. "It's the scene of our first kiss."

"Such a romantic."

The hum of the plane changed pitch.

"It's starting to make a dive run," Parker said. "Damn, I was hoping you and I had time to have a little moment here."

"You pick the strangest places," Eric said. He peeked his head up out of the rocks to try and spot the plane.

"Hey, I take them where I can get them," Parker said, sticking his head up as well. "I cherish these moments away from Margaret the Meddler."

"That's not very fair," Eric said, scanning the horizon. "She got us together in the first place."

"And she's been trying to keep us apart ever since," Parker said. He pointed to the south. "There it is."

Eric squinted to see. "Looks like a twin engine job," he said.

"Small cargo plane," Parker said, nodding.

"Margaret and Alice have spotted it as well." Eric nodded toward the two women hiding in the trees several hundred yards away.

"I hope they stay put this time," Parker said.

"Do you think it was such a good idea to drag them up here?" Eric asked. He settled back down in the rocky niche beside Parker.

"There wasn't time to waste back-tracking to the station," Parker said. "I want the drug shipment and Bledsoe, both."

Another rumbling of the fast approaching thunderheads echoed off the rock face above them.

"Looks like you're going to get more than you bargained for," Eric said, sniffing the presence of ozone in the air. "Margaret's already pissed off about her shoes. If she gets her hair wet too, she'll blow a gasket for sure."

"Stop trying to cheer me up," Parker said. He grinned at Eric. "Gee, do you think she'll get all muddy too?"

"What goes round comes round," Eric said, shaking his head. He looked up. "In coming!"

They watched as the small cargo plane came low over the cliffs. It banked a turn to the east, and an indistinct object fell from its belly and plummeted toward the rocks below. A small parachute billowed up from the object. The plane banked once more and headed south.

"Looks like the storm made them change their direction," Eric said.

"Keep your eyes on the birdie," Parker said, standing. "The wind's coming up and no telling where that thing is going to land."

The increasing winds from the approaching storm carried the falling object over the cliffs above their heads and out onto the open grassland. It came to rest in a puff of dust midway between the cliffs and the tree line. Parker and Eric remained concealed in the rocks until the small plane was well on its way south.

"Well, let's see what the stork brought," Parker said. He climbed out over the boulders.

"That's a pretty good size package," Eric said, following.

They sprinted across the tundra to the object. Margaret and Alice had already left the protection of the trees and were headed toward them. Parker knelt beside the oblong bundle wrapped with burlap and rope. It was about the size of a small filing cabinet.

"Where's that knife of yours?" Parker asked as he untangled the parachute lines.

Eric pulled the large blade from a sheath attached to his boot. "Here let me," he said. He cut the lines with one pass of the razor sharp knife. "You want to have a look at the contents?"

"Yeah," Parker answered. "But I want to be able to put this thing back together before our good friend, the Superintendent, returns."

Margaret and Alice finally made it to the spot.

"Well," Margaret said, panting for air. "What's the verdict?"

Parker wrestled with the knots in the rope. "I'd say we're looking at about twenty-five to thirty kilos of real fairy dust here."

"Manna from heaven." Margaret whistled.

"How much is it worth?" Alice stared wide-eyed at the crudely wrapped bundle.

"Several million, at least," Parker said. He got the first knot open. "Old Bledsoe was planning to retire in high style."

"Maybe you can find him a nice friend in prison to keep him company on all those lonely nights," Eric offered.

They all laughed.

"Eureka." Parker loosed the last knot and pulled the burlap open. "Shit," he said, discovering an over-sized, stuffed duffle bag inside. "I hate over-wrapped presents." He fumbled for the zipper and opened the bag.

They stared down at the brick-size blocks, neatly wrapped in plastic and tape.

"Now that's a lot of smack," Margaret said. "About thirty years to life."

Parker zipped the duffle bag shut and pulled it free of the burlap wrapping. "Okay, we don't have much time," he said.

A loud crack of thunder gave them all a start.

Parker stood and pointed to the fir trees beyond. "Everyone to the trees and grab up as much pine straw as you can carry," he ordered. "I want to fill this package up again."

He hoisted the duffle bag up onto Eric's shoulder. "Very convenient having such a strong, young buck close at hand," he said.

"How come I have to carry it?"

"Heavy lifting is husband's work," Parker replied, patting the younger man on the rear.

Eric started for the trees with Parker helping to keep the heavy bundle balanced. The women ran on ahead to begin gleaning straw. Eric deposited the bag well into the stand of trees and joined his friends hauling arm loads of straw back to stuff into the burlap.

When it was full, Parker quickly retied the ropes. "That looks pretty good," he said, standing. "You girls take a minute to get your bearings. You may have to lead law enforcement to find this thing."

Both the women nodded.

Parker motioned for quiet. "Listen!"

They listened to the distant, metronomic hum of helicopter blades.

"You girls get back to the trees," Parker said. "Drag that bag as far into the brush as it will go. Then get down to Bear Lake as quick as you can. Alice, do you know the other way down through the woods?"

"Sure." She gave Margaret a worried expression. "It's a little more difficult going."

"Hell, don't worry about me!" Margaret threw her hands up. "What could one more hike do to this suit?"

"All right." Parker rolled his eyes. "Just get down there as quick as you can. Put in a call to the sheriff . . . what's his name?"

"Sheriff Jenner," Margaret said.

"Yeah." Parker nodded. "Have him get up here with every man he can spare. Now get!"

"What about the two of you?" Margaret asked, not moving.

"Eric and I have to welcome our guests." Parker adjusted the blood stained cap down over his eyes.

"Alone?" she asked.

"Margaret!" Parker glared at her. "Get your butt down this mountain before I kick it down!"

"I'd like to see you try," Margaret said, backing away.

"Come on, Margaret," Alice said, pulling her along. "The sooner we notify the cavalry, the sooner we'll save *their* butts."

Margaret followed her reluctantly.

Parker waited until the women had run into the trees. "I thought they'd never leave," he said to Eric. "Now grab your dick and look menacing." He unstrung the Uzi from his shoulder and brought it up to ready position.

"If you don't mind, I'd rather grab this," Eric said, readying his own Uzi.

"Whatever." Parker gave him a smile. "You stand about ten feet that side of the package and I'll be opposite you there." He pointed. "Keep your head down and look like you're standing guard."

"Yes, ma'am." Eric dodged Parker's foot and went to

his position.

The roar of the helicopter became suddenly deafening. It appeared as if from nowhere over the top of the cliffs and hovered a few hundred feet directly over Eric and Parker's position. The two men kept their heads down. Parker gripped the bill of his cap to prevent it from blowing away in the vortex of air and dust kicked up by the chopper blades.

After a moment's hesitation, the chopper began to descend, coming to rest at a safe distance. Even over the sound of the chopper's engines, Parker could hear Eric cursing vehemently about the damage being done to the surrounding ecosystem. For a second, Parker feared that Eric's ecological outrage might override his own sense of survival. The two men exchanged glances and Parker gave Eric a reassuring wink.

"Cover our back," Parker said loud enough for Eric to hear him. "I'm going in."

Eric nodded and kept his back to the chopper. He watched the surrounding tree line for any surprises.

Parker ducked his head and started for the chopper. He tried to look as non-threatening as possible. The chopper door swung open.

"Go bring the goddamn package, you idiot!" Superintendent Bledsoe's unmistakable, gravelly voice yelled from the cockpit. "We've got to beat that storm."

Parker raised his head and brought the Uzi up, fanning its barrel at the helicopter's occupants. "Hello, Superintendent," he said and flashed his teeth. "Special Agent Parker White, Federal Bureau of Investigation. You're under arrest . . . as if you didn't know that."

Bledsoe instinctively sat forward. He was caught short by the sight of the Uzi and sat back growling.

"Wise decision, Superintendent," Parker said. He turned to the pilot. "Shut it off." He aimed the Uzi at the pilot. "Now!"

A switch clicked and in a matter of seconds the rotors stopped spinning and there was a moment of frozen silence. A crashing burst of thunder shook the tundra beneath them.

"All right." Parker stepped back from the door. "Everyone out. Keep your hands where I can see them."

Bledsoe, the pilot and one other man climbed out of the chopper.

"Get your hands up!" Parker raised an eyebrow. "Hi, Stan," he said to the pilot. "You don't look too good. Altitude sickness?"

"Fuck you!" Stan spat at the ground.

"Careful, Stan." Eric swaggered up to the chopper. "The boyfriend is listening."

Parker grinned at Eric. "How long before we hear something from Margaret and Alice?" he asked.

"Give it another fifteen minutes," Eric answered.

"Right." Parker turned back to the three felons. "In the meantime, everyone has the right to remain silent." He sighed with boredom. "Anything you say can and will be used against you in a court of law."

"Let me," Eric interrupted. "I've always wanted to do this."

"Be my guest," Parker said, cocking his head to one side.

"You have the right to an attorney," Eric said with relish. "If you cannot afford an attorney, one will be appointed to represent you." He looked at Parker for approval.

"Do you understand these rights as they have been

given to you?" Parker added, giving Eric a nod. He looked at the three men, questioning.

"You're going to regret this, White," Bledsoe said through clenched teeth.

"Somehow I doubt that," Parker responded. "Everyone turn around, hands up against the chopper, feet spread!"

The three men complied, but not without much grumbling.

"I'm going to make a weapons search," Parker said to Eric. "If anyone moves, shoot first and ask questions later."

"My pleasure," Eric said. He leveled his Uzi at the three men.

Parker began to pat down each of the men, removing a pistol or two from each one. He tossed the offending items far from the chopper. A sprinkle of rain enveloped them as the black thunderheads rolled in above them. The light had dimmed to an almost twilight state and the dark clouds boiled with flashes of lightening and the increasing wind.

Parker stood up. "Looks like we're going to get soaked."

"We'd be safer in the chopper," Eric said, looking up at the clouds.

"It barely holds three people, much less five," Parker said.

"I just don't like the—" Eric stopped suddenly, feeling the tingle of static electricity raise the hair on his arms and the nape of his neck. "Shit!" He grabbed Parker's arm. "Everyone head for the rocks, now!" He jerked Parker with him. "Run!"

The urgency in his voice made Parker obey without a

question. Besides, he felt the electric charge himself.

The pilot and the other man began to react, but Bledsoe stopped them. He threw open the chopper door and climbed in. The pilot started to follow.

Parker and Eric had barely gotten fifteen feet away when they were knocked off their feet by a powerful percussion wave, followed a split second later by an ear-splitting explosion behind them. The powerful lightening strike suffused the surrounding air with ozone.

"Jesus-Fucking-H-Christ!" Parker managed to yell after hitting the ground hard. He rolled to his side and looked back at the chopper.

One man lay unmoving on the ground beside the small helicopter. Parker thought he could see steam rising off the body. Bledsoe and the pilot had made it into the safety of the chopper, but had been momentarily stunned by the force of the lightening strike.

Parker scrambled to his feet and was relieved to see Eric do the same next to him. "There's another one I owe you," he said and gave Eric a slap on the back.

"We're losing them!" Eric gestured to the chopper.

The two men in the chopper had recovered quickly and the rotors were already beginning to turn above the roar of the engine.

"Goddamn it!" Parker brought his Uzi up.

Parker felt a bullet whiz past his cheek before he heard the gun report. "Hit the dirt!" he yelled to Eric.

Both men dropped to the ground.

Eric wrestled with his Uzi. "How many guns do these bastards have?"

"My fault." Parker spat on the ground beside him. "I should have checked inside the chopper."

"We've got to stop them," Eric said. The chopper

had begun to lift off.

Parker nodded. He rolled onto his stomach. "If I miss at this range, I need glasses." He aimed the Uzi at the chopper's tail.

The small machine gun spat a lethal spray of bullets that struck the small maneuvering rotor on the helicopter's tail. The steel blades and most of the supporting structure shattered. The small chopper began a slow gyration, no longer able to maneuver in a forward direction. Parker took aim at the bubble of glass that enveloped the front of the cockpit as it spun in and out of gun-sight. He held his fire and waited for the chopper's occupants to figure out that their get-a-way was totally screwed. The helicopter sat back down on the tundra with a heavy jolt. Parker started to stand, but Bledsoe dove out of the chopper and fired a volley of shots with his own Uzi.

Parker dropped face down in the dust beside Eric.

"Maybe you'd like to reconsider your stand on gun control at this time," Eric said.

Parker ignored him and fired a few shots of his own in Bledsoe's direction.

Eric concentrated his fire on the cockpit of the helicopter where Stan, the pilot, had taken refuge behind the seats. The bubble of safety glass exploded into a thousand pieces as Eric's bullets found their mark.

Parker crouched down in the rocks and pulled the ammo clip from his Uzi. "Try not to waste any shots," he called out to Eric. "We just have to keep them pinned down until the cavalry arrives."

Eric nodded. "Right now," he said. "I think it's a toss-up as to who is keeping who pinned down."

"Let's try and establish a crossfire," Parker said.

"Move off to the right and I'll make my way over there." He pointed to a couple of man-size boulders about fifty feet to the left.

"Sounds good to me." Eric climbed over the rocks.

"Keep your head down!" Parker fired off a few rounds to cover him.

When Eric was in position, Parker moved off to the left. A barrage of bullets splintered the rocks about his head. Eric popped up from his position and strafed the helicopter with covering fire until Parker was safely behind the huge bounders.

"He's making a run for it!" Eric yelled.

Parker peered around the boulder. Bledsoe was running away from them down the slope of the open tundra in a zigzag fashion toward the drop off to the tree line. Before Parker could say anything, Eric jumped from the safety of his position in the boulder field.

"Cover me!" Eric yelled and darted out onto the tundra in pursuit of the Superintendent.

"Wait!" Parker knew his words would go unheeded. He quickly turned his weapon on the helicopter, but not before Stan managed to fire off a few shots at Eric.

Parker blanketed the chopper with bullets and watched relieved as Eric adroitly dodged Stan's hastily fired rounds. Parker kept his aim steady on the chopper as Eric parroted Bledsoe's zigzag escape. Eric dashed by the helicopter, keeping a good distance away. Parker saw Stan's weapon come up from behind the seats. Once again he strafed the cockpit with bullets.

Suddenly Parker's weapon went silent. "Oh, shit!" He slammed a fist into the side of his weapon and quickly ejected the ammo clip. It was empty. He saw Stan's Uzi come up from behind the helicopter seats once again.

"Eric!" he cried out.

Eric started to turn and at the same instant the helicopter pilot's weapon spat out its deadly missiles. Parker watched in horror as Eric's body twisted in the sudden illumination of a lightening flash high overhead. The redhead's arms groped into empty air and Eric fell hard onto the ground, rolling several feet from the forward momentum.

"No!" In an act of desperation, Parker hurled the Uzi into the air at the helicopter. It landed far short of its goal.

He leapt over the surrounding boulders and jerked his pistol from his ankle holster. He made a mad dash for the helicopter, emptying his ammunition clip into the sides of the chopper. The moment his pistol emptied, the pilot threw open the cockpit door, jumped out and raced off in the Superintendent's direction.

Parker's lungs felt as if they might explode, but he continued to run at an all out pace. Unable to look, Parker dashed between Eric's fallen form and the helicopter. He concentrated his blinding anger on catching the pilot and killing him with his bare hands.

The rain went abruptly from a light sprinkle to a hard downpour. Above the natural noise, Parker heard the shout of voices and gunfire. He careened to a stop at the top of the hillside and looked down to see a line of heavily armed sheriff's deputies in khaki rain parkas. They crouched at the edge of the trees, keeping their weapons trained on the Superintendent. He was sprawled back on the hillside, clutching the remains of his left shoulder. Stan, the pilot, had stopped midway down and dropped his weapon. He stood with his hands above his head.

Oblivious to the danger, Parker barreled down the

hillside. He crashed into the back of the pilot and both went down. Parker got him by the throat and repeatedly slammed the man's head onto the hard ground.

"Motherfucking son-of-a-bitch!" Parker yelled into the rain. He slammed a fist into the almost unconscious pilot's jaw.

Deputies raced up the hillside. It took three of them, but they finally managed to pull Parker off the pilot.

"Don't hurt him!"

Parker recognized Sheriff Jenner's voice. "Fuck you!" Parker shouted. "He shot Eric. I'm going to kill the son-of-a—"

"Calm down, son." Sheriff Jenner clamped a hand on Parker's shoulder. "I'm talking to my deputies, not you."

Parker became aware of the heavy rain for the first time. He wiped the mud from his face and tried to rein in his hoarse breathing. The adrenaline drained from him and he let rising despair and grief fill him in its place.

"Parker!" Margaret cried out. Wrestling with a large umbrella, she burst through the deputies and grabbed Parker's arm. "Parker, are you all right?"

"He shot Eric," Parker said weakly, his voice trembling. The rain masked the wash of tears.

"What?" Margaret looked at him in disbelief.

Parker's head lowered. He covered his face with his hands.

"Oh, no!" Margaret's arms went about his neck. "No!" She hugged him tightly.

"He went after Bledsoe," Parker said, almost stuttering. "I couldn't stop him." He felt Margaret's hold on him relax suddenly.

She jerked his head up. "Are you saying this to me just to be mean, or what?" she asked angrily.

"What?" Parker looked at her, blinking.

"I mean, here I am worried sick about the two of you. I come racing back here with the police, and you give me this crap about Eric being shot." Margaret looked like she might slap him. "I believed you there for a minute, you asshole!"

"What?" Parker pulled away from her.

"This is in pretty poor taste, Parker White!" Margaret's eyes flashed with the lightening.

Parker shook his head violently, trying to reset the picture to one that made sense. "The son-of-a-bitch shot Eric!" He began to recover his anger. "I saw it. What the hell are you—"

"He shot Eric, huh?" Margaret's free hand went to her hip.

"Yeah, goddamn it! Are you listening?"

"Then who the hell is that?" Margaret pointed up the hillside.

Parker jerked his head around. In the dark and heavy rain, he could barely make out a tall figure silhouetted against the black sky, standing at the top of the hill.

"Who . . ." Parker blinked his eyes and wiped away some more of the mud. Lightning flashed again and Parker caught a glimpse of strawberry-blonde hair. "Eric!" He heard his own voice scream out.

The figure stood waving, favoring one leg.

Parker broke away from Margaret and stumbled up the hill. "Eric!" he shouted once more.

The figure had disappeared. Parker crawled up over the top of the hill. He stared at the young man seated on the muddy ground, massaging his ankle. Parker couldn't believe his eyes and moved in closer, his mouth agape.

The man with Eric's face looked up at him and

grinned.

"I tripped," Eric said, wincing. "Just call me Grace."

Parker tried to speak but nothing would come out.

"Are you all right?" Eric looked at him with a worried expression. "You look like shit."

Parker screamed like a mad man and leapfrogged onto a surprised Eric. "Goddamn it!" Parker shouted over and over again. He locked his arms about Eric's neck and smothered him with one kiss after another.

Eric fell back, laughing. They lay in each other's arms as the rain pelted down onto them. Parker felt Eric's arms tighten about him. He raised his head up and looked down, forcing his tear-blurred eyes to focus at Eric's mud-splattered face. He couldn't remember ever having seen anything as beautiful.

"Eric?" Parker said, finally.

"What, old man," Eric answered, smiling up at him.

"I . . . I just . . ." Parker stared down into Eric's laughing, hazel eyes. "You're all right . . . you're all right!"

"Of course I'm all right," Eric said. He pulled Parker's face to his own.

"You'd better be," Parker said, his tears falling onto Eric's face. He felt Eric's hands on his buttocks, pulling him closer.

"Agent White?"

"Yes, Ranger Borenson?"

"Is that a gun in your pocket or are you just glad to see me."

Parker brushed his lips over the tip of Eric's nose. "That's the worst Mae West I've ever heard," he said.

Their lips parted, then joined while the lightning flashed above them. The sheriff's posse moved in closer, watching Eric and Parker with reactions varying from snickering to exclamations of disgust.

"Take a good look, you sons of bitches!" Margaret stood in the rain, hands on hips. She shouted at the assembled posse. "That's how real men do it!"

CHAPTER 18

Parker stretched out in the tub and let the water jets massage the small of his back. Normally he would have jumped in the shower to scrub the mud off, but when he saw the Jacuzzi bath, his aching muscles called the shots. He reached for his wine glass and took a long sip of the dark ruby merlot. He held it in his mouth, savoring it behind a satisfied smile, and looked up through the clear skylight overhead. Eric's attention to the details of function and space had made his tiny cabin a sanctuary of comfort.

He took another sip of wine and wiggled his toes up through the foam. The mouth-watering aromas filtering in from the kitchen added to the romance of the moment. A warm bath, a delicious meal, stimulating conversation, and then . . . He chuckled to himself, feeling the geyser of bubbles tickling over his groin. He adjusted his position in the tub. After all, if he walked out of the bathroom wrapped in a towel and sporting a big hard-on, he might seem overanxious.

"Well, don't you look the picture of decadent luxury?"

"Wha—" Parker almost dropped the wine glass into the tub. "Margaret! Dammit, you scared the shit out of me."

"Don't mind me," Margaret said from the bathroom door. "I just came in to borrow the mirror." She sauntered over to the oversize mirror fronting the sink.

Parker watched her in disbelief. "Margaret, I'm taking a bath."

"Is that what you call it?" Margaret gave him a wink as she touched up her lipstick. "Looked like foreplay to me."

Parker felt his face flush. "Everything looks like foreplay to you." He gave her a hard look. "What the hell, may I ask, are you doing here?"

"Alice and I stopped by on our way to paint the town." She turned and pulled at the hem of her revealing, black satin dress. "And to show you boys what you'll be missing."

"So you're not hanging around," Parker said a little too quickly.

"You are such a misogynist bitch." Margaret smirked.

"I'm not a misogynist." Parker offered her his wine glass as a peace offering. "I would just like to finally have an evening alone with Eric."

"Of course you would, dear." Margaret took the glass along with a healthy swig of its contents. "Who wouldn't?" She handed the glass back. "Now just relax. You're going to get your wish. Alice and I are off to the singles bars in Denver to do a little man hunting of our own."

"Man hunting?" Parker frowned at the lipstick smear

on his glass. "From the looks of that dress, I'd have thought man killing."

"Aren't you sweet?" Margaret said. She knelt down beside the tub and grabbed up a loofah sponge. "Sit up and I'll do your back."

Parker sat forward in the tub and rested his chin on his knees. "Do you think little Alice is ready to go for the big game with an experienced brush beater like yourself?" He sighed as Margaret massaged the sponge over his shoulders.

"Are you kidding," Margaret said. "She's wearing this little red, strapless number that even made Eric's eyes bulge."

Parker laughed.

"I'm not kidding." Margaret set the sponge on the back of the tub. "You would never have known it from that awful uniform she was wearing today, but that girl's got boobs to beat the band."

"Can you stand the competition?" Parker asked.

"Competition, my ass." Margaret stood. "She's just added bait. Together we make one gorgeous, irresistible black widow."

"There will be meat on the table tonight," Parker said lightly.

"Enough of this lolling about," Margaret said, grabbing a towel from the rack. "Now get out and let's all have a drink together before our various and separate festivities begin."

Parker took the towel from her. "All right." He started to stand, but changed his mind. "Turn around."

"What?"

"You heard me," he said again. "I said turn around."

"It's just us girls." Margaret looked wounded.

"Margaret!"

She rolled her eyes. "Oh all right." She turned to the door. "Such modesty."

Parker stood with his back to her and dried off a little. He glanced back to find Margaret admiring his backside and quickly wrapped the towel about himself.

"Like I've been saying . . . nice ass, G-Man." Margaret nodded appreciatively.

Parker retrieved his wine glass. "Girlfriends don't admire each other's asses," he said with a smile.

"I'm a lesbian," Margaret said, batting her eyelashes.

"More like a gay man in a woman's body," Parker said with a smirk. He caught sight of Alice talking to Eric in the other room. "You should be so lucky to be a lesbian," he said with a whistle. "You weren't kidding about Alice."

"Come pour us a glass of that delicious wine," Margaret said. She drifted into the living room. "Alice, look what I found floating in a bubble bath."

"Hi, Alice." Parker checked to make sure the towel was securely fastened about his waist. "Nice dress."

"Thank you," Alice said with a slight curtsey. "Margaret made me wear it."

"It's a nice choice." Parker headed for the wine on the kitchen cabinet. "But don't listen to everything Margaret tells you. You can get into all kinds of trouble with her."

"I'm counting on it," Alice said.

"I wonder how Dan's getting along with his cellmate this evening." Margaret sighed.

Eric stood at the stove in a terry cloth robe, checking on the contents of one of the steaming pots. "I'm not sure the Superintendent has a choice in the matter," he said brightly.

They all laughed.

"What plans do you and Margaret have for the evening?" Eric asked.

Alice took a glass of wine from Parker. "We're going to eat dinner at Farinelli's first—"

"Load up on carbohydrates before the real action." Margaret accepted a refill from Parker.

Alice giggled. "Then we're going to this club in Denver near the University," she said. "What's it called? Quincy's?"

"Not Quintin's," Eric said.

"Yeah," Alice nodded. "Quintin's. That's it."

"By the looks of your face, you seem to question the appropriateness of Margaret's selection," Parker said. "What is this place, a male strip club? And then, how do you know about it?"

"Don't be ridiculous," Margaret said. "It's a perfectly respectable dance club, full of perfectly respectable people."

"You lying slut." Parker wrapped his arms about Margaret's waist and nuzzled her ear. "Tell us the truth."

"Stop that." Margaret tried to push his lips away. "It's a nice club."

"Full of college students," Eric said. "Nothing but young . . . very young guys."

Alice's eyes widened.

"And what's wrong with that?" Margaret nestled back into Parker's arms. "They're all legal age."

"Barely," Parker said.

"They're sweet, homesick—"

"Horny," Parker interrupted.

"—fun-loving, fun to talk to, hunky men," Margaret continued. "It's true they need a little seasoning. That's where an experienced, beautiful woman, such as either of us," she said, giving Alice a wink, "has the upper hand."

Alice took a large swallow of wine.

"Now you've got her all scared." Margaret slapped Parker's hand. "Don't let him fool you dear," she said to Alice. "He didn't exactly raid the old folk's home for this exceptionally beautiful man." She smiled at Eric who blushed almost immediately.

Parker returned the slap, but on Margaret's backside. "Drink your wine, Margaret," he said. "The sooner you finish it, the sooner you can snare one of those poor, unsuspecting schoolboys."

Margaret took a sip of wine. "Parker . . . sweetheart." Her smile became a razor's edge. "You're always trying to get rid of me."

"Margaret, honey bun," Parker parroted, "it's just your overworked imagination."

"I'm going to miss you when you go back to Washington." She looked up at his sudden change of expression. "When will you be going back? Tomorrow? The next day?"

Parker glared down at her and mouthed, "Bitch."

Eric had turned away and busied himself at the stove. Parker watched him and willed his hands not to resist the impulse toward Margaret's neck.

"Of all the things you could have avoided saying," he said under his breath into Margaret's ear. He released his hold on her and went to the stove.

"Just wondering," Margaret said lightly. She raised a triumphant eyebrow at Alice.

"Actually, I'm not going to be leaving anytime soon," Parker explained.

Eric turned to check the contents of the wall oven.

"Is that so?" Margaret blew Parker a silent kiss.

"Yes." Parker made a threatening gesture to her with one of the pot lids. "I've requested a temporary posting with the Denver office. There are a lot of loose ends to clear up about this smuggling operation. It could take several months." From the corner of his eye, he thought he saw Eric smile.

"Several months," Alice said. "How wonderful! You and Eric will get to spend a little more time together."

"I hope so," Parker said truthfully.

"Surely you're not going to stay in the motel all that time?" Margaret said, ever helpful. "You know I have a spare bedroom that you're welcome to use."

"Aren't you sweet?" Parker glared at her.

She set her wine glass on the cabinet. "Well you think about it. It would be fun." She turned to Alice before he could answer. "Alice, I'm famished. Let's go for the gold."

"I'm ready if you're ready." Alice finished off her wine and put the glass on the counter.

"Honey, I'm always ready." Margaret brushed past Parker to give Eric a kiss. "Don't stay up too late, beautiful. It causes wrinkles."

Eric grinned at her. "Have a good time, Margaret," he said, giving her a wink.

She turned and wrapped her arms about Parker's neck. "I'll see you tomorrow, tall dark and handsome." She gave him a long kiss and whispered in his ear. "And I want to hear ever nasty, sordid, delicious little detail."

"Go away, Margaret." Parker smiled at her despite himself.

"Come on Alice," she said. "We've overstayed our welcome."

"Bye, guys," Alice said following Margaret to the door. "Wish me luck."

Parker followed them and shut the door with a sigh of relief. "Finally!" he said, turning the lock. He sipped his wine and took a moment to try and recapture the ambience he had been enjoying in the Jacuzzi bath. He heard a crackling sound and followed it to the large, stone hearth across the room. "Is that a fire going?" he asked, making a beeline for it.

"It's going to get pretty cool outside tonight." Eric grabbed his glass of wine and joined Parker by the fire. "I like having a fire at night."

"I've never had a fireplace before," Parker said. "Nothing but central air and heat. I'm usually off working a case somewhere or just too busy to enjoy it, anyway."

"We're a little more laid back up here in the mountains." Eric turned off the lamps, giving the firelight dominance in the room. "That's better."

"Much." Parker watched the flickering light from the fire dance about Eric's face. "I could almost get used to the pace of things up here."

"Oh, you'd probably get bored real quick." Eric smiled into the fire. "Like you said, you like to stay pretty busy."

"I think that's just been a symptom of loneliness." Parker reached up and absentmindedly toyed with a tress of hair over Eric's ear. "And there's sure nothing like you back home."

Eric turned to Parker. He traced the outline of Parker's bare biceps with the tip of his finger. "So, are you going to take Margaret up on her offer?" he asked.

Parker watched the finger. "Unless I get a better one," he said.

"Do you snore?"

"Not loudly," Parker said.

"Want to stay with me?"

Parker took Eric's hand and brought it to his lips, kissing the finger that had been lightly brushing over his bare skin. "That's a much better offer." He looked down at his growing erection, straining against the confines of the towel. "We can discuss the arrangements later."

"I hope Alice knows what she's getting herself into," Eric said. His hands slid up to Parker's chest and he began to massage Parker's right nipple with his thumb.

Parker caught his breath. "Do you know what you're getting yourself into?" He closed his eyes as Eric's hand traced its way down his chest to his belly button.

"Not a clue," Eric said, leaning in to nibble the top of Parker's ear. "Want to talk about it?" Eric's tongue retraced the route his hand had taken as he dropped slowly to his knees.

"Not right now." Parker threaded his fingers through Eric's thick hair. "Maybe later." He felt the towel loosen about his waist and looked down to see it drop to the floor.

"You looked like you'd be more comfortable this way," Eric said, standing to run his hands up Parker's bare back.

Parker pushed the robe off Eric's freckled shoulders and it joined the towel on the floor. He glanced down at what Eric's garment had been hiding. "I'm glad to see I'm not the only one here having unclean thoughts," he said.

Eric looked down, too. "Oh, that," he said. "It's been bothering me all day. Must be a change in the weather."

"Hmmmm." Parker ran his hand over the object in question. "I can see how this would be a problem."

"What do you suggest?" Eric exhaled raggedly.

"How long before dinner's ready?"

"About twenty minutes, why?"

Parker pulled Eric down onto the braided carpet in front of the fireplace. "That should be just time enough," Parker said, continuing his ministrations.

Eric stretched out on the rug. "Twenty minutes?" He moaned as Parker's lips began a line of kisses from his neck downward. "Is that all?"

"Tonight will be a dining experience." Parker paused to pull a curly red hair from his tongue.

"Do tell."

"We begin," Parker said, licking his lips, "with the appetizers."

The pot on the stove finally reached a simmer.

www.ingramcontent.com/pod-product-compliance
Lightning Source LLC
Chambersburg PA
CBHW030027180626
46810CB00001B/241